The Acolyte

John T. Hitchner

For Beverly and Don Thomsen, Larry and Sara Moss,

and Steve and Janet Simmerman: long-time friends

.

ACKNOWLEDGMENTS

I thank the people who read this novel in its many phases and offered suggestions and wisdom about the story. First and always I am grateful to my wife Pat and to my son John for their patience and support of my work. Sincere thanks, also, to Dawn Andonellis, Patrick Armstrong, David Chase, Jack Coey, Steve Hall, Charlie Hansel, Ernest Hebert, Jeanie Kahus, Jerry Kaufman, Norman Klein, Sean McElhiney, Tim Napier, Katie Parker, Kenneth Schalhoub, and Jerry Whelan: kind, knowledgeable, and witty readers all.

Finally, my thanks to Kenneth Schalhoub for technical assistance, to Ernest Hebert for crafting *The Acolyte*'s cover, and to John R. Hitchner for the photograph of the author.

PART I: A FATHER'S HANDS

1

Happy Birthday: May 1956

When I was fifteen, Ralph Malloy, my best friend's father, reminded me of an aging heavyweight boxer: broad-chested, paunched, a smoker, drinker.

On this particular May afternoon in Lorrence, New Jersey, Mr. Malloy, as I addressed him out of the respect my mother and father had drilled into me, didn't appear ready to go ten rounds; instead, he looked like a big man at ease and intent on lawn tasks. He knelt on one knee on the square patch of dull green grass along his gravel, pebbled driveway, black-bladed grass clippers in one hand. A white T-shirt clung to his chest and back. Curls of hair black as the wavy hair on his head crept above the shirt's collar below his neck. He rubbed his shoulder against the side of his head.

"Davy! How's the lad" he greeted me. "Gonna be hired help for Lizzie's party, eh?"

"Yeah, that's me," I replied.

"How's Mom and Dad, Davy?" he said, and jiggled the clippers. "Don't see'em around much. See your dad at the bank and once in a while he comes in the store. Haven't seen your mom lately. She still at that woman's shop?"

"Yeah, still there."

Mr. Malloy's comments and questions made me uncomfortable. I wanted to be polite to him but I was in a hurry to see Skip and find out our duties for his sister's birthday party that afternoon. Mr. Malloy probed as if he wanted more of a relationship with my parents than "Hello, how are ya?"

Last summer when I suggested to my parents that we "all go out to dinner," my father pursed his lips and caught my mother's eye for a sign. She shook her head in a secretive way, but I caught her meaning anyway. "Maybe sometime," Dad had said to me. "Not this weekend."

Sometime never came.

And Dad had never mentioned to me that he had gone to the auto parts store where Mr. Malloy worked.

"Think those Phillies're gonna do anything this year?" Mr. Malloy asked me.

"I dunno…Maybe. If they get some good pitching," my answer the same point of view as my father's.

"Roberts can't do it all," he said, noting the success of the Phils' ace Robin Roberts. "They'll need a few more strong arms, don't you think?"

"That's for sure," I agreed matter-of-factly.

Ralph Malloy concentrated again on snipping the grass evenly an inch or so near the driveway's edge.

At the stucco-sided house directly across the street, a man and woman—Mr. and Mrs. Arvidson—came out to the porch, newspapers in hand, and sat on wicker chairs. Skip had gossiped to me the Arvidsons had no children. Mr. Arvidson—an engineer at the Kenner's Point oil refinery on the Jersey side of the Delaware River, his wife a secretary for a Lorrence lawyer—spent two weeks and occasional weekends every summer at their cottage in Cape May. From where I stood, Mr. Arvidson's mustache looked like a thin slice of tar. After he handed a newspaper section to his wife, he waved to Mr. Malloy. Mrs. Arvidson looked in Mr. Malloy's direction, but she didn't wave.

"One of these days, Davy," Mr. Malloy spoke up, "maybe you and your dad and me and Skip can see a Phillies game, huh? Tickets aren't cheap, I know, but your dad and me could swing it, don't you think? Wouldn't that be fun?" He shook the clippers in my direction.

"Sure. I'll see what my dad says," I replied. My head signaled Dad wouldn't go for it. Not the four of us. It'd be "Maybe sometime, but not this weekend" again.

"Atta boy…Thanks." Ralph Malloy regarded me as if I had already given him a pair of box seat tickets. "Eighteen today, Lizzie is," he continued. "And a senior! Gonna graduate next month. Time to celebrate Lizzie with a good party." He shifted his attention to his lawn task. "Skip's waitin' for ya', prob'ly in his room lis'nen to that rock 'n roll junk you kids like."

The metal shears clashed like dueling knives.

———————

Skip's bedroom was only two footsteps beyond the top of the stairs. Centered on the door was a plywood sign he had carved and lettered in red: NO KIBITZERS: ENTER AT YOUR OWN RISK. Through the closed door Little Richard shouted "Well it's Saturday night an' I jussa got paid!"

I announced myself with a 'shave-and-a-haircut-two-bits' knock.

"Come on in, numbnuts!"

Phillies pennants, including one from the 1950 Whiz Kids season, thumb-tacked the wall to my left. A glossy color photo of the Philadelphia Eagles NFL Championship season team was above his bed. Rosary beads looped around the front bedpost. A St. Christopher medal and chain hung from a peg on a mirror above Skip's bureau. Lizzie's senior picture framed on the bureau, her yearbook smiling face planted somewhere among the sports souvenirs. A 45 RPM portable record player propped on the lid of a scratched and dulled toy box just inside the door. Little Richard blaring "I'm gonna rip it up, an' ball tonight!"

And Skip sitting on the floor beneath the window that looked down on the back yard.

"You see the old man? What's he up to?" he demanded.

I explained his father's lawn care activity, nothing about seeing a Phillies game.

"He have any beer?"

"Not that I saw. Why?"

"Just checkin'. Shut the door. Need privacy."

I swung the door closed with my right foot.

Skip and I had been best friends ever since he became "that new kid" in fourth grade. We were the same age then, the same age now and the same 5'6", but he bulked chunkier, 15 pounds heavier than me. Thick-lensed glasses bulged his brown eyes. When Skip grabbed your attention, you notioned a cartoon figure; in Skip's case, Alfred E. Newman. This likeness, and the fact that he didn't fit in made my best friend an easy target.

"Whud'ya' see, it's Alfred E.!" and "Here comes What Me Worry!" had plagued my friend ever since *Mad* hit the magazine shelves. Skip defended himself against the mockery by using fists first, words afterwards. He never won. His "wise-ass" and "pathetic-jerk" reputation was like a black cloak over his shoulders, too heavy to shake off.

"I know who I look like," he had confided to me one afternoon in eighth grade after a rough and tumble pick-up game of touch football, "but I wish to God those bastards'd lay off."

Skip could live with the fact that he wasn't a "native" of my hometown of Lorrence. He could live with his looks. He could not abide being bullied—mocked and pushed and pinned against high school locker room walls, and having his face slapped and glasses knocked off. He flailed at "those bastards" who laughed at his wild, vengeful punches and obscenities. After the melees the instigators walked away proud, their secretive laughter a bruise on Skip that wouldn't fade away.

The oafs grew tired of fighting with him, but hey still wisecracked Skip and me in gym class, the hallway, and at Saturday night dances. They gawked and snickered at us as if we were discarded trash. We tried to keep our cool. We didn't retaliate.

"They're not worth it," I had told Skip.

I understood him. It came home to me one day when we rode our bikes around town. Skip churned his legs fast as if with each revolution he pumped his anger into the street. The rest he kept inside him. Maybe that's why he was such a wise guy. He didn't quite know the right thing to do and when to do it.

Now another 45 slid down the record player's stem. The machine's arm swung to the disc, the needle clicked onto a groove. Elvis complained "Well my ba--by left me, never said a word…"

"Too bad, Elvis. Gonna turn you down." Skip lowered the volume. He sat on the edge of his bed.

I took a stand at the open window. "Your mom and Lizzie're getting some stuff ready," I said nodding down at the yard.

"Like what?"

"Settin' up picnic tables."

"The old man oughta' do the heavy work. Lazy ass bum."

Skip's mother and Liz lifted and moved three picnic tables and benches into a triangle. "There, that looks all right, doesn't it, honey?" Mrs. Malloy said to Liz.

"Looks fine, Mom."

It was natural, I thought, for Mrs. Malloy to call Liz "honey." I had never heard her use an endearment for Skip. I had always heard her call him by his nickname, not William, his real name; his full name was William Thomas James Malloy.

Mrs. Malloy and Liz walked out of my sight line toward where I knew wooden stairs led up to the back porch. I heard Helen Malloy say, "Tell your father he needs to set up the grill."

Beyond the tables the yard stretched a grassy rectangle—our imaginary football field where Skip and I had tossed a football last fall, or the outdoor arena where we had challenged each other to one-on-one, making our fair share of jump shots through the backboard's net bracketed above the garage door at the end of the driveway. The door gaped open now, the trunk and rear fenders of Ralph Malloy's black '53 Ford like a crouched, metal chest-protected catcher.

Skip seemed focused on his own thoughts. He made a pfft sound through his lips. "I hope the old man doesn't make an ass of himself."

"How?"

"Tryin' to impress the girls," he said without his usual sarcasm. Then, he shrugged and smiled out of the corner of his mouth. "If he does, Lizzie and my mom'll put him up Shit's Creek without a paddle."

Little Richard replaced Elvis Presley on the turntable. "Well Long Tall Sally she's built sweet, she got everything that Uncle John needs, oh baby...Yeah, yeah, yeah, ba-a-by..."

Footsteps plodded up the stairs, thumped softly on the hallway carpet, stopped outside the closed door. The metal knob turned, the door jarred opened, and shook as if in fear.

"I'm havin' me some fun tonight, yeah!" wailed Little Richard.

"Jesus, Mary'n, Joseph! Turn it down! You want the whole neighborhood to hear that stuff?" barked Ralph Malloy. He gripped a beer bottle belt level, the bottle top aimed at his chin. The breadth of his upper body allowed only fist space between his chest and arms and the doorway molding. Perspiration glistened his face.

"What's *wrong* with it?" Skip asked in an unsmiling challenge.

"What's wrong with it?" The big man's eyes flicked from me to Skip. "You're playin' that junk too loud, that's what. You can't hardly understand a word that guy's sayin'. So would you be so kind as to turn it off and get outside to decorate. And while you're at it, gimme a hand with the ice and sodas in the coolers. Your sister's havin' a party, remember?"

Skip stayed where he was, our elbows an inch away from each other on the window sill. "Aye aye, sir," he gave a single nod to his father.

Mr. Malloy had apparently calmed, probably because I was there.

Skip continued as if the air between them had eased. "Lizzie wants the record player for the party. I'll use an extension cord to plug it in inside the back door."

Mr. Malloy included me in his point of view. "You don't call that stuff music, do you, Davy?"

"It's not that bad," I replied, an honest answer, the answer I had given my parents when they complained about the rock 'n roll high volume on my radio.

"Bless and save us. Give us peace," pleaded the aging-like boxer with a smile. He blessed himself, sipped the beer, turned his thick body toward the stairs.

The same solid body and strong hands, and the same blessing of himself I had seen one night last month when Skip had invited me to stay for dinner. My parents and my grandfather had gone to the hospital to visit Nana, my grandmother, who'd been terminally ill with cancer. Helen Malloy, a stout, kind woman who labored to keep a clean and presentable house, had prepared a meatloaf dinner with mashed potatoes and green beans. Mr. Malloy and his wife presided at opposite ends of the table, and we three kids filled the middle chairs across from each other.

Liz Malloy in my sights: Had I done some good deed? I couldn't think what that blessed favor was. Liz was one of many senior girls I had daydreamed slow dancing and holding hands with. In those fantasies I talked as persuasively as Alan Ladd, Cary Grant, or any other handsome Hollywood leading man; in real life I only stared and stumbled. On this night I gazed at Liz Malloy's blond and creamy-complexion and prayed to God I wouldn't trip over my words if and when I talked to her.

Before we ate that evening, Mr. Malloy said Grace. Then he, Mrs. Malloy, Liz and Skip blessed themselves and followed with "Amen." Omitting the sign of the Cross head to chest, I uttered a soft "Amen."

Mr. Malloy added a postscript that drew snickers from us: "Amen, Brother Ben shot a turkey in the pen. Yay God!", the kind of remark my father never made after he or I offered Grace at our dinner table. Dad was not the kind of man who made jokes of religious matters. Hearing Mr. Malloy's quip, I wished my father could be a little more like Mr. Malloy.

Skip's dad passed the plate of sliced meat loaf to Liz and simultaneously asked me, "You're an acolyte over at St. Thomas's, aren't you, Davy?"

I replied that I was.

"Don't you make the sign of the Cross during your Mass?"

"No…I didn't learn it," I said.

Ralph Malloy's tone turned serious, as if the gesture of blessing myself was an obligation I should respect and perform during Holy Communion and after Grace. That I was not taught, therefore not required to do so made my best friend's father pause and frown.

"You don't? What's goin' on with you Episcopals up high there on Willowyn Terrace, huh? Too sophisticated to make the sign of the Cross during Holy Communion or a simple meal like we have here?" He smiled but I had not heard a smile in his voice.

Mrs. Malloy reached out and laid a hand on my arm. "Don't worry, David. My husband should be should be more polite." Directly to Mr. Malloy she said, "Maybe David wasn't taught what we were taught about when to bless ourselves, and that's all right. Let's enjoy our dinner, Ralph. Pass the mashed potatoes, please."

"In my own good time, Helen. In my own good time."

Mr. Malloy sighed and then flexed his fingers before he passed the potatoes and green beans. The conversation the rest of the meal focused on the Senior Prom (for juniors and seniors only) the first Friday in May, the Sophomore Hop (for freshman through seniors) less than 24 hours after the Prom, and Liz's birthday party the weekend after the Hop. Liz mentioned that she and Lorraine, one of her girlfriends, still hadn't found prom dresses. Skip and I, two "single" freshmen, didn't think it would be worth it to go to the Hop.

"I'll dance with both of you if you go," Liz said. She winked at me, not at her brother.

I felt a blush creep into my face.

"David, you're turning so red! Oh my god, that's really cute."

I remembered Liz's smile and my blush before I fell asleep that night. I remembered, too, what I had seen and heard that night after dinner.

Mr. Malloy had stood in the kitchen – living room archway, his arms folded across his chest like a foreman watching his crew. Skip had gone to the bathroom, I was clearing the table, and Mrs. Malloy and Liz were washing and drying dishes.

"You think you're goin' out gallavant'n' two nights in a row—your prom and that Sophomore Hop thing?" Mr. Malloy had challenged Liz. "You got Mass Sunday morning after, you know."

"It's Prom weekend, Daddy. My senior year. It's a special time."

"We'll talk about it," Mr. Malloy said.

"You mean *you'll* talk about it but I have to listen."

Liz strode from the kitchen. I heard a door slam after she went upstairs.

"She's gettin' pretty sensitive if you ask me," Mr. Malloy had said.

Mrs. Malloy shook her hands over the sink and turned to her husband. "But I think she's right, Ralph. It is her senior year after all, and she has a lot on her mind. I'm sure she's thinking about next year, too. Where she's gonna be, school and all. She's thinking about that Pierce Business School in Philadelphia, you know. She was looking through one of their catalogs the other day. I think it's something we could help her afford."

"We'll see," Mr. Malloy said.

His attention wasn't really on what his wife had explained. He glanced at me and then turned toward the cellar door behind him. "I'll be downstairs," he mumbled. He closed the cellar door.

I said a quick thank-you-for-dinner, first to Mrs. Malloy and then to Skip after he came out of the bathroom. Walking home that night, I had visualized Liz's closed bedroom door. Would it stay closed for the night, or would she and her father have a nice father-daughter talk before he kissed her goodnight?

Compared to the Malloy's day-to-day life, mine was ordinary; the routine of usual dinner table conversation— my mother's job, my father's tasks at the bank, his appointments for the Plymouth's 3,000-mile oil change, Mom and Dad taking my grandfather grocery shopping (Granddad didn't drive, neither did my mother; Dad was the family chauffeur). Scenes without excitement were my life.

Now in Skip's bedroom I looked out the window at the undecorated backyard. Then I eyed the empty doorway where Mr. Malloy had stood. The stairway was silent, and the hallway's cream-colored wallpaper of mint-green leaves and vines, an ordinary pattern, showed no action, no surprises.

———

"Hi, David. My dad treating you and my brother all right? I heard him bark about Little Richard." With a half-smile, Liz looked toward the house.

Before I had a chance to answer her, Skip said, "Same as always."

He and I had decorated the clothes line poles with blue and pink (Liz's favorite colors) streamers. Skip had carried the record player, I had brought the discs to the picnic table closest to the house.

Lizzie now thumbed the player's narrow power tab to ON. The turntable spun.

"Good!" she grinned her little victory. "Let's see what you brought me, David."

I scooped up and bestowed on her a handful of 45's in their record-label sleeves.

"Thanks." She pecked me on the cheek and kidded me about the sudden blush in my face.

"Where's *my* kiss?" protested Skip.

His sister obliged.

I didn't know much about love, but I whenever I was around this eighteen year-old girl with green eyes, blond hair in smooth waves above her ears and neck, and blond down like fair gold on her arms, I felt giddy. Not the same giddiness I experienced the first time my father had taken me to a Phillies game; not the same joy as when I had laid eyes on the first set of American Flyer model trains my grandfather had bought me for Christmas when I was ten; rather, a shy but playful happiness slid into my body and voice. This afternoon Liz wore a robin's egg blue blouse, the first two buttons unbuttoned, her neck a blush of pale pink, the blouse's hem worn outside a pleated white skirt. White sandals, her toes pink nail-polished. In my fifteen-year old heart I loved her.

"I'm gonna sneak in Fats Domino," she said. She fanned out the sleeved records like a set of playing cards. "I'll put him in the middle of the stack. Dad won't know what he's hearing." She looked back at the house again. The inside back door was open. We heard heavy steps soften as they descended the cellar stairs. "What's Dad up to?" she wondered to Skip as well as to herself.

———

They came with cards and with wrapped gift boxes in pink, white, and blue bows. They dressed in dungarees, pedal pushers, and skirts; yellow, white, and robin's egg blue short-sleeve blouses, and white sleeveless sweaters. Sockless or in white bobby socks. Black and white saddle shoes or white sneakers. They all would receive official Lorrence High School diplomas the second Friday night in June.

Skip and I leaned our arms on the back porch railing. We watched.

Liz opened presents to Charlie Gracie singing "You Butterfly" and to

Kay Starr's "Rock 'n Roll Waltz." She showed off new earrings to her mother, who stood behind two of Lizzie's girlfriends. "What do you think of this, Dad?" she posed as she displayed a record album titled *Elvis Presley*.

Standing next to his wife, Mr. Malloy smiled and muttered, "They say he's polite to grown-ups and a good son to his mom and dad. I guess I can put up with it. Just play it in your room and be sure you close the door."

Lizzie's girlfriends chuckled. Mr. Malloy nodded and offered "Thank you, ladies."

He nudged and winked at one of Liz's friends. "That's my girl," I heard him say.

After Liz opened presents, her father strode to the charcoal grill Skip and I had fired up. Mr. Malloy smacked his hands and clanged a spatula against the grill's bowl underbelly. "Your attention please!" he bellowed. "Doggies and burgers'll be ready soon! First in line gets a kiss from the cook." He smacked handfuls of hot dogs and hamburgers onto the grill, listened to them sizzle, uttered a satisfied "Ah!" He reached into a cooler at his feet, withdrew a bottle of beer, "church-keyed" the cap, and tilted the bottle's lip to his mouth. He swallowed, the muscles in his neck moving piston-like up and down, up and down.

Mr. Malloy then raised the bottle in the direction of Mr. Arvidson standing hands on hips a third of the way down the driveway. "Hey neighbor," he called, "wanna join the party?"

Mr. Arvidson waved "No thanks, Ralph. Maybe some other time." He paused a few seconds and then walked up the driveway toward the back of his house.

"Suit yourself, you stuffed shirt," Mr. Malloy mumbled, clear enough for his audience, including Skip and me to hear it.

"Let's get some grub and go upstairs," Skip said.

We crouched again at the back window of his bedroom, late afternoon sunlight a gloss upon the grass and party voices. Skip's Phillies memorabilia reminded me that my father took me to Connie Mack Stadium at least once, sometimes twice a summer. Usually Dad bought us grandstand seats on the first base side; last year he had sprung a few extra bucks for two box seats seven rows up from the third base side Phillies dugout. That Saturday afternoon the Phils beat the Pirates 6 to 5 in the ninth inning on a run-scoring double by Richie Ashburn.

"We'll make a day of it!" Dad always said the night before our excursion. Images in my head of the teams taking batting and fielding practice, it was always hard for me to fall asleep.

How would he react when I raised the idea of the Harper and Malloy fathers taking their sons together to a National League baseball game in Philadelphia?

Skip flicked on the black table model radio on the night-table beside his bed. Out from the speaker came "Well, Be Bop a-Lula, she's my ba-by, Be Bop a-Lula, she's my ba-by…"

"Your dad like this?" I asked of Gene Vincent's hit.

"One of his all-time favorites," Skip replied.

We munched our first of two hot dogs apiece, washed them down with root beer.

Lizzie's friends lined up for burgers and hot dogs.

"Don't forget to kiss the cook!" Mr. Malloy, grinning, reminded them, and shook the spatula in his right hand. He basked in sunlight, he basked in girlish, gigglish reception and kisses on his offered cheek.

"Here you are, special treat for my birthday girl," he said, handing Lizzie a hamburger.

She didn't smile, didn't giggle. She offered her father only a perfunctory kiss that didn't touch his face.

I didn't wonder why Liz walked head down back to her table. I knew her father had embarrassed her.

Skip breathed, the sound of his breath like my own when I had seen Mr. Malloy try to cuddle Liz in the kitchen last month.

"The red-head. She's nice," I said. "The way her hair comes over her collar. Nice shape, too."

"You're not getting a boner yet, are ya' Harper?" Skip chomped the first bite of his second hot dog.

"Not yet. Every morning, though, soon's I wake up it's right there."

"Ten hut!"

"That's about it."

That was the last time he and I laughed that day.

"I like Lorraine Wyles," Skip said. "Tight white sweater. Next in line."

"Yeah, I've seen her around. Likes to wear sweaters. Cheerleader, right?"

"Right. You've heard the rumor? 'While away the hours with Wyles?'"

"Yeah...Maybe she'll cheer for us someday."

"You wish. She's spoken for. Some guy from Haddonfield, goes to Rutgers. She got accepted at Douglass. Sorry, numbnuts. You lose."

Gene Vincent groaned "...my baby doll, my baby doll, my baby doll. Let's go, cat!"

"Check out the bottles the old man's set up," Skip said out of the corner of his mouth.

Two empty beer bottles stood like trophies on the grass in front of the grill. I thought of my father. Dad drank beer on hot summer days after he mowed the lawn and did other yard chores, which I sometimes helped him with...Not often enough, he complained. But he had let me take a couple sips of beer, too. I had shaken my head at the bitter taste.

"Good," he had smiled at my reaction. "Beer's not something you want to get used to at your age."

Ralph Malloy scooped a hamburger, slid it between the bottom and top of a roll, kissed the top, and handed it to Lorraine Wyles, but not before he presented his cheek to her. The white-sweater girl pecked him with a kiss. In return, he put his mouth close to Lorraine's ear and seemed to kiss her.

She laughed and spun away. Mr. Malloy shook a spatula in Lorraine's direction. I couldn't hear what he called out to her.

"Wonder what your dad said to her."

"I dunno...Thinks he's a ladies man."

Liz sat with her back to the house. Skip and I couldn't see her facial expression when her father had pulled Lorraine against his chest. She flipped over the records on the record player's spindle now, pushed the power tab, and watched the lowest record drop onto the turntable.

The Four Lads began to sing about standing on a corner, watching all the girls go by.

"Last chance to get goodies from the grill!" announced Mr. Malloy.

"Thank you, boys, for helping me get things ready for the party, and for helping clean up," said Helen Malloy. "David, you didn't have to do any of this, you're a guest. Then again you're practically family. I appreciate your help. Lizzie does, too."

"You're welcome," I said.

Helen Malloy sat at her usual place at the table, the chair closest to the back door. She smiled a closed-mouth smile and wiped her hands on the yellow and white-check apron she had been wearing since I had arrived at four o'clock. The flesh of her upper arms hung loosely, in contrast to my mother's athletic swimmer's arms.

The porcelain cherub-faced clock on the kitchen wall between the cabinets and refrigerator read five minutes after eight. The twilight-shaded sky had dissolved into purple night. In the glow of the back porch light, Liz and her friends chattered at the picnic tables and jitterbugged to Elvis, Pat Boone, and even to Fats Domino and his bluesy band of solid bass, horns, and percussion. Mr. Malloy had sauntered away from the grill. We didn't hear him putter in the cellar or mumble upstairs. Maybe he was rearranging things in the garage, an activity my father sometimes performed when he and my mother disagreed on an issue, which was not often.

Skip uncapped two bottles of root beer, plunked one in front of me. "One for the road," he said and sat down across from me, in the same chair he had scraped back when he had confronted his father last month.

I tipped the bottle to my mouth.

"I'm sorry again, David, about your poor grandmother passing away," Mrs. Malloy expressed. "How's your grandfather doing? He must miss her terribly."

"He's doing all right." I had read the sympathy card Mrs. Malloy had signed 'Ralph and Helen' Malloy and family,' the card's message about "the blessings of cherished hopes and memories," and "the power of faith in God." I kept my memories of Nana in a place I wanted no one to invade. In the days after the funeral I had not visited Granddad. I didn't want to go into a room without seeing her reading a newspaper or listening to the radio or knitting a scarf or asking me "How did you do on the algebra quiz we practiced for?" The day I finally stopped in to see Granddad, I could still smell Nana's powder she had used to smooth on her face and neck. Nana was a presence in the house, a presence that I brought home with me that day like a gift I didn't want anyone else to know about.

"Are you still an altar boy at St. Thomas, David?" Mrs. Malloy asked.

It was then I noticed a bluish-purple bruise in the crook of her arm. Meanwhile, I told her I was still an acolyte. "I'm tired of it, though," the same complaint I had voiced, with no success, to my parents. I had not, however, revealed to them or now to Helen Malloy my doubts about God, His existence, His supposed almighty powers. Where was the evidence?

Why couldn't You have saved Nana?

"It's nice for you to do," she continued. "I'm sure your mother and father like it when they see you helping Father…What's his name?"

"Hepplewhite," I answered.

She repeated the name. Then she began "I wish Skip—"

"Forget it, Mom."

"It wouldn't take you very long to learn…"

"I don't *like* Latin, Mom. It's all mumbo-jumbo. Harper's got it easy. You didn't have to learn a new language, did you, Harper."

"You see what I'm up against, David?" Mrs. Malloy had a warm smile, as warm as her hand on my arm. She drew her hand away now and fingered the bruise on her arm. "Are you going away on vacation this summer?" she asked me.

"I don't know…Maybe. I hope so, but I haven't heard my parents talk about it yet."

"Tell'em to go off by themselves. You stay home, take care of the house, we can have a party." Skip's eyebrows lifted as he swigged his soda. "Or sneak off to Philly, catch the Fizz Kids," he said, using the sarcastic name for the Phillies, who had since fallen from National League heights after their pennant-winning season of 1950.

"Need money for that," I said.

"We'll cash in empty beer bottles," he recommended. "Got plenty'a those in this house."

Helen Malloy squeezed her eyes shut. Seconds later she opened them. She didn't look at Skip, though, when she said, "You didn't have to say that. Come on, now. It's still Lizzie's birthday. Let's not spoil it."

He made the pfff sound through his lips again.

She put her hands on the table and pushed up from her chair. "I'm going in to lie down for a little while. Let me know when Lizzie's friends start to leave. I want to thank them for coming." As she walked behind me she patted my shoulder. "Thank you again, David."

Liz's girlfriends departed at eleven o'clock; some, who lived on the west side of Lorrence and didn't drive a car were picked up by parents; others, their homes within walking distance, left in twos and threes.

As her friends were leaving Liz asked them, "Did Lorraine already leave? I was looking for her."

"I think I saw her walking home. She doesn't live that far away," one girl replied.

"Oh, okay," Liz said.

She and her mother thanked everyone and bade goodnight to the last group of three, the girls' footsteps and voices like a popular song's fade-out.

Liz gave her mother a thank-you hug and kiss and turned to go upstairs.

"Nothing for me and Harper?" Skip, not-so-kiddingly, objected.

"How could I forget?" Liz slung one arm around Skip, the other around me.

The touch of her lips on my cheek, as sisterly and perfunctory as the kiss was, was only one of several significant memories for me of that party. Ralph Malloy's complaints about rock n' roll, and seeing Liz's kiss not touch his cheek, yes. And the soft wave of her blond curls as she jitterbugged with her friends, yes.

That I temporarily lost my wallet became a personal turning point for me that night. An eighth grade graduation present from Nana and Granddad, and in which they had tucked a congratulatory fifty dollar bill: I didn't find it between the seat cushions of the living room chair I had slumped in while Skip and I had watched TV, nor was it anywhere in Skip's bedroom, negating the possibility the wallet had inadvertently slipped out of my hip pocket.

"I cannot tell a lie: I am not a pick-pocket," Skip joked. "Tell you what: I'll check the cellar where we stashed the empty sodas, you check around the tables outside. I'll turn on the back porch light."

The back yard seemed smaller in the porch light's dull glow. Picnic tables, clothesline poles and rope, like traps, mysteriously and silently had inched closer to the house. Even the garage, its sliding door a dark open mouth. I didn't know if I should close it or leave it open. I debated the issue for maybe five seconds. I stepped forward. My right foot pressed a cushion-like object. I bent down, picked up my wallet, and slipped it into my left back pocket. "Thanks, Nana," I whispered.

———

In the six blocks to my house, I knew the names of the families who lived on both sides of Willowyn Terrace. I knew the makes of cars they drove, the jobs they had and the businesses and industries where they worked. Those people lived in a world not so different from mine. Behind their darkened windows and doors they lived safe, unthreatened lives. They would awaken in the morning and mow lawns, plant flowers, sweep sidewalks—ordinary spring weekend routines accomplished since they had moved into those houses. Sunday morning I might see them kneel at the communion rail at St. Thomas Church, open their hands to accept the white wafer, touch the chalice as they sipped the wine, and then return to their pew to give thanks or just wait for our rector Father Hepplewhite's final blessing. Some might duck out before the recessional hymn. Things to do, places to go. They wanted to beat the traffic.

One block from my house I approached St. Thomas' on the corner of Willowyn and Woodholm Avenue, the Episcopal parish my parents and I belonged to and where I was baptized, and where I at age twelve was confirmed by the bishop of the Episcopal Diocese of New Jersey to receive Holy Communion; the white wafer tasted dry but the cream sherry wine tasted sweet; I liked it then, I liked it now. Sipping the cream sherry from the chalice offered me by Father Hepplewhite was about the only good thing about being an acolyte.

I shifted now from jog to walk. St. Thomas' granite facade glistened in the glow from two spotlights beneath the front lawn shrubbery. The spotlights didn't breathe life into the stained glass figure of Jesus the good shepherd centered in the granite façade. The whites, greens, and blues of Jesus and his flock that looked down upon the congregation Sunday mornings, now on a late Friday night, appeared dull, without the hope that prayers and Father Hepplewhite's sermons invoked to his congregation.

I shivered. In the glow thrown from the light on the church façade, I spoke to someone whom I had spoken to since my grandmother died; someone I wasn't even sure would hear me.

Are You for real? I'm just wondering. You didn't help Nana when she was sick, so I don't even know if You're real or not. So what is it? Where are You?

I waited. No voices came from nearby houses or from inside the church. No sounds came from the trees behind the church, either.

But as I started walking again toward home, I heard the rising, gunning acceleration of a car far down Willowyn Terrace, a force of motion that grew fast and bold in its approach, a black Ford, I realized under the streetlights, one just like Ralph Malloy's. The Ford dipped, its under-carriage bumped across the intersection and gained greater speed as it passed the house where I lived a half block away. In five seconds the car and its red taillights leaned out of sight, not out of sound, not until I began walking again.

Ralph Malloy behind the wheel? I wasn't sure. The Ford's speed so fast, I was unable to read the license plates. If it was Skip's father, where was he going and why? Lizzie was home, her friends had left, and he would help clean up and put tables and chairs away.

Too many questions.

I had no answers when I entered 422 Willowyn Terrace.

2

Sanctuary

The living room—same as always. Mahogany desk with the globed lamp lit; three-cushioned sofa, empty fireplace (We didn't use it because my mother feared fire.); table model TV, archway posts, my height lines penciled on the white enamel by Mom; Dad's chair where he watched TV and read the paper, Mom's upright piano...She hadn't played a note since Nana died.

"David?" my mother called down from upstairs.

"Yeah?"

"Are you all right?"

"Yeah."

"How was Liz's party?" my mother asked. "Did you have a good time?"

Typical questions; typical as seeing my mother's bare ankles and pink-slippered feet come to the upper landing. Ordinary as her pink terrycloth robe with its matching cloth belt, which she tightened as she came down the stairs...

Ah, not much, Mom, my imaginary sarcastic self remarked. *Just that Mr. Malloy flirted with a bunch of Lizzie's friends.*

I had already started across the path from living room to dining room to kitchen, the refrigerator my destination. I wasn't ready to face my mother. I glanced out the kitchen window to investigate for a black Ford. Nothing.

"What are you doing?" she asked.

"Grabbing a beer...Thought I'd go out for a cigarette and a cold one," an attempt to deflect my unease with sarcasm, a voice I could control.

"Don't be silly," her standard rebuttal to many of my adolescent wisecracks.

She stationed herself—arms folded, inquiry in her eyes—in the kitchen – dining room archway.

I kept my hands busy, my focus on a favorite creation: Lebanon bologna and Swiss cheese sandwich on white with mayonnaise; my beverage a glass of chocolate milk. I put the sandwich on a paper napkin.

"Did everybody have a good time?" my mother asked.

"Sure…Okay…"

"Did Liz get some nice presents?"

I activated my imagined sarcastic self again: *Holy shit, Mom! Do I have to tell you everything?*

I chewed my sandwich, swallowed some chocolate milk while I reported the gifts I could remember.

"Are you all right?" my mother asked. "You keep looking at the window. What's the matter?"

"Nothin'. Just lookin' out the window, that's all."

"You look tired."

"I'm all right." I flashed two empty beer bottles lined in the grass beneath Mr. Malloy's grill and the Ford that roared by St. Thomas Church. I tried to imagine Mr. Malloy as the driver, but the only things clear to me were the clunk-clunk of metal over the intersection's pavement and the red taillights like eyes in the distance.

Like a good boy I dropped the paper napkin into the wastebasket next to the sink, rinsed my empty glass and placed it upside down in the dish strainer on the counter.

"Where's Dad?"

"He's asleep."

I kept my back to my mother..

"Did you want to tell him something?"

Her face expressed curiosity, an inquisitiveness that would change to worry if I delayed my response any longer.

"No…I was just thinking about some things, that's all."

I switched off the kitchen ceiling light. The living room desk lamp threw a pond of weak light toward the stairs. My mother walked ahead of me, her familiar scent of powder and perfume a memory of Nana, weak comfort at best. Sheet music she had played days before Nana died still lay open on the piano.

"Don't forget you're scheduled to serve at eight o'clock Sunday," she reminded me.

"How could I forget."

———————

My bedroom—my sanctuary— gave me meager reprieve.

Skip and I had shouted the word in jest after we had watched *The Hunchback of Notre Dame*. "Sanctuary!" Quasimodo had cried of the cathedral's belfry, his refuge from the callous Catholic cardinal. At St. Thomas' the red-carpeted space where I performed acolyte duties in front of the altar was the church Sanctuary, a holy area where my fasted stomach gurgled, and where I noted, as they knelt at the Communion railing, the figures of college girls home for weekends and holidays.

"Sanctuary!" I had exclaimed in my imagination as I watched those girls take the body and blood of Christ, close their eyes, and bow their heads.

A holy place indeed.

My bed where I slept and fantasized about Liz Malloy naked, and where I remembered the Lorrence High School girls touching the round white Communion wafer with their lips and tongues, this was my safe sanctuary.

On the night-table beside my bed was a wall of Major League baseball yearbooks, each one a gift from Granddad. I had read all ten of them, learned about the "jury box" bleachers of old Braves Field and about "Duffy's Cliff" before Fenway Park's outfield was made level. I had studied field dimensions, outfield angles, and neighborhood houses beyond outfield walls. Tonight I didn't open any of those yearbooks. I didn't want to. They were a barrier, one not strong and thick enough to prevent the penetration of other scenes and voices into my head.

No speeding car had shot by the house after I came in. My mother had not asked me if I had seen the car, had not even commented on its noise. It probably wasn't important, I thought. Just some crazy Lorrence High School upper-classman showing off to his girlfriend.

Glossy color pictures from *Sport Magazine* and *Sports Illustrated* decorated my walls. Willie Mays' over-the-shoulder catch of Vic Wertz's drive to the Polo Grounds deep center field; Rocky Marciano smashing Ezzard Charles against the ropes; Duke Snider swinging for Ebbets Field's upper deck; Eagles end Pete Pehos leaping for a pass. Pros all. They and other heroes I had thumb-tacked around the room, all athletes in motion toward victory. I had never met them. I didn't know the sound of their voices, but I had memorized their faces. I wanted to meet them someday. Someday they might call me by name, shake hands with me. For now they watched over me in the dark as I slid under the covers.

I shivered under a sheet and cotton blanket.

Lizzie: Her warm lips when she had kissed me, her arm around me. Would she ever dance with me? Would she ever let me hold her close, let me kiss her on the mouth the way I fantasized? What about Lorraine Wyles? Pointy breasts beneath her white sweater. I didn't know her, but what would she feel like in my arms? Would she ever let me touch her breasts?

It wasn't wrong to think about these things. I thought about that mysterious feel every ten seconds in school, out of school, anywhere. It was natural to wonder about the shape and feel of breasts. It was acceptable to dance close to a girl if she let you. Some girls I had slow-danced chest-to-chest at the high school's Saturday night canteen, their breasts like little hard cushions or soft pillows. Some nights I had fallen asleep reliving those sensations. Did those girls know how excited I was when we slow-danced close to each other? Did they think about me the way I thought about them?

Skip and I had talked about the facts of life. He had told me that Liz had explained to him that putting your hand on a girl's breasts (which I hadn't experienced) was acceptable if you were serious about each other. "When the girl doesn't move your hand away," he had said.

You know what I'm thinking about? So what? I don't care if you do. Nothing wrong with thinking about girls. So if You're out there, You know something more about me. You probably know I don't say my prayers anymore, either. No more "Now I lay me down to sleep." No more "Our Father who art in heaven," except in church. Nothing happens. What's the use?

You'll see me there Sunday but I'd rather sleep in. No chance of that, though.

3

Return of the Prodigal Sons

Skip and I were born two months apart; he in January, me in March. The Saturday afternoon after Liz's party my best friend looked older than fifteen. No gray threaded his thick black hair, no worry lines cut his face, no tremors in arms and hands, but age beyond his fifteen years pitted his voice; the sound of trust gone bad, of a heart split in half.

"I dunno what hell it is but somethin's goin' on," he said on my back steps.

"The old man went out last night, hasn't come back, and Lizzie went to Ocean City to apply for a summer job. Mom and me, we're holdin' down the fort."

"What time did he go out?"

"Few minutes or so after you left."

"I think I saw him."

I described the sound of black Ford as it passed the church. I couldn't tell who the driver was, but—

"Probably the old man. He drives like a bat out've hell when he's got somethin' on his mind. I don't know if Lizzie told him she was goin' to the Shore or what."

"You think he'd been drinking?"

"Prob'ly. He's got a bug up his ass about something."

I wondered. Just the effect of beer? Maybe beer makes him flirty with Lizzie's friends? Maybe he was upset with Lizzie about going out two nights in a row, the Prom and the Sophomore Hop. But driving like hell because of that? Dad liked a beer once in a while, but it never affected him, not that I had ever seen.

"The old man's always been like that," Skip said after I asked him if his father drank a lot. "When he gets ticked off, when he just feels like drinkin' a few. Loves his beer."

Skip added that his mother had once confided to Liz and him that "your father was a skirt chaser when we were growing up in Pennsylvania. One of the sweetest men you'd ever want to meet, a good father but after one too many beers, a silly fool."

She had married him, Skip explained, because he was nice looking, he treated her with respect and, in the coal mining region of Pennsylvania where they had lived, there weren't a lot of men who had "my old man's charm, if you can believe that. He was a beer drinker when he was a kid and he started on Scotch then, too. My mom thought she could change him, she thought having Lizzie and me around would change him. Now she says, 'I just do the best I can.'"

He sniffed, and rubbed his shoulder against the side of his face the way his father had done yesterday afternoon. Skip didn't look at me, he didn't look straight ahead. He kept his focus on the backyards of neighbors, where trees shaded clothes lines and fireplaces. A shine of wetness was visible beneath the lens of his glasses closest to me.

I thought of my mother and father: high school sweethearts who had postponed their wedding five years because of the Great Depression and had decided to stay in Lorrence because they had grown up here, made friends here. I had never heard Dad ridicule Mom, had never seen him flirt with other women. Mom would have chastised him for that kind of behavior, perhaps served him an ultimatum: change your behavior, or leave. Without Dad the house would have been just a place of rooms and walls. A place without the familiar slap of his car keys on the glass-top desk, and without his familiar voice and footfalls. It wouldn't have been a home.

"I have no idea where the old man is," Skip said. "His car wasn't in the garage when I rode over here. For all I know he might be wracked up somewhere...Get your bike. Let's get the hell outa here."

Skip was already pumping away on his Rollfast down Willowyn Terrace when I swung onto my trusty Schwinn.

That afternoon the strain and push of Skip's legs on his bike was enough evidence of how much anger churned through his heart.

Past orchards and vegetable farms in Lenape Township west of Lorrence, the apple and peach blossoms "gone by," an expression of my grandfather. Rows of tomatoes and beans, squash and corn already in stem and leaf, stalk, vine, and hill. Barn doors open, a woman hanging laundry on clothes lines, kids younger than Skip and me pedaling two and three-wheeled bikes in driveways. My parents and Nana and Granddad had bought vegetables and fruits at farmers' stands on Sunday drives, the stands and sheds now closed until the produce "came in." Things and people in wait, but for Skip and me that afternoon it was good to be in motion. Good to have the May sun on our backs, sun and sky harbingers of the school year's end and the start of summer vacation.

From Lenape Township Skip and I swung to Forgeville, the college town directly south of Lorrence. Forgeville "wet": Tadaro's Bar and Restaurant across from the Forge Theater, Joe-Frank's Pizza, Beer, and Subs a block from the college, and the Forge Hotel and Bar across the street from a Methodist Church. Lorrence "dry" due to Blue Laws created at the turn of the century and still in effect ("No bars on the streets but a bar in every cellar," Skip and I had joked of our town.). So strict the stern, dark-suited and dark-bearded men (they certainly appeared grim-faced in the town's history text) that their Thou Shalt Not-like commandments forbade even Sunday train service in Lorrence prior to World War I. Post war, freight and passenger service resumed. Sales of alcohol, though, remained illegal.

Was Mr. Malloy home by now…sobered up? I wondered.

North, past woods where small-game hunters used scattershot against rabbit, quail, and pheasant in the fall. Past Teal Lake, where my parents as high school sweethearts had gathered with friends for winter cook-outs and ice-skating parties. "I proposed to Mom at one of those parties," Dad had confided to me the winter day he had taken me skating on Teal Lake. I was seven.

I'm not sure what I said after he had told me. Maybe I smiled, maybe nothing at all. That night, though, before I fell asleep I remembered the firm grip of his hand as he led me onto the ice, and the way his voice lifted when he saw me shakily stride out on my own: "That's the way! Now you've got it!"

As Skip and I pedaled by the lake, I thought that when I passed my driver's test and got my license, I'd bring my girlfriend (whoever she was) out here. We'd build a fire, cook hot dogs, drink soda, then make out by the fire. We'd have the freedom to be by ourselves there, at least for a while. Until we had to go home and wait until the next time we could be together.

"Time out," Skip yelled over his shoulder to me at the junction of Teal Lake Road and Riversea Drive, the two-lane highway link between the Delaware River and Atlantic City.

We straddled our bikes, our feet secure on pavement. In front of us Riversea Drive traffic whisked north and south.

"I better go home, find out what's going on," he said.

"I'll come with you."

He grinned back at me. "Come at your own risk, numbnuts. Don't say I didn't warn you."

No one sat on the Malloy's screened porch. The inside front door hung as if someone intended the door be closed but had left it open. No noise through the screened windows and porch door. A push mower whirred behind a house down the street. Neighbors' properties in quiet uncertain wait. Had the Arvidsons and other neighbors heard Ralph Malloy's Ford roar out last night? How could they not?

Maybe Dad—

Skip angled down his kickstand on the graveled driveway opposite the back porch. The three picnic tables still formed a triangle on the grass. Mr. Malloy's Ford, its front grill aimed at Jessup Avenue, loomed outside the garage.

"Want me to wait out here?" I asked.

Skip swung his head toward the house. "Come on in. You'll be moral support." He did not grin.

I walked behind him into the kitchen. The cherub-face clock read ten minutes after three. Sweat still dampened my back, my legs wobbly from pumping miles of roads and streets. Two cups and saucers sat rinsed in the sink.

Skip called out "Mom?"

As if on cue Mr. Malloy stepped from the hallway into the living room. His beard a shadow, black hair slick to his scalp, he wore baggy gray khakis, navy blue t-shirt, and black sneakers. He nodded toward the hallway at his and Mrs. Malloy's bedroom. "She's lying down," he said softly. He eyed us as if wondering what he would say next or if Skip or I would speak. I did not want to say anything.

" Ah, the return of the prodigal sons," he nodded. "Well, where the hell were you two?"

Skip replied that we had been bike riding.

"Oh really? Where?"

"Outside of town, down to Forgeville," Skip said.

"See anything interesting?"

"No."

During these questions and answers, I hadn't focused at all on Skip. My eyes had skimmed from the living room's floor-model TV to the window looking out to the porch and to Mr. Malloy. His eyes nailed me as he said, "David? You haven't said a word. How're you doin'? You have a good ride?"

"Yeah."

"Thanks for your help at Lizzie's party." His smile questioned how I might answer his next question. "Good party, huh? Lizzie had a good time, didn't she."

"I guess so."

"You just guess so. You were present and accounted for, weren't you, David?"

What're you trying to do, cross-examine me?

"Never mind, I know you were there," said Mr. Malloy. He sniffed and then rubbed his hand under his nose. "What mischief you boys plannin' for the rest of the day?"

"Just gonna listen to some records. Let's go up." Skip shoulder-bumped me toward the stairs.

"Keep it turned down," his father's words more threat than polite request.

Not until I was pedaling Willowyn Terrace on my way home that afternoon around five o'clock did I again see my best friend's father. I heard the Ford's steady, unthreatening engine, saw the right front black panel, tire and hubcap followed by the rolled-down window. "Pull over for a second, David," Ralph Malloy ordered, his hitch-hike thumb jammed toward the curb.

I braked. In view one block away stood the gray granite of St. Thomas Church, my father's boring gray Plymouth in the driveway of two blocks away from where I leaned forward, hands on the Schwinn's black grips.

Mr. Malloy levered into neutral, let the Ford idle. He scrunched to the passenger side, his right arm across the top of the seat.

"You see anybody around here last night? Anybody walk home with you?"

"No."

"You sure? No girls from Lizzie's party?"

"Nobody. I walked home by myself."

"Huh. And you didn't see any girls who live in that new development up Willowyn?"

"No."

What was going on? Who was he talking about? I wondered.

Across the street from St. Thomas', my grandfather turned the corner and walked toward 422. Since Nana had died, he had wanted our company, so he often came over for dinner.

I thought about telling Mr. Malloy I had seen a car just like his shoot by the church. How would he react to that information? I wondered. I decided to say nothing about it.

Mr. Malloy shifted back to the driver's seat. He ducked his head and looked out at me. "Okay, just checkin'."

I didn't push off on my bike until his Ford was out of sight.

————————

I'm supposed to help Father Hepplewhite at eight o'clock Communion tomorrow. I guess I'll be there. Not that I'm crazy about going. I'm not sure You know it or not, but Skip's got stuff he's trying to figure out. Me too. I'm okay but Lizzie might be in trouble…maybe Skip and his mom, too. So, if You can help them…

4

Communion

My arms stuffed through the narrow red cassock sleeves and wide white floppy cotta shoulders. "I'm a red and white penguin," I mumbled Sunday morning as I flapped my arms and checked my appearance in the St. Thomas parish hall choir room mirror.

"In this cor-nah," my playful self announced, "wearing a red cassock and white cotta, a lightweight weighing in at one hundred twenty-five pounds, Da-vid Harper!"

So the Friday night fights announcer would introduce me. If: If I had stamina to go ten rounds. If I went into training. If Skip would be my manager.

No training this morning. No ringside applause. No **'David Harper'** printed on a fight card. No take-home pay for what I'd have to do for Father Hepplewhite. Big deal.

For self-satisfaction I crouched, jabbed with my left, slammed a right to an invisible body. *He goes down…Ralph Malloy goes down, ladies and gentlemen…*

The cassock's hem hung the width of a football above my ankles, the cotta's shoulder seams tight as a jacket I had outgrown. I don't need this stupid penguin outfit.

But I made the climb: I trudged up the parish hall stairs, peered through the lobby windows—no black Ford in sight—then I entered Father Hepplewhite's Sacristy, red cassock rubbing like a skirt against my khakis.

"Good morning, David, nice to see you," smiled Father Hepplewhite as

I entered.

Greetings, Bread Man, my playful imagination returned the greeting.

Father Hepplewhite: our tall, loose-jowled rector, handshake soft as white bread, hair a sticky grayish-black mat combed right to left across his scalp, his wide forehead smooth and shiny. Today—one of the Sundays after Trinity, I couldn't remember which number—'the good Father,' as Skip and I had nicknamed him, wore a white robe tied at the waist with a green sash. I didn't know Hepplewhite's exact age, maybe fifty, probably older. All those hours of writing sermons, kneeling to genuflect and pray, visiting the sick and dying…He had sat at Nana's bedside the afternoon she died that past April. "Grant her welcome into Your kingdom, O Lord," he prayed after Nana had closed her eyes and drawn her last breath.

Where are you now, Nana? Give me some proof. I need it.

Father Hepplewhite's morning breath reeked sour milk when he asked me, "Got you up early today, huh?"

"Yeah, kind of," I replied in the near whisper I had adopted from older acolytes. There in the Sacristy, ten steps from the altar, you raised your voice only in song. Low voices and whispers offered prayer, confidences and confession.

'The good Father' handed me a book of matches and a maple-wood candle-lighter that looked like a shepherd's staff. I lit the wick, adjusted its length to three or four inches. Holding the staff with both hands diagonally in front of my chest, I walked out to the Sanctuary.

Where I had to be without breakfast: (*Thou shalt not eat any breakfast before taking Holy Communion early Sunday morning,* my Catechism teachers had impressed upon me). Where I had to be because the St. Thomas Church Acolyte Schedule listed me for the 8:00 AM Holy Communion service, the second Sunday in May. Therefore, I should not have been thinking of Lorraine Wyles in a tight white sweater. Not imagining her without the white sweater.

So, concentrate on lighting the candles, Harper. Concentrate.

That morning the Sanctuary of St. Thomas' was a place of almost holy quiet; yellow glow from the overhead conical lights and from sunlight through stained-glass windows. *And now, ladies and gentlemen, on my right we have Adam and Eve naked in the Garden of Eden—fig leaves in the usual places; on my left there's Jesus, the Good Shepherd, tending His sheep.*

And is that God's holy sunlight shining through the windows upon us? Oh, what a beautiful morning! Oh what a beautiful day! I've got a wonderful feel-ing, not a heck of a lot is going my way!

This quiet was interrupted by the foot-shifting, throat-clearing of the eight o'clock regulars. I felt their eyes try to peer into me as I lit the altar candles. Older men in shiny blue or tan suits too heavy for summer, older women in raincoats even though it wasn't raining this morning...What other Sunday outfits did they have?

The St. Thomas rich didn't attend eight o'clock service; if they were not in sunny Florida or on business trips in Philadelphia or New York, they came to eleven o'clock. Older women wearing gray felt hats and white straw hats with netting they lifted when they received Communion. Widows and widowers. Older couples. Some older parishioners had attended Nana's funeral last April. I had shaken hands with them—"A sweet woman, David." "We'll miss her very much." They drove pale blue or gray Chrysler New Yorkers and black Buick Roadmasters that never seemed to collect dirt or newspapers the way my father's three year-old Plymouth did...I wish he'd trade it in, get a better looking car.

Finished lighting candles, I bowed in front of the altar and returned to the Sacristy.

'The good Father' stood hands clasped in front of his vestments bureau. He now wore white cassock and red and gold chasuble. His face and stance reminded me of Pope Pius XII, whose photograph hung in the Malloy living room. The silver chalice Father Hepplewhite used for Holy Communion rested on the bureau; a white veil-covered the front of the chalice, a white cloth-covered pall sat on the chalice rim like a square cardboard plate. I imagined an empty picnic plate.

Checking his watch, 'the good Father' said, "Well, shall we begin?"

He followed my lead out to the Sanctuary.

But all I thought about was the taste of cream sherry I'd get.

"Almighty God, unto whom all hearts are open, all desires known, and from whom no secrets are hid..."

Hepplewhite's church voice always surprised me. Chant-speak in front of the candlelit, cross-dominated altar. "Thou shalt love the Lord thy God with all thy heart and with all thy mind..." Perhaps in those days 'the good Father' was sort of an actor. A split personality: half minister, half performer, who believed without question the prayers he half spoke, half sang: "...vouchsafe, we beseech thee, to direct, sanctify, and govern, both our hearts and bodies, in the ways of thy laws and in the works of thy commandments..."

In my head I heard Hepplewhite break into "You ain't nothin' but a hound dog, cryin' all the time!" *Go, Father, go! You'd get more people here if you'd move those hips.*

"Here endith the Epistle," he announced. He kissed the open Scripture and laid the book upon its gold pedestal.

I bowed, stepped to the altar, and carried the gold metal pedestal and the Scripture from the Epistle side to the Gospel side.

My head drifted away from the Gospel. I remembered no New Testament book title, no verse numbers. Scrambled eggs, bacon, grape jelly-smeared toast—that's what I'd attack at breakfast.

If Lorrence police didn't show up to ask me questions...Did police investigate crimes on Sundays?

Gospel finished, I mumbled the "Nicene Creed" as if I was listing inventory of the glove compartment of my father's Plymouth. I delivered the collection plate to the volunteer usher and then brought the silver box of communion wafers to Father Hepplewhite. "About seventeen," I said, my estimate of this morning's congregation.

"Thank you," he replied, and counted out 20 thin wafers and spread them on the paten.

Tiddlywinks—Boing!

I handed Father Hepplewhite the crystal cruets of water and wine. I smiled to myself as he poured both into the chalice...a little more, Father, a little more. He was generous with the cream sherry. Skip joked about his priest's fondness for whiskey. "My old man gave Father Bradeen a fifth of bourbon for Christmas. Bradeen, he practically kissed the old man's hand."

"For in the night in which He was betrayed…"

The Last Supper: pictures I had colored in third grade Sunday School class, sweating, pressing my crayon to be neat, to stay within the lines, Christ in white, disciples in brown, my Sunday School teacher bending over my shoulder to compliment "Very nice, David," even though I knew my jerky flicks of color had crossed some lines; even though I knew I could have done better.

"The Body of our Lord Jesus Christ, which was given for thee, preserve thy body and soul unto everlasting life. Take and eat this in remembrance that Christ died for thee, and feed on Him in thy heart by faith, with thanksgiving."

I knelt in front of 'the good Father,' accepted the wafer in my cupped hands, and brought my hands to my mouth. The wafer tasted dry, like paper. I wondered if heaven this dry and dull? What was on heaven's menu? Hoagies? Milk shakes? Whatever they served there, it had to taste better than those wafers.

"Drink this in remembrance that Christ's Blood was shed for thee, and be thankful."

I swallowed the water-diluted cream sherry. I felt no special change in me… didn't feel blessed, didn't feel saved. I didn't know how it felt to be special or blessed or saved. My feet didn't feel fuzzy either. The truth was I felt warm, as if the sherry settling in my empty stomach had been pumped to my head...

Am I getting light-headed?

Now Father Hepplewhite beckoned the less than two dozen congregants to Communion.

I stood up again, folded my hands belt-level, and took my place in front of the stained-glass window of Adam and Eve. Why did artists cover up Adam and Eve's "privates"? What was the sin in showing the naked body? Eve's breasts were hidden by her long, chestnut-colored hair. She looked pretty well built. Had Adam ever touched her breasts? I guess he had when they'd made love…

"Almighty and ever living God, we most heartily thank thee…"

Mom and Dad would be up by now, I thought. Breakfast ready, then she and Dad would go to 11:00 Morning Prayer and afterwards drop in on Granddad. They would probably tell me to visit him, too. Maybe I would, maybe not. I'd check in with Skip first.

"We heartily thank thee for thy humble doings…"

Yes, I heartily thank thee, too, God, for these holy mysteries, this bread, this wine, these seventeen regulars, let's really hear it for them, ladies and gentlemen, the blessed company of all faithful people, yeah, every one of us heirs to Your kingdom, wherever it is. Wish I knew, save me a place, I beseech You, well not really beseech You, that's weird as 'vouchsafe,' whatever the heck that means, but I'm wondering in this holy fellowship holy fellows holy smokes fellows world without end yes, on earth peace, good will towards me, Merry Christmas and a Happy New Year we wish you a Merry Christmas we wish you a seat at the right hand of God, is God right or left-handed, who's on the left, who's on first, no, what's on second. Okay, let's go!

"Thank you, David," Father Hepplewhite, shaking hands, expressed in his soft, Sacristy voice.

"You're welcome." I helped him remove his chasuble, the red, gold, and white garment like a heavy carpet in my hands. Father Hepplewhite smoothed the chasuble across the top of the bureau and let the vestment drape down across the bureau's drawers.

Braced to the wall above the bureau was the square cabinet where bottles of cream sherry were stored.

"See you next month," he said.

Would I have the guts to kick my once-a-month acolyte duties goodbye? I wondered.

Father Hepplewhite departed the Sacristy to greet the congregation.

I took the long-handled candle-snuffer and returned to the Sanctuary. Coughs and foot-scrapes chuffed from the pews. I bowed to the Cross.

I don't know if You're there or not. I need proof You know what's going on.

I extinguished the candles, bowed again, and left the Sanctuary.

I didn't leave church right away. While 'the good Father' greeted the faithful parishioners at the front entrance, I opened the communion wine cabinet and sneaked a couple sips of cream sherry.

Father Hepplewhite met me as I left the Sacristy.

"Thank you again, David," he said.

"You're welcome," I replied, turning my head away.

No suspicious vehicles lingered at St. Thomas' when I headed home. In the stained-glass front window, Jesus the good shepherd appeared a silent, indifferent caretaker of His sheep.

---

422 Willowyn Terrace: a two-story red brick and white clapboard house one block from St. Thomas Church. Mom and Dad weren't rich, they weren't poor. They made ends meet on two paychecks. I didn't know the exact amount of their combined pay. All I knew was that it covered food and other bills, including payments on Dad's four-door gray Plymouth, insurance, and one three-day weekend each summer in Ocean City.

I liked our house: full-length front porch where we watched the annual Fourth of July parade, backyard deep enough for Dad and Skip and me to toss a baseball or football. It embarrassed me that Mom and Dad didn't own the house. The Malloys owned theirs (but how much longer?), the MacAdamses (Jack, a friend of mine) owned the big stone house with a backyard swimming pool on West Crosstown Avenue, plus a beach house in Ocean City. Our neighbors were homeowners, too. My parents Philip and Grace Harper were renters, the only family on the block who paid a landlord every month. Young, anxious, I tried to keep my embarrassment to myself.

"Someday," Dad had promised, his voice trailing off like a leaf caught in a brief wind gust whenever I raised the subject "When're we going to have our own house?"

I loved my parents. They worked hard. I admired them for that and for their caring about me. My friends respected them; so did their moms and dads. Weekends, though, instead of looking at empty building lots or houses for sale, Dad puttered in the yard or cellar, and took Mom and Granddad grocery shopping (Granddad didn't own a driver's license.

Neither did Mom.)

"Stagnant," I thought of their life and mine that spring of '56.

Another difference between my friends and me was that I was an only child. Skip, of course, was Liz's younger brother; Jack MacAdams the oldest of three sons. Most of our soon-to-be sophomore class had brothers and sisters. Not me. When I was five or six I had asked my parents if I could have "a little brother." Surprised, they had laughed. "We'll see," my mother's answer. When I was twelve I approached my only-childness again. My mother explained the reason: a heart murmur. Her doctor had advised her after I was born that it was best she did not become pregnant again.

The irony of the heart murmur was that, prior to her marriage to Dad, my mother had been one of the strongest athletes in Lorrence High School history; she had varsity lettered in field hockey, basketball, and swimming. Field hockey and basketball now in her past, she swam laps without stress every summer, every time she and Dad went to local Halcyon Lake. Except for a once-a-year common cold, she remained healthy.

And so I was by myself. It didn't bother me. I had friends. I wasn't lonely. Being an only child was as normal as B's and C's in five major subjects on my report card. I did achieve A status but Phys. Ed. was not a major subject.

Lawn sprinklers, front doors open, no one in the doorways, no one on porches. *Anybody home?* Same as last year, same as the year before that. Predictable, safe. That's what I thought of Lorrence, the town where I had lived since I was born and where streets were named after trees and dead presidents. That's what I thought of the neighborhood where I lived as I walked home from church that Sunday. And I knew what to expect at home.

Skip didn't know what to expect when he woke up every day.

This morning Mom and Dad ate toast and drank coffee at the kitchen table and scanned the *Philadelphia Sunday Bulletin*--Mom the "South Jersey News," Dad comics and "Sports." Granddad had joined them. I was glad to see him. Now I had an excuse not to drop in on him today. More time for me to check in with Skip.

Granddad lifted a cup of tea to his mouth and made a sucking sound as he drank. "Ahh," he said and raised his eyebrows. "Good hot tea on a hot morning. Idn't that right, Davy?"

"Guess so," I replied, noting that on this hot morning Granddad wore his standard summer outfit: long-sleeve white shirt—cuffs folded back over the wrists--, navy blue slacks, and brown and white wing-tip shoes. I had never seen Granddad—my mother's father—in a short-sleeve dress or sport shirt or a polo shirt. Even now in retirement, on a warm summer morning, he dressed as a casual professional.

My mother pushed back the sleeves of her pink terrycloth robe. Her chestnut brown hair hung in limp waves over her forehead and ears. Her slippers scuffed the linoleum floor when she handed me a plate of scrambled eggs and bacon.

Good protection from cream sherry on my breath.

Before I sat at the table I switched on the radio on the counter near the stove.

"Many in church?" Dad asked, not taking his eyes from the exploits of Dick Tracy.

"About seventeen." I jounced my left leg in sync with Fats Domino's "I'm in Love Again."

"You and Mom going to Eleven o'clock?" I asked my father.

She continued to read the paper. Dad turned to 'Beetle Bailey.' "I don't think so," he concluded. "I want to get some things done around here."

"How come you and Mom don't go but I had to?"

It didn't get an answer. I knew it wouldn't. I just had to let them hear a jibe of my quest for independence from church.

To myself I smirked at his outfit of a white T-shirt and khaki shorts that couldn't hide his thin arms and legs. Dad wasn't muscular, his body wiry like a coiled spring. He could throw a spiral pass and a medium speed fastball down the middle.

"What about you and Mom go house-hunting today?"

"David, turn that down, please?" my mother asked looking at the radio. "Or find something nice we can all listen to."

I shifted the dial from Fats to Jo Stafford singing "You Belong to Me."

"That's better," Dad said. "I couldn't understand a word that other guy was singing."

I returned to house-hunting: "What do you think? Look for a house?"

My father's expression signaled he realized my impatience. "Maybe…We'll see. It may not be the right time, though," he said.

"So when'll be the right time?" I asked.

His eyebrows hooded.

Granddad saved Dad and, probably, me. He leaned his left elbow on the table, cupped his chin in his right hand, and asked, "What can you do to that music you had on there, Davy?"

"Dance to it."

"You ever dance to it?" he said.

I felt myself blush. I didn't like being pinned down with questions about music or dancing, but because Granddad, one of the nicest older men I've ever known, had asked the question I replied, "Once in a while."

"Now *that* I'd like to see sometime," he laughed, a mix of hisses and chuckles, softer than Nana's laugh. I wondered if he ever thought about Nana's laughter.

My mother put a slice of buttered toast on her plate. "Granddad's got a favor to ask you," she said, another change in subject that saved Dad from my curiosity.

Not another chore, I thought.

Just by her tone and raised eyebrows I caught the idea that the favor was something I must do today. *No thanks. No interruption to my plans today.*

I wolfed down scrambled eggs and took a bite of bacon. "What?" I said.

"Don't talk with your mouth full," Dad reminded me.

"Mmm. *What?* Skip and I might take a bike ride," not quite a lie, not quite the truth.

Granddad winced. I didn't want to take back what I had said, only how I had said it.

"It doesn't have to be today, Davy," Granddad added. "Just whenever you have the time."

I continued to set a fast pace with the scrambled eggs and bacon.

"I've got some photographs to show you," he explained. "They're kind of special...Nana, your mom when she was just a little thing, and some people I don't think you've ever met. I'd just like you to take a look at them, keep'em for a while. They'll be yours someday anyway."

I didn't say yes, didn't say no. I just wasn't in the mood to look at pictures. It wasn't because I didn't love Nana. I just didn't want to remember her when she was dying last winter. It was almost summer now. Time for doing whatever I felt like doing, even if it was absolutely nothing.

"Maybe one've these days soon?" Granddad asked.

"I guess," I said.

Granddad finished his tea. Before he left, he patted me on the shoulder and said, "You have fun with your friend today."

Quiet returned to the table. While I finished breakfast I wished someone else would talk. Dad switched from comics to sports; the pages slapped as he turned them. My mother washed and rinsed dishes at the sink. Dad scowled, his eyebrows close together. What was coming? Phil Harper was even-tempered most of the time. Dissatisfied with my grades or one of my flippant remarks, his complexion reddened. I loved my father, but I wanted him to be more than he was. Jack MacAdams' father was a lawyer. I wanted Dad to be more than a bank teller.

His complexion reddened now, and he bit his lower lip.

I pushed back my chair and stood up.

"Stay here," he said, an order, not a request.

"What?"

"Sit down."

"What'd I *do*?"

"Sit *down*,' I said!"

I did as I was told.

He folded the sports section, placed it between us on the table, and smacked the front page. "What do *you* think?" he said.

"About what?"

"You don't know, do you."

"*What?* All I did was sit here and eat breakfast. What the heck's wrong with that?"

My mother dried her hands on a dish towel and let it fall on the plastic strainer next to the sink. She pushed her bathrobe sleeves toward her elbow. "The way you spoke to Granddad, and the way you're talking now," she said.

"What'd I say that's so wrong? I said I'd look at the pictures."

"The *way* you said it."

She was serious, but her calm, firm voice wasn't angry like Dad's.

"We don't ask you to do much around here," he said, a familiar argument. "And quit that wise-guy attitude right now. It's about time you showed more consideration for us and Granddad. The way you looked when he asked a favor of you, you looked like you couldn't have cared less about something special to him."

I didn't answer. I didn't want to.

"Don't you ever, *ever* act that way in front of him again. You've got a few things to remember about being polite."

I wanted to stare them down. Maintain control. Instead, I stared at the edge of the table where perforated tips of the sports pages pointed at me. I'd see Granddad soon, when I was ready. In my own good time.

I burned to say more: I didn't want to be an acolyte anymore. I didn't want to do this damn chore and that damn chore the minute they wanted it done. I'd get things done when I *damn well felt it*.

Mom switched off the radio and put away plates and juice glasses in the cabinets, the sounds of porcelain on porcelain and glass on shelves like warnings.

Dad let out a breath. He sat back in the chair; signs his anger had passed. He narrowed his eyes and calmly asked, "Has Ralph Malloy ever offered you a drink, David?"

"You mean beer?" I asked.

"Beer, wine, hard stuff? Has he?"

"No."

I had to be on guard. I had to protect myself and Skip, *especially* Skip. The only time his house was probably quiet was when hand Liz and their parents were asleep.

My father's face seemed to shift from worry to curiosity. His tone indicated a man-to-man talk with me. My mother folded her arms and leaned back against the sink counter. She watched, listened.

"Has Skip offered you anything?" Dad asked me.

"Skip? No."

"Does Skip drink?"

I waited a couple beats: "No."

My father sought a silent opinion from my mother, as if she would verify my answer.

"What's goin' on?" I asked both of them. "Why all the questions?"

"Has Mr. Malloy ever yelled at you? Gotten rough with you?"

No, my imagined truthful self replied, but he probably had too much to drink Friday night.

"No," I said. "He gets a little loud sometimes, but…"

"What do you mean?" Dad asked, his dark eyebrows worming closer to each other.

"Yells at Skip…sometimes Liz and Mrs. Malloy."

Dad glanced again at my mother. He bit the right corner of his lower lip. His voice gentled when he said, "Be careful, David. You tell us if Ralph Malloy *ever* offers you anything other than iced tea or soda, or if he tries to do anything he shouldn't. Tell us."

"What about Mrs. Malloy?" my mother asked. "Does she seem all right when you're there?"

"Yeah, she seems all right."

More to herself but clear enough for Dad and me to hear, my mother said, "I wish I could help Helen Malloy—"

Dad looked at the floor between himself and my mother. "You're better off staying out of it, Grace," he said.

"I feel sorry for her."

"So do I but—"

"Stay outta what?" I asked them.

"Never mind," Dad said to me.

"Thanks. That really helps."

What did Mom and Dad know about what went on at the Malloys'? *They must know something I don't know about.*

"What about Mrs. Malloy?" he asked again.

He waited. I waited.

"I've told you: That's all I know," I said, and shifted in my chair at the admission of the lie.

My mother then said something I never expected: "We don't want you going to Skip's house anymore…Not for a while, at least."

"*Why?*"

"We're concerned about what might be going on over there," Dad explained. "We don't think it's good. We don't want anything to happen to you."

"I'm not a *baby*. I can take care of myself."

"It's for your own good," Dad said. "Mom and I have talked it over. Be friends with Skip, he's welcome here, we just don't want you going over there for a while."

"So what do I tell him? 'My parents say your house is off-limits'? Come on. It's not fair."

"Tell him to meet you here," my mother said.

"So how long's 'a while'?"

"We'll see," Dad said.

"I've heard that before."

Upstairs I used the phone on my parents' night-table to call Skip's number. No answer.

I changed into jeans, T-shirt, sneakers. Not telling Mom and Dad where I was going, I rode to Skip's house. The Malloy black Ford was not in the driveway. No one answered my knocks at the back or front doors.

I relieved my frustration and worry and pumped my Schwinn west of town limits into Lenape Township. Not the same roads Skip and I had followed the day before. Today past the 18-hole Lorrence Country Club, where my parents had attended parties and dances before I was born. Mom and Dad hadn't been members of the country club then, they weren't members now. Maybe because of the expensive dues, maybe they didn't see themselves as part of the country club set. It didn't matter; neither of them had swung a golf club since I was in kindergarten.

A mile beyond the country club to a grove of birch and oak trees where a murder had occurred one summer night five years before. I braked, pulled off the sandy shoulder and stopped at the rutted trail into the grove. A seventeen-year-old girl walking home from her job as a diner waitress had been abducted, brought to this grove, raped, tied to a tree, and strangled to death.

Was it the birch tree at the end of the path about twenty yards in? Is that where it happened?

I had seen newspaper pictures of the crime scene. I had read articles about the girl, a high school junior about to start her senior year; her father a farmer, mother a housewife, a younger brother and two younger sisters. On the radio and in newspapers I had followed the manhunt, seen pictures of the accused murderer, a 23 year-old "handyman" from Camden. "Hello, Mother," it was reported he had "mouthed silently" to the woman in the first row behind him and his defense lawyer. The accused murderer did not make eye contact with his victim's family and relatives. Hearing the guilty verdict, the man's mother shrieked and wept. He remained "passive" as he was led from the courtroom. Three months later he was pronounced dead in the electric chair at Trenton State Prison.

Could Ralph Malloy be a rapist and murderer? Could Lorraine Wyles be his victim? I asked myself that afternoon on that quiet country road where, a mile away, golfers teed off, putted, and compared scores.

Maybe Lorraine Wyles already was a victim. So was Skip. So were Mrs. Malloy and Liz.

I pushed off, the grove of trees behind me like a setting for a picnic, not a murder.

On my way back to Lorrence I passed a farm Skip and I had not biked by in our fury the day before. A man steered a tractor out of a barn; a little boy, maybe five or six years old, sat smiling, apparently giggling, on the man's lap. As I pedaled home, and as I tried to fall asleep that night, I thought about that boy and his apparently natural joy. I wanted to be that happy kid protected by his father's arms.

PART II: WATER AND SPIRITS

5

Halcyon June

Skip and I chain-locked our bicycles in the Halcyon Lake bike rack.

"Shirley here?" he queried me about the most beautiful girl in our sophomore class.

"We'll find out," I said good-naturedly. I scouted the beach crowd. "Maybe she's still eating lunch."

"I wish she'd make *my* lunch."

"You wish."

"So do you, numbnuts."

School year finished, we were officially sophomores ready and eager to play at Halcyon Lake on a warm and bright June afternoon, the sun pricking warmth on our backs.

Halcyon was Lorrence's only lake, thumb-shaped and safe at the end of a two-mile, tree-shaded bike ride from Skip's house. A good leg-stretch along Crosstown Avenue—past Lorrence High School, through the Crosstown – Park Street downtown intersection, under Crosstown's canopy of elms and oaks, and past Hobe's Ice Cream & Sandwich Shop across from the lake, and over the Crosstown Bridge, a thirty-five-foot drop to Halcyon's spillway into Lenape Creek below the bridge.

Today our goal was the same as last summer's: admire the female scenery, especially Shirley Brackett, brunette goddess of our sophomore class.

Towels over our shoulders—Skip and I in a white tee shirts, he in navy blue swim trunks, me in red and white small checked trunks—we walked from tree-shade to the wide sun-bright curve of Halcyon's beach.

"How's Lizzie?" I asked.

Skip explained that she was now living in an apartment two blocks from the Ocean City boardwalk and the restaurant where she was a waitress. He was grateful she had moved to the Shore. "Mom and me—we miss her, but at least she won't have any more tug-of-wars with the old man," he said. "He doesn't like her being out of the house but he can't do anything about it. She's a big girl now. He'll just have to put up with it."

Packs of our fellow Lorrence High School population had already staked out territory on the sun-baked beach and on the tee—a 45' by 35' anchored wooden platform fifty yards from shore. Shirley Brackett—queen of last fall's inaugural Freshman Fling and the object of practically every guy's lust—sat with the Taggart twins on a blanket about five yards from the life-guard chair. Shirley wore a white bathing suit sleek as a Ford Thunderbird. When she saw Skip and I approach, she crossed her legs. My eyes dipped to the bathing suit's little white triangle where her legs came together. The freckle-faced Taggart twins, Melinda and Janice ("the Back-ups," Skip and I had coined them), shared a plastic container of sun tan lotion. Hal Chauncey, Lorrence High School's varsity football quarterback, presided in the chair.

"...and sitteth at the right hand of God," I thought as Skip and I planted our towels and butts a yardstick away from Shirley and the Back-ups. He removed his glasses, slid them inside an eyeglass holder, and wrapped the holder in a corner of his towel. Chuck Berry chugged through "Maybeline" on the portable radio among them. Wherever Shirley went, Melinda and Janice were sure to follow. The Taggart sisters were not identical twins; Melinda brown-haired, Janice reddish blond. Melinda the quiet, Janice the social. Skip and I fantasized about Shirley. We didn't drool over the Back-ups.

"Hi ya'll," Skip greeted them.

No answer.

To the girls and Chauncey, Skip and I were peons. In their provincial brains we required permission to swim and enjoy the sun. When Chauncey saw Skip, the-worshipped-by-females lifeguard turned his half-responsible gaze back to young swimmers in the roped-off kiddie area.

Shirley and the Back-ups huddled together, skidded looks at us again, and showed us their backs, not their fronts.

Undefeated, Skip persisted. "How's the water?"

"Wet," replied a Back-up.

Shirley finger-combed her hair and adjusted a strap of her bathing suit. As she tugged the strap, her right breast jiggled.

"I guess borrowing your radio is out," Skip said to Back-up Melinda, who pretended to search for something in her beach bag.

"You guess right," she said.

"Thanks," his sarcasm hot as the sand under our feet.

"You're welcome," Melinda Taggart replied.

Janice the social scolded her sister "You didn't have to say it like that." Melinda the quiet retaliated: "Mind your own business, creep."

More of the same crap for Skip, I thought.

"I'm goin' out to the tee," I said to him.

Not many kids at Lorrence High School liked Skip Malloy. Even though he wasn't the new kid in town anymore, his cartoonish face, thick glasses, and wise-guy attitude worked against him. I was one of his few friends, perhaps his only friend.

Freshman class president Jack MacAdams had asked me at my locker one day last fall, "How come you hang around with that wise-ass jerk?"

I felt threatened, challenged. In front of honor roll student and three-sport athlete MacAdams, I wanted to match his control and confidence.

"He's a friend," I had said, proud I had defended Skip.

MacAdams had slid his eyes away from mine, had shaken his head (His brown hair fell like curled wool over the middle of his forehead), and walked away: dismissive actions of someone who strode the halls of Lorrence High School assured in his own skin.

My skin wasn't as tough as Jack MacAdams' skin.

I jogged to the water, waded in to my knees, dove and stayed under in the hollow-sounding wavy dark for about thirty seconds. I broke through the surface and strong-armed toward the tee—the floating, bobbing playground minus adult supervision. Not that we needed any. The tee fulfilled two purposes for LHS students on summer vacation: we caught up with friends and lay open for summer tan. Today Jack MacAdams and Guy Ross, MacAdams' compatriot, played one of their manly games: stalk and towel-slapping each other while hop-stepping over couples interested in the sun and in each other. I did not see Lorraine among the tee's crowd.

"Do you have to do that here?" complained one girl, shading her eyes.

"Yeah, we do," laughed Ross. He turned to snap his towel against the girl's bottom. MacAdams shouldered him into the water.

"Hey Harper," Jack greeted me as I climbed onto the boards. He yanked his foot away from Guy Ross's hand creeping like a spider up over the edge of the tee.

MacAdams asked me why I was a no-show for Babe Ruth League baseball this summer.

"Decided to take time off and rest my bat." I tried to laugh off his question without telling the truth. I had known at last summer's season's end what the score was for me: two years of bench-warming until the last couple of innings, more ground balls to the infield than base hits, more strike outs than walks. My spike shoes were still shiny when I had dumped them in my closet.

Guy Ross gripped the tee's edge with both hands and spouted water on our feet, an action that saved me more embarrassment in front of MacAdams.

"Ross, you idiot!" MacAdams grinned, straight white teeth in a yearbook smile. Legs together, he arrowed into the lake feet first.

"Beat you across," Ross challenged him, blond crew-cut slick to his scalp.

"Naa! Saving my strength."

Guy Ross dared people. He would swim towards the center of Halcyon until the lifeguard's whistle shrieked him back to shore. He would sneak out at night and roam streets on his bicycle "just to see what this dull burg's like at night." On one of his after-midnight adventures he had thrown stones at my window until I woke up.

"Come on out, Harper!" he had challenged me.

I had refused, afraid of my parents' reprimand if they discovered my empty bed.

"Chicken," Ross had sneered at me at school the following Monday. "Mommy an' Daddy's boy."

Since that night I regretted turning down Ross's dare. Consequently, I felt the same way around him as I felt with MacAdams: inferior.

Ross's smile displayed a symbol of another past adventure: his left front tooth chipped from a spill on the Thomsen Elementary School metal fire escape during a fire drill. Skip had thumped down the iron stairs directly behind Ross; Ross had accused Skip Malloy of pushing him. Skip had always denied it.

"I never touched Ross," Skip had told me as we walked to his house that afternoon three years ago.

I had walked ahead of Ross in the drill line. I believed Skip.

Now Ross jerked his head, one-handed gripped the tee, and wiped water from his face. "Malloy, you asshole, get the hell away from me!" He kicked out with his legs.

Skip brashed to the surface, shook water from his head like a dog, and held to the tee with one hand.

"Warning you, Malloy: keep your friggin' hands off." Ross turned to me as a witness against Skip." How come you hang around with that prick?"

"He's my friend." I gripped the edge of the tee with one hand. I dared Ross to come up and stand face-to-face with me: "You don't like it, tough. Come on: I'll smash your mouth right now."

"Some other time," Ross replied, smiling.

Ross and MacAdams stroked to the side of the tee closest to the beach. Over his shoulder Ross accused "Alky!"

Skip slithered out of the water and sat next to me. He gritted his teeth. "Sonova bitch Ross."

"Not a good idea, whatever you did," I said.

"You heard what he called me. Sonova bitch'll be sorry someday."

"I'll be glad to take a few swings at him myself." I tried to divert his attention away from trouble. "How's Shirley?"

He squinted toward the beach. "Hot for Chauncey. He asked her to file his toenails. Fool, she did it."

"There's always the Back-ups," I said, figuring, too, I was nobody in Shirley's eyes. Hal Chauncey had it made.

"Snobs. Last year one of those carpenter's dreams turned me down when I asked her to a CYO dance… Looked at me like I was scum."

"Maybe she was trying to tell you something, Malloy."

I didn't recognize the male voice and didn't survey the tee's population for the speaker. This afternoon I wanted no more threats. My stomach turned in on itself.

"Yeah, Malloy," said a girl's voice. A second girl chimed in "Yeah, Malloy," followed by another boy: "Yeah, Malloy."

Skip waited until the laughter died down. He closed his eyes for a long moment, then opened them. Holding his right hand close to his chest so that no one but me could see, he raised the middle finger and said, "Forget this shit. I'm going back."

I followed him. The applause behind us drove my arms hard for the beach.

We made sure our bikes' tires had not been deflated (It had happened last summer twice; possible witnesses "didn't see anything," culprits suspected, never accused), then we bought Cokes at the refreshment stand. Side-by-side we sat on the cloddy grass beyond the beach sand and leaned back against a shady poplar.

Skip put his glasses back on, swigged his soda and blew train whistle notes on the bottle's open end. "The old man calls this stuff 'rust remover.'"

I remembered something Skip had described to me on our ride to Halcyon. "What happened to the living room wall?" I had asked him.

He had snickered. "The old man pushed my head through it."

"*What*? You serious?"

"No. Come on…No…We were moving furniture," he had said, as if he was telling a story. "I just elbowed the wall too hard, that's all. I'll patch it when I get home."

Now Skip dug into both side pockets of his bathing suit and pulled out two kiddy-size medicine bottles. Both contained a tannish-gold liquid.

"Try somma this." He inched closer to me, uncapped one bottle, and poured the contents into my Coke bottle.

"What is it?" I asked.

"Scotch whiskey. Puts hair on your chest."

"What the hell? Where'd you *get* it?" I scanned parents nearby watching their children and talking with other mothers and fathers. For now, we were safe.

"The old man's favorite hiding place." He checked for spies left and right. "What the hell," he said and poured the contents of the other bottle into his Coke. "Here's to us." He drank more than a sip.

"To us," I said, and followed suit.

"Whud' ya think?"

"Not bad." I took another drink. "Strong."

"Supposed to be, numbnuts. You'll live."

He saw the question and challenge in my eyes. "Why the hell not. Be*cause*! Come *on*, nothing's gonna happen. Drink up!"

We studied the tee. Faces alive with smiles, frowns, or near sleep. Kids I had known from kindergarten and first grade. Kids who had tolerated Skip since fourth grade when he was 'the new kid,' kids who despised him. Kids who seemed to like me. Not a damn one of them knew we had just finished off a scotch and Coke, a dare none of them knew about.

"Feeling anything?" Skip asked.

I grinned. "I'm okay." Maybe I was, maybe I wasn't. Stomach warm, not queasy, not ready to vomit. Whatever was down there—bacon, scrambled eggs, toast, and this new-to-my-system beverage—was in negotiations to either stay a while or leave via one of two outlets.

Good thing Mom and Dad aren't here, I said to myself. I'd probably be jailed at home for the rest of the summer.

My father had given me a taste of beer on my fifteenth birthday this past spring. My mother hadn't voiced objection. "Better you have it in front of us," she had reasoned, "than you sneak it behind our backs."

The beer had tasted bitter. Mom and Dad weren't upset when I told them so. I didn't confess I had liked the taste of sherry better than beer.

"You really like this?" I asked Skip, tilting the Coke bottle toward him.

"Goes down all right," he replied.

"Your dad mix Scotch with anything?"

"Lighter fluid." He nudged my chest. "Just kidding, numbnuts. Just kidding. Sometimes he mixes, sometime drinks it straight." He looked at moms and dads in beach chairs, at kids digging in the sand and in the roped-off kiddie area…Liz, not their parents, had accompanied Skip to Halcyon before both of us were twelve and allowed to be on our own here.

I returned our own not quite empties to the refreshment stand. Skip wrapped his fingers around the empty little medicine bottles and dropped them one at a time in a trash barrel next to the bicycle rack.

My legs felt warm, feet swollen and fuzzy. "My feet aren't growing fur, are they?" I asked Skip when we walked back to our towels. I immediately laughed loudly.

He knelt on the clods of grass, peered at my feet and toes. "No. I see no sign of growth here. You need coffee to sober up. I'll buy."

He bought two coffees black at the refreshment stand. I stood by and stifled my giggles.

"Easy does it, numbnuts. You'll get us arrested you don't quit that stupid giggling. Drink your coffee."

I drank the ten-cent black. It wasn't the first time. Wouldn't be the last time I'd try to sober up, not that I was flat-out smashed. Only a fuzzy bit. No pink elephants. Over the next half hour my furry feet lost their fur, my sliding stomach settled down, and my "stupid giggling" stopped. The coffee slid a weird sensation into my head: I watched myself finish what was left in the cup. I felt time pass in slow motion. As the sun pricked through the skin between my shoulder blades, I watched myself stretch out and look out toward the tee.

"You back to reality now? Whud you wanna do?" Skip asked.

"No more Scotch."

Skip blessed himself—hands folded prayer—and bowed his head. "Bless me, Father, for I have sinned," he said in his usual voice. "I have led my best friend David Harper astray. I gave him an alcoholic beverage, which seemed to make his feet grow fur.

"Say three Hail Marys," Skip continued in a stern low voice. "Thou shalt not give your friend anymore Scotch, but buy me a bottle of that good stuff next time you're someplace where you can buy booze. Forget Lorrence. It's dry. Here's a ten. Bring me the change."

I har-harred at his little skit. My mind floated to the hard blue sky, the warm Halcyon sand, and to an older girl I still had a crush on. "Any news from Liz?"

"Not much. She likes her job, likes her friends…"

"You think she'll come home soon?"

He snickered. "Maybe to do laundry, if she knows the old man's not gonna be here."

We looked out at the tee. Voices from there seemed as far away as picnic grounds on the other side of the lake.

I wanted to swim out to the tee. I wanted to lay beside Shirley Brackett, see the swell of her breasts cupped in the top of her white bathing suit. I wanted to stare at where her legs came together. I'd look, nothing more. Nothing like what Mr. Malloy did.

I wanted Guy Ross to challenge me, wanted to dive from the tee and swim across the lake as far as the spillway, swim back, heave myself up onto the tee, and have Ross shake my hand. I wanted to have Shirley Brackett put her arms around me and say, "What a great swim, David! I'll go out with you." I wanted to walk her home, have her invite me inside (Her parents would be out.). We'd stretch out on the sofa. "*It's all right, nobody else is home,*" she'd whisper. "*It's all right.*" She'd tickle my neck with her fingers the way she did when she danced with Hal Chauncey. "*Does that feel good, David? I want you to feel good.*"

And I wanted Skip to have a day without insults. A day without worry about anything.

Shirley and the Back-ups splashed into the water, giggled like five-year olds, and swam out to the tee, Shirley in the lead, the Back-ups paired behind her like ducklings.

"My head's tired," I mumbled to Skip. "My mouth's dry."

"Come on, numbnuts. Sober up."

We gathered our towels. "What're you doin' tonight?" he asked.

"Don't know. Watch TV, I guess. How about you?"

It was his parents' wedding anniversary, he said. His mother and father would go out for dinner. Skip mocked the notion of a happy anniversary.

"They're going out? Are you kidding?"

"Far as I know. We'll see what happens."

Skip slung his towel over his shoulder and said, "Nothin' much doin' here. Let's go." I did not follow Skip to his house. I didn't want to risk an encounter with Mr. Malloy.

———————

Dad was mowing the backyard when I got home. He and Mr. Malloy were around the same age—their early forties—but my father, in tan Bermuda shorts, white T-shirt, sneakers minus socks, still looked as youthful and athletic as the quarterback, pitcher, and first baseman Phil Harper pictured in the Lorrence High School yearbook,: head cocked in a smile, pigskin tucked under one arm; one foot on first base, body stretched, arm extended, glove ready for the ball. *He's out!*

When he saw me lean my bicycle against the side of the house, he halted the push mower and called out "Hey, you wanna have a catch?"

"Sure!"

After the World Series had ended last fall, my father, Skip, and I had tossed a football in the backyard. Now I couldn't remember when Dad and I had pulled on our baseball gloves and thrown a baseball.

I brought down my ball and glove—'Robin Roberts' inscribed on the tan leather heel—from my bedroom closet, while Dad grabbed his old and scarred fielder's mitt from a storage bin of bats and balls and a football inside the back screen door. He jogged in tight short steps to his usual spot in front of the lilac bushes at the deep end of the yard, 60' 6" from where I stood, a bald spot ten feet from the back steps.

I shook my head to clear away the last of scotch-induced fuzzies, then lobbed the first pitch to him. He caught it one-handed in the pocket of his glove. He smiled, rocked back, strode out on his right leg, and delivered a medium-speed fast ball. I snagged it shoulder high in the web of my glove.

"You still got it, Dad. You gonna play in the Old Timers' game this year?"

"Ha! I'm out of shape for that."

"Wouldn't take you long to get back in. It'd be fun to see you pitch again."

The last time Dad had pitched for the Lorrence Old Timers was eight summers before. I was seven. My mother, Granddad and Nana (My grandparents were spry then and certainly knew their baseball), and I had watched that game from wooden bleachers along the third baseline at Morgan Field, Lorrence's Babe Ruth League and American Legion teams' home turf. Before the recording of "The Star Spangled Banner" had sounded over the PA system, Granddad had nudged my shoulder. "Phil Harper throws three speeds, Davy," he chuckled. "Slow, slower, slowest."

He was right. Dad threw three innings of off-speed fastballs, slow curves, and change-ups, stuff that looked easy to hit; stuff the first six Forgeville Old Timers nearly screwed themselves into the dirt trying to hit solid line-drives that wound up strike-outs or infield grounders.

That's what Dad threw to me now. That's why I didn't have to move a yard and a half to snag his pitches. My father's easy and lazy motion expressed he wasn't worried about anything in the world. The sunlight shading through the trees in the yard behind ours put him in a glow, as if he was a special personality.

"Do you miss it?" he asked me after he threw me a slow curve.

"Miss what?"

"Playing ball."

"I didn't play that much."

I threw him a pitch with two years of frustration in youth baseball on it. The ball slammed the pocket of his glove. He winced and lobbed the ball back to me.

"Build up your arm and get it shape. You'll do fine."

"I'll get in shape for football, not baseball," I said.

"Swimming'll build up your wind for football."

For ten minutes we had an easy catch; Dad in his slow, relaxed delivery, me in pitches that Little League and Babe Ruth teams had roped to the outfield and beyond.

"Good pitch," he said when I caught the inside or outside corner."

"I could've teed off on that one," I told him when one of his pitches cut the heart of an imaginary home plate. It was fun having a catch with my father again.

A black Ford—Ralph Malloy at the wheel—slowed in front of our house. Mr. Malloy hunched forward to peer at me. Spotting Dad behind me, he eased the Ford toward the corner one house away from ours at a calculated speed. At the corner he turned and drove out of sight.

At the bottom of the back steps Dad handed me my glove, the baseball in the pocket. I didn't realize I had dropped the glove on the grass. Dad held his fielder's glove in both hands.

"What was that all about?" he asked me.

Images swirled through my head. I didn't describe them to my father. I only said "I dunno," and went inside.

My mother was mixing potato salad at the counter when we came into the kitchen. In white shorts, a yellow polka dot sleeveless blouse, she looked youthful, as if she could swim Halcyon's width back and forth without rest. "Well, did you have a good time at the lake?" she asked me.

"It was okay."

She asked about Skip. He seemed all right, I told them. I didn't rat out my best friend, nor his father.

I didn't want to rehash the Mr. Malloy or Guy Ross situation, either. I just wanted to eat a hot dog, my mother's potato salad, sliced tomatoes, and go upstairs and listen to a ball game or some music. Anything to take my mind away from if and where and when I might encounter Ralph Malloy again.

Shirley on the beach, Shirley in a white bathing suit controlled my mind before I fell asleep. Radio off, evening dark beyond my windows, I imagined Shirley's curves beneath that suit...

Do You know what I'm doing? Maybe it's wrong but it doesn't feel wrong. A lot of boys do it. Skip does, and I do. It doesn't hurt us, it doesn't make us cross-eyed, it feels good, especially...

"Nobody's home, David. Just you and me. Let's lay down on my bed. There...You can touch me. There, yes...Does that feel good when I touch you? I want you to feel good...There...There. Yes...yes..."

6

Photographs and Fireworks

At noontime on Fourth of July, after the last band and float had lumbered by our front porch, Granddad, at ease in a wicker rocking chair, leaned toward me. The clip-on sunshades attached to the lenses of his regular glasses made his face appear pale. The cuffs of his long-sleeve white shirt were rolled back from his wrists. He rested his arms on his legs and folded his hands.

"I brought those pictures I told you about. What you say we take a look at'em."

I had agreed with Mom and Dad to keep Granddad company while they prepared for our annual "Fourth" backyard luncheon. I didn't want to be the reason for a "discussion" about my inconsideration, selfishness, and laziness. Granddad was good company when he didn't talk about missing Nana.

With both hands he carried two large gift-size boxes to my room, his footsteps slow and deliberate on the stairs. He wheezed as he set them on my bed.

"Up here's nice and quiet," he said. "Won't be in your mom and dad's way. Be back in a minute. Gotta see a man about a dog," his favorite expression for needing to use the bathroom.

He closed the bathroom door, but I heard his stream first trickle, grow stronger, and trickle again. Then, nothing, but enough time for me to wonder if he had become sick. Would I find him collapsed, sprawled on the floor?

The toilet flushed, water ran in the sink. In another minute he appeared at my door. One lens of his clip-on sunshades peeked above his shirt pocket.

"Not as fast as I used to be," he chuckled.

He studied my bedroom walls—my personal gallery of photos I had scissored from *The Sporting News* and *Sport Magazine*. "You put up a few more pictures. Willie Mays, huh? He's a future Hall of Famer. You wait and see."

"I'm not waiting, I think he is already." I wanted to sound as confident as he sounded, but I heard my wise-mouthed teenaged self again. I wished I could have said it differently.

"Could be, could be," Granddad said. He paused, and tilted his head back in front of a black and white picture of Richie Ashburn sliding into home plate. "Is that a real honest-to-goodness autograph? Did Ashburn really autograph this for you?" He peered at the signature.

"Got it last month," I said.

"How about that!" he smiled. "Good for you."

I had found the return, self-addressed stamped envelope in the mailbox. Mom and Dad had encouraged me to tell Granddad the good news. Now I felt ashamed I had kept the news to myself.

I wasn't sure if I should get off the bed and stand with him. He looked strange and alone and thin in his familiar stance--left arm across his chest, left hand cupped under his right elbow.

I felt trapped in my sanctuary. The pictures on my walls, the two boxes of pictures he had placed at the foot of my bed, and Granddad standing beside me now—everything too close. I didn't want to run out on Granddad; I didn't want to upset him or Mom and Dad anymore. I stayed.

"Here," Granddad said. He removed the lid of one box, drew out a newspaper-wrapped object, and slowly removed the newspaper. "This is Nana. It was taken a few days before we got married," he said. He didn't take his eyes away from the photograph. Neither did I. The woman in the bridal gown and veil became the woman who had put dollar bills in my birthday, Christmas, and Easter cards, had watched me play Little League baseball, and who had told me a few days before she died, "You study for those Algebra tests."

The woman in the bridal gown could have been my mother, I thought.

"I always said your mother looked just like Nana the day she married your dad." He cleared his throat and set the picture aside. He unwrapped another: a framed black and white photograph of Nana and Granddad; Nana in a polka-dot dress and holding a purse in both hands; Granddad in a double-breasted dark suit, white shirt, and necktie. In the background the United States Capitol. "That was taken the year before you were born...the year before the war started."

He unwrapped a third frame, a brownish-tinted photograph of a stiff unsmiling boy in a dark suit and high collar. "I'z about your age," he said, and reminisced about when he, a boy from Maryland visiting relatives in Pennsylvania, met Nana at a church picnic. Every weekend that summer he traveled by train to West Chester to see her: "To go a-courtin'," he grinned. The following Christmas he proposed to her, she accepted. Early spring that year they married. "That darn wool suit was the itchiest piece of clothing...made me squirm in church."

Voices called to each other now from downstairs. I heard the front screen door open and clack shut, and then Dad shouted a greeting to my aunts and uncles.

"Guess company's here," Granddad said. "You're gonna have other things to do."

He wrapped the framed pictures and put them back in the first box. He removed the lid of the other box and said, "In here's the old photo album you used to look at. I thought you'd like to have it."

"To keep?"

"Nana wanted you to have it. It's yours now." He closed the lid of the box and tapped it twice. "Well, that's that," he said. "You got company."

"You're gonna stay, aren't you?"

Later in the afternoon, after Granddad had finished Mom's angel food cake topped with whipped cream and strawberries, he stood up slowly from the backyard picnic table and said his thanks and goodbyes.

The protests of Mom and Dad and my aunts and uncles didn't change his mind.

"David, you walk Granddad out front," my mother said.

"I don't need a nurse, Grace," he protested.

"Thanks for the pictures," I said as Granddad and I reached the front sidewalk. I had been thinking that I had never seen a photo album in Skip's house. Nana and Granddad had kept one, so had Mom and Dad, theirs on the low shelf under the coffee table in front of the sofa.

"You're welcome, Davy."

"You going to the fireworks tonight?"

"Too crowded there for me," he replied, no harsh complaint. "I'll stay home and go to bed early. You have a good time for me. See you later."

He walked slowly to the end of the block. Now and then he hitched his left shoulder and crooked his head to the right as if he had a stiff neck. When he turned at the corner and went out of sight, I didn't return to the picnic table. I went inside, took the stairs two at a time to my room, and opened the photo album.

The first picture I saw was of Mom, Dad, and me on the Ocean City boardwalk. Nana's ink printing stared at me at the bottom of the photograph: "David, 3."

My father's hand holding mine, my squinting eyes toward the camera...I didn't want to see myself anymore as a child in need of anyone or anything. I snapped the album shut. Guilt knifed down through my chest. Guilt for more than slamming the cover on Mom and Dad.

Halcyon Beach hissed pinwheels, whistled twirls and sprays, and the thrum-crack-boomed rockets. After the big show, Skip and I jostled through the crowd on the Crosstown Avenue Bridge. Loud-muffflered Chevys and Fords shifted gears and chugged by. Skip hollered "Grind me a pound!" and "Check that fart!" Mothers and fathers gaped at us but kept on walking with their kids.

"Too loud for ya'?" Skip called to them.

One father swung around to face us. His shoes scraped sand on the sidewalk. To both of us the man said, "Too loud and impolite, the two of you. We've got children here."

"Congratulations! My compliments to you, sir," retorted Skip. "I'm sure they'll grow up to be model citizens." To me he urged, "Come on, numbnuts, let's cut through this crowd."

We jogged to Hobe's Ice Cream and Sandwich Shop. We maneuvered around kids—juniors and sophomores munching candy, puffing cigarettes, lolling around in general on the wooden plank steps. I expected wisecracks—*Hey, Alfred E., buy one for me!*—but no one gave challenge or slurred insults. We bought ice cream cones and sat on the upper step. Our company sneered over their shoulders, inhaled, and shuffled down the steps into a gray '50 Ford that took them away.

"Friendly sorts." Skip and licked the edge of his vanilla fudge cone.

"How'd the anniversary go?" I asked. Since that afternoon at Halcyon I had avoided mention of his father name-calling visit with me.

Skip kept his eyes on the car and pedestrian traffic. "Okay."

I looked at him, expecting him to add detail.

"I said *okay*, you jerk off. It was fine and dandy, shots and beer, just a wonderful happy anniversary. Many happy returns an' all that shit."

He gobbled more vanilla fudge and then, leaving at least two mouthfuls of it, fired the cone to the sidewalk: splat! Luckily no one was walking by.

"Stupid shit," he mumbled. "Don't sweat it, numbnuts, I didn't mean you."

I changed the subject. "I been thinking of trying out for football this year."

"Go ahead. Get your ass creamed."

"I prob'ly won't make it, not even jv, but—"

"Never heard of anybody being cut from Lorrence football, Harper."

An aqua-blue T-bird convertible slowed in front of Hobe's and idled at the blinker light. I didn't recognize the driver, had never seen that particular T-bird around town. A woman in a white dress sat beside the driver, the dress pulled above her knees, *creamy skin*…The driver revved the engine twice and then gunned the T-bird up Crosstown Avenue.

"Nice," I said and worked on my chocolate cone.

"So's she."

"Think they'll have a good time tonight?"

"More than you and me, for damn sure."

Hobe's screen door kicked open, rattled, and slapped shut.

"Well well, what do I see but Alfred E. and com-pa-ny. How's it hangin', Al?"

"Hard as ever, Zanger. How's yours?"

Jerry Zanger's local fame boasted being a nineteen year-old senior next September. He also drove—his buddies whooping and hanging out the passenger windows—a two-door maroon '53 Mercury he backfired in front of the Lorrence Police station as many nights as he felt like it.

Apparently alone tonight, Zanger clunked down one step, the cuffs of his jeans stuffed into ankle-high boots. He frowned at Skip.

My stomach tightened, as it had when Dad had quizzed me about Mr. Malloy's behavior.

Zanger leaned close to Skip's face.

"Need some help?" Skip asked.

"With what?"

"I dunno. You tell me."

"You think I need help?"

Zanger inched closer to Skip. I wondered what smell Skip caught on his breath.

The local outlaw waved his hand in front of his face. Then he leaned back and uttered, "Whew. S'at beer on your breath, Malloy?"

Skip squinched his eyes, hissed through his teeth, shook his head. "Just hard stuff. Too hard for you. You definitely need help, Zanger. Definitely."

Jerry Zanger sighed, puffed air through his lips, and straightened up. "You know, Malloy, you are one wise ass. Someday I'd love to smash your face in."

"I'll sell tickets," Skip said.

"See what I mean?" Zanger challenged me. "A little wise ass." He swung back to Skip. "Don't know when to keep your mouth shut. It's a big mouth, idn't it?" Zanger laughed, and clunked down the steps.

"Bastard," Skip whispered.

Less than a minute later the '53 Mercury, Zanger at the steering wheel, swerved around the corner and *wha-wha'd* in front of Hobe's front steps. "Someday, Malloy!"

"You bet!" Skip yelled back.

The driver saluted with a raised middle finger, the Mercury's *wha-wha* manifold ridiculed support.

Skip shouted "Your age or IQ, Zanger?" Then he mumbled "Bastards. Let's get the hell out've here."

––––––––––

The front porch light at Skip's house glowed yellow. Lamplight shone through a downstairs front window. A stranger's car, a light-toned Chevy, slouched in the driveway.

"Wonder whose that is," Skip said, and let himself in the front door.

I didn't go in with him. I heard the door's lock snap shut.

I stood guard ten yards away. The porch light blinked off. Laughter trickled from a neighbor's window, a voice across the street called out "In a minute!" Voices undisturbed, peaceful as maple leaves rustling above my head. I walked four steps away and listened. Nothing.

A young woman's shouts inside the Malloy house broke the peace. Her words as clear as the pictures from Granddad. "No! Get *off* me, Daddy, you dirty sonova bitch!"

Liz.

Fights sounds: furniture shoved, grunts, and "You stay away from her! You touch her again and you'll regret it the rest of your life. She's never coming back here,"—a man's voice I didn't recognize.

I waited. Where was Skip? The sobs I then heard must have come from Liz and Mrs. Malloy. I didn't hear Mr. Malloy, I didn't hear Skip.

The Arvidsons' front door opened. Either Mr. or Mrs. Arvidson—I think it was Mr.—leaned out toward the Malloys' and then spoke to someone behind him. I stood still, not wanting to draw attention to myself.

Mr. Arvidson stepped onto his front porch and walked to the sidewalk. Putting his hands on his hips, he looked in my direction and called out, "You know what's going on in there?"

"Not for sure," I replied softly.

"Doesn't sound good," said Arvidson.

A door clacked shut. The Malloys' back door.

I waited. No more sounds from the neighboring houses. No more sounds of a fight from Malloys'.

Silence: silence that made my stomach tense the way it felt when my mother had told me last spring that Nana wouldn't have long to live. Cold silence like the chill that had made me shiver the night of Liz's birthday party.

Maybe it was an hour, maybe only a few minutes. Mrs. Malloy, Liz, Skip, and a tall man walked out from the screened porch to the Chevy. The man carried a bundle he tossed into the back seat. Mrs. Malloy and Liz put their arms around each other. I couldn't hear exactly what they were saying. I only heard sniffles.

"Are you *sure* you don't want me to stay?" the tall man said to Mrs. Malloy and Skip.

"I'll be all right. You two go. I know what I have to do."

"Mom, please?"

"Skip will be here with me, honey. Now, go."

The tall man walked around to the driver's side and got in. The start of the engine was the only sound on the street.

As I left my spot within the bushes, I heard "Helen?" and saw Mr. Arvidson walk across the street to Mrs. Malloy and Skip. Mr. Arvidson mumbled something I could not distinguish.

Mrs. Malloy shook her head no. Then she clearly said, "Thank you just the same."

"Helen, are you absolutely sure? Do you want me to call anyone?"

"No, don't do that, Walter. Things are all right now."

Skip mumbled words that sounded like disagreement with his mother.

Arvidson countered, "Look: if something else happens you can stay with Vivian and me, you know that."

"Skip and I will take care of things, we'll be all right," she said but had already begun to walk back to her house.

Skip stayed with his neighbor.

I did not hear any of what Mr. Arvidson said to him. I saw Skip nod and then return to the porch. Mrs. Malloy put her arms around him; together they walked into the house.

After perhaps a minute to two, Mr. Walter Arvidson crossed the street to his house. This time he went inside but did not close the door.

Home: I didn't feel like eating my usual night-time snack of Lebanon bologna sandwich and chocolate milk. My mother had waited up for me. She looked older tonight than she had while we had watched the parade. Maybe it was the pink terrycloth robe and pink slippers, or maybe because she wasn't wearing any lipstick that made her look over fifty when really she was only forty-two. She sat on the sofa two cushions away from me.

"How was Skip?" she asked.

I didn't know how to answer or what to say except, "Okay." I didn't want to describe the scene at Malloys'. Maybe later I might change my mind, maybe I'd tell Mom and Dad in the morning. Right then I wanted to stay in control, keep everything I'd seen and heard to myself to deal with it the best I could.

I changed the subject. "We going anywhere on vacation?"

"I don't know…Dad and I haven't talked about it yet. We'll see."

"We'll see" in those days meant that she and Dad would determine whether or not they could afford a week away, probably in Ocean City. Maybe we could drop in to see Lizzie, I thought. When school began again in September, I wanted to tell my friends I had been "someplace cool" on vacation.

"Could Skip come with us?" I asked.

My mother waited a second before she answered, raising her eyebrows, "Are the Malloys planning to go away this summer?"

"They never go anywhere." My stomach curled. Voices and sounds I remembered snarled in my memory.

My mother tightened the cord of her bathrobe. "That was nice what you did for Granddad today," she said. "Dad and I thought it was very considerate of you. What pictures did he show you?"

I described the framed photographs and the photo album.

"Take good care of them." She stood and turned toward the stairs. As a casual reminder she said, "Don't forget you're serving at eight o'clock tomorrow morning."

Religion was just the subject I didn't want to hear about. "Why do you and Dad go to church? What do you get out of it?"

Church doesn't help the people who really need it, I thought.

My mother stepped away from the stairs. Walking in slow steps toward me, her face inquisitive, her tone controlled anger, she said, "We go because we want to. We believe it's important."

"You and Dad really believe in God?" I wondered.

"Yes, we do."

She and I stared directly at each other like two opponents. I believed she had told me the truth. I wanted her to say more but didn't want her to spout off a bunch of commandments or a sermon. I wanted her to tell me something I had not heard before; something that sounded believable.

"I don't get it. God and heaven, and He's supposed to be almighty and see and know everything? Where the heck's the proof? Do you know where Nana really is?"

"I know she isn't in Hell, David. She was a good person. You know she was. I'm sure she's in Heaven."

"How do you know?"

"It's something I feel. You should, too." My mother wasn't close to anger now. She pulled her bathrobe cord tight again and sat beside me.

"I guess she's in Heaven," I said. "I don't like to think of her as just being in a cold grave."

"Neither do I. Her body's only one part of her. You know that. We've taught you about the soul. So has Father Hepplewhite and your Sunday School teachers. Nana had a good heart, she has a good soul, so we have to believe she's in a good place."

"How do you know she's really there? How do you know there's really a Heaven?"

My mother faced me. "I don't really know for sure if Heaven's there or not, David. I don't *really* know if Nana's there. I have faith she is. That's something you should have, too."

She sounded truthful and sincere, as if she believed every word she said. I didn't want to ask her anything more tonight about church. It would have been like trying to understand a language I knew nothing about.

"It's getting late," she said, patting my shoulder. "You should go to bed. You have to get up in time for church."

———————

Sunday afternoon Skip and I sat on the back steps of my house. He had stayed for dinner, we'd had a catch with Dad before my parents had gone to visit friends.

"Thanks for a good dinner, Mr. and Mrs. H," Skip had told them. "You two come home at a reasonable hour."

He said nothing more until they had driven away. Then Skip filled me in.

"Lizzie came back home to get some more summer clothes. This guy Marty drove her. The old man snored his head off as usual in the living room. Lizzie and Marty and Mom were talking in the kitchen, tryin' to be quiet…

"The old man woke up, came out to get a beer. He says, 'Who the hell's this guy?'

"Lizzie introduced Marty. Then it started: 'You takin' advantage of my daughter? Nobody does touches my daughter, nobody 'cept me.'

"What!"

"The old man tried to prove it and it got worse. Marty and me against the old man, and Lizzie shaking likes she's freezin' cold, Mom bawlin' her eyes out.

"The old man didn't last long. Marty and me threw him down the back steps. He slept outside, came in this morning."

"You mean your Dad—"

"That's right, numbnuts. It makes me wanna puke and cut his balls off."

At first I didn't know what to think, what to say. I knew some things about life—how life began and how and why people died. I had held my grandmother's cold hand the night she had died. I knew that my parents could not yet afford to buy a house, and I knew that I was still, deep down, embarrassed about it. And I knew that Jack MacAdams was popular because his parents had money, a nice house and swimming pool, and because he was class president and sported brown wavy hair like a young recording star. That's how things were in Lorrence. And I knew that Skip Malloy was not treated very well by a lot of kids because he wasn't good looking and because he acted like a wise guy. And Mrs. Malloy—What was it my mother had said to my father about her? Something about wanting to help her? And Mom felt sorry for her?

"Stay out of it," Dad had told her.

Stay out of it. Out of the mess of things. The mess that Ralph Malloy had made. And still making. The truth, I figured, was that Ralph Malloy was a man I could not trust anymore. No one should.

Skip squinted at our backyard and then stretched his neck side to side, as if he needed to loosen some muscles. He took some short breaths, swallowed, and then a deep breath.

"How's Lizzie?" I asked, in almost a whisper.

He rubbed the heel of his right sneaker on the concrete step. "Mom talked to her on the phone this morning. Okay for the time being. I don't think we'll see my sister for a long time. I told Mom either the old man leaves or she and I do. I don't know where the hell we'll go but somewhere."

7

Saturday Night Push and Shove

Skip strode like a soldier in cadence when I met him in front of Our Lady Queen of Heaven at the corner of Willowyn Terrace and Lorrence Boulevard. He only said "Let's go." He ignored the church.

I fell in beside him. Our destination: a dance at Sunrise Auditorium on the west side of Lorrence.

I kept pace a half step behind him. Our polished cotton khakis whisk-whisked as we walked up Lorrence Boulevard through the warm July twilight. Sunlight slanted into our faces through lower branches of oaks and maples on the lawns of older homes, the houses like mysterious rich people who didn't want to live close to the street. Long walkways led to empty porches.

All the while I flicked glances at Skip, waited for him to explain how things were at home.

He was tight-lipped.

Lorrence Boulevard crested at the railroad. We crossed the tracks and then cut left into Memorial Park. Old men on benches smoked cigarettes, puffed pipes, chatted about this 'n that, and gazed across the park's grass and walkways. In the center stood the Lorrence Roll of Honor, a tall, wood-trimmed glass case that displayed the names of World War I and II and Korean War deceased soldiers in white plastic letters on black felt. The summer I was seven, my father had walked me through the park to the Roll of Honor after a Fourth of July parade. He had pointed to the names of World War II veterans he had known and told me where they had been killed in action. "I want you to remember the names of these men," Dad had said to me that morning. "It's very important."

As I grew older I wondered if he regretted not being a soldier; if he regretted working at the shipyard in Philadelphia and handling a rivet gun instead of hefting an army or marine weapon. I could never think of the right words to ask him for fear of embarrassing him or making him angry.

Skip slowed his pace and bit his lip as we came out of the park and crossed Park Street to Long Avenue. Tears slid behind his thick glasses.

"What happened this time?" I asked him.

"Never mind." He reached into both side pockets of his khakis, pulled out two mini bottles of Cutty Sark, and handed me one. "Have one on the old man," he said.

"Where'd you find'em?"

"The cellar, up on a shelf behind his tool box. Drink up. Don't make a big deal out of it." He swung his head left and right as if he was avoiding a fly around his face.

We downed the contents in two swigs.

I squeezed my eyes shut. "Ow, that's *strong stuff*!"

"Puts hair on your chest and around your gonads, if you need some there."

"I'm fine, thanks." I coughed to clear my throat.

We began the four-block climb up Long Avenue to Sunrise Auditorium. "What happened? You okay?"

Skip looked straight ahead toward the top of the hill. "Never felt better. Well, maybe not. 'Cept for one of the old man's good-for-what-ails ya' left to the shoulder and a right to the ribs, I never felt better."

A duel-exhaust '52 Chevy and a '49 Ford gunned by us. Would Jerry Zanger chug and backfire by Sunrise Auditorium in his maroon Mercury?

We dumped our two empties in a trash barrel beside the auditorium steps, paid the fifty-cent admission for three hours of dance, food, and sodas. We walked onto the vein-like cracked concrete floor of Sunrise Auditorium, an airy, open-sided local landmark where the town Youth Counseling Committee sponsored summer dances for young people. Tonight the dance space showed a wide concrete garden of sun-tanned girls I had eyed at Halcyon's beach and tee, girls now in tight white, scoop-neck blouses or tight yellow blouses; wide skirts and tight skirts; boys with long blond or brown hair in slicked-back ducktails, cigarette packs in shirt pockets. Onstage at the far end a man at a table sorted packs of 45 RPM records, removed some from their sleeves, slipped them over a record player spindle. In the alcove left of the stage a group of men and women grilled hot dogs, stashed bottles of soda in a red cooler, and unwrapped cartons of candy.

"Any beer in the cooler up there?" I grinned to Skip.

"You kidding? In this dry burg? How dare you suggest such a thing! Better buy some gum to take away our Scotchy breath."

In empty lots on both sides of the auditorium, grade school-age kids played tag and tossed footballs. The humid summer night air felt like warm scarves and shirts around us.

I want to stay, I said to myself. *Stay a long time and not think about trouble. Slow dance with a girl and pull her close.*

"One two three o'clock, four o'clock rock..." shouted through the auditorium amplifiers: Bill Haley and his Comets had shot off the dance.

"Gonna be a good one tonight, my boy," Skip predicted in a near growl that echoed his father's sarcastic anger. "Shirley's back, and no Chauncey. Look over there."

Shirley Brackett stood near a roof support post, her aqua-blue pedal pushers tight as tubes, her white pullover top like a big marshmallow that showed off her Marilyn Monroe-like figure. Back-ups Melinda and Janice Taggart, like maids, stood beside her. I studied the slim curves of the Back-ups, the full curves of Shirley Brackett, and immediately imagined slow-dancing with Shirley, close enough to feel her warm cheek against mine, her breasts crushed against me.

One dance with her, I begged in my young lust. *Just one.*

Skip and I roamed the floor and checked out the rest of the crowd. Pencil-thin and barrel-fat seventh and eighth graders yacked and danced as if trying to imitate older brothers and sisters. Jerry Zanger and his honchos marched in behind the stag line; a row of outlaws as they leaned back against the metal railing connecting two roof support pillars. We kept our distance.

Reconnaissance complete, Skip and I stood about a first down away from Shirley Brackett.

"Here goes," said Skip when The Platters crooned "My Prayer" through the speakers.

Skip walked right up to Shirley.

I watched her withhold a smile as she told him "No thank you."

Arms-length away from me like deputies—I hadn't noticed them pay their way in—Guy Ross and Jack MacAdams winked at each other as if they loved a joke they had just overheard.

"Attaway, Malloy! There's a boy who knows what he wants," Ross nudged MacAdams. "What, him worry? Hey Alfie, get me tall cool one, will ya'?"

I debated personal retaliation against Ross: *Tell him to shut the hell up? Punch him in the mouth, knock out a front tooth?*

I did neither because I'd be tossed out of the auditorium, thus denied my chance to dance with girls of my choice, especially Shirley Brackett.

Skip walked Back-up Melinda to the dance area where he drew her close, her face and slim body touching the front of his shirt. She did not pull away.

What the hell, I thought, and promptly repeated the dance request to Shirley. Refused, I settled for Back-up Janice, her freckles like tiny islands on her face, and her arms sunburned pink. She had bunched her reddish-blond hair in a yellow ribbon. I steered Janice away from laughter while Elvis Presley wailed about wanting and needing the woman he loved.

"Having a good summer?" my first attempt at conversation.

"It's okay," she answered, her voice thin as her hand. "Are you?"

"Yeah, it's okay," I replied, wondering if my chewing gum had masked the scotch.

Halfway through the song, Jack MacAdams escorted Shirley to the dance floor. What would he dream tonight?

Janice and I avoided conversation in favor of slow-walk dancing. My right hand had detected through her blouse the clip of her bra. She didn't balk when I pressed my hand against her back; she came in against my chest, her breasts like little cushions without pins. "I Want You, I Need

You, I Love You" ended just as it would have become embarrassing for me to hold Janice any closer to me.

"Thanks," she smiled when I walked her back to her sister. Skip went on mission to the refreshment stand. Melinda regarded me with suspicion: what were my intentions toward her and her sister? I looked away.

Outside the auditorium the dusky sky shaded dark. Tag players and footballers shuffled to the sidewalk where they watched the dancers and admired our freedom to dance and stay out later than they would be allowed. Chopped and channeled hot rods chugged and growled by while "Be Boppa Lula" hiccoughed over the speakers.

For the next two hours I wandered and wanted. I concluded that root beer tasted better than Scotch but not as good as cream sherry. I wished the two hot dogs I had downed were cheeseburgers. I danced with Janice Taggart to "I Almost Lost My Mind" by Pat Boone, and "No, Not Much" by the Four Lads. Janice felt light and warm in my arms and didn't pull away when I pressed my hand on her back for her to step closer to me. Maybe she wanted to be right up against me, I thought. Maybe.

After Janice I tried to work up courage to dance with suntanned girls, who smiled and put their hands on the arms of junior and senior boys who smiled at them and swung them onto the dance floor. I fantasized how those girls would feel in my arms. Maybe they wanted to be as close to me as I wanted to be to them. They didn't. They turned me down; some with "No thanks," some with a shake of their head. Their rejections didn't bother me, though. What still bothered me was Mr. Malloy touching his daughter, the possibility of him doing the same with Lorraine Wyles, and Skip taking the brunt of his father's fists. Those touches and punches frightened me.

Janice didn't say no when I asked her to dance again.

"You gonna try somebody else besides the Back-up? Wearin' it out, aren't you, Harper?" asked Skip when we met later around ten o' clock.

I knew, as a lot of us did, that with Skip it was mostly talk. I knew of no girl who had gone out with him. Maybe that would change. Maybe he'd get lucky. Maybe we both would.

When I heard the piano lead-in to "Since I Met You, Baby," I scanned toward Janice and Melinda. They sat on the auditorium front steps. Were they waiting for a ride home? The hem of their skirts looked like a No Trespass border across their knees.

Meanwhile, Skip asked a black-haired girl I had never seen before to dance, her figure as curvy as Shirley's. They hadn't taken five steps when Jerry Zanger tapped him on the shoulder. Skip ignored him. Zanger tapped again, smiled, even bowed to the girl. She put her hand over her mouth and laughed, couples dancing by watching them. "You gonna," Zanger seemed to say to Skip, then shoulder-nudged Skip aside, took the girl in his arms, and danced away with her.

The look on Skip's face was the same one I had seen earlier that evening. More than anger, more than hurt, he carried it into the crowd where I lost sight of him. Let it go, I thought. It was all I could come up with. 'Let it go,' the only answer I had to questions that swirled again in my head.

"Since I Met You, Baby" faded into crowd conversation. Unanswered questions pressured around my shoulders as they had after Lizzie's birthday party. I walked the edge of the auditorium, hunted for Skip. Couples side to side and chest to chest, guys who never danced but hung around and smoked or swigged sodas, even the committee parents at the refreshment stand—Did they know I was looking for Skip? Did they know Zanger had wise-mouthed Skip on Hobe's steps? My mouth felt dry, the same way it had felt at Nana's funeral and at Lizzie's party. I couldn't see Skip anywhere.

"This is the next-to-last dance," one of the committee fathers announced, "the next-to-last dance."

Bill Haley's news about "Well I saw my baby walkin'" flung dancers onto the floor. Only the smokers and watchers along the side railing stayed put.

I stopped between the front corner of the stage and railing. Smokers and watchers flicked looks at me and then turned their heads toward what I saw in the half-light of the empty lot: a fight circle.

"Your pal Malloy's kinda busy right now!" a watcher yelled to me. "He's kinda going 'round in circles." The other watchers' and smokers joined his laughter.

I strode to the railing, away from them so that no one could touch me or hold me back. About twenty feet in front of me, where tag and football had been the twilight games, Jerry Zanger and his gang pushed and shoved Skip like a human medicine ball across and around inside their circle. Skip swore, they jeered; he swore again; they jeered again as if they scored points every time they pushed him. Skip's glasses winked like little flashlights in the glow from the auditorium.

Zanger grabbed Skip's shoulders and spun him off balance. Skip's legs buckled like a tired boxer's, and then he heaved, collapsed, and lay on the ground like a beaten animal.

The sight of his body humiliated me. I scissored my legs over the railing and charged the circle.

"Watch it!" one of them shouted.

Like a lineman I slammed shoulder first into some kid's butt and knocked him down. "Skip, come on!" I yelled, and drove head first into a stomach and knee-groined somebody else, and then I ran, open air around me, threats, swears, and Skip's footsteps behind me. He caught up to me at the sidewalk.

"Go, go!" he shouted.

We sprinted down Long Avenue, darted looks at cars passing us, expecting Zanger's Merc to swerve to the sidewalk, his gang to jump out and pummel us, toss us into the trunk. I flashed Skip and me blindfolded, driven out of town, shoved onto some dark dirt road, left to find our way home, or worse.

At the bottom of Long Avenue, Skip huffed, "This way." He cut onto Carpenter Avenue below the railroad embankment. We slowed to a walk, hands on hips. A runner's stitch knotted my right side.

Skip bent, vomited, once, twice, his shoulders heaving, the ground spattered.

I lay my hand on his shoulder.

He groaned again, retched again. Nothing more dripped from his mouth. "Oh, son--o--va *bitch*!" he moaned.

I scanned Long Avenue for prowling cars: none.

"Oh shit," he mourned. "I'd love to have some Scotch right now."

We climbed the railroad embankment and crossed the tracks.

Under a streetlight I squinted at Skip.

"Your glasses," I said.

"Stomped to shit. Zanger'll pay for this." He puffed, his breath sour air in my face. "I dunno what the old man'll do about it but he'll do somethin'."

Sweat slid down my ribs. The bottom of my shirt felt damp inside my khakis. We zig-zagged streets toward Willowyn Terrace. If Jerry Zanger threatened us any more, we'd make a run for my house. Houses ignored us, porches and windows dark. Quiet bedrooms, maybe not so quiet. Bushes good hiding places. I checked over my shoulder for cars. Zanger and his gang could attack from anywhere.

I glanced at Skip as we approached a corner a block away from Willowyn, his face tearless. He was used to punches to his shoulder and ribs…Mr. Malloy couldn't control himself. Too much booze. I asked myself what would happen to Skip and me if we kept sneaking stuff. It couldn't catch up with us. We wouldn't let it.

Maybe Skip should have retaliated against his father, done something. But he had walked away, probably chose to, didn't want to make it worse for his mother.

Dad and I never had fights, I reassured myself. *Little arguments, never fights.*

"Christ, Harper, maybe you *should* go out for football," Skip laughed. "You plowed those bastards like a tank."

We laughed together, our laughter too loud among the quiet lawns and houses.

Just beyond the streetlight we heard a car rumble behind us.

"In here," Skip whispered.

We plunged through a hedge and crouched behind it. The car prowled closer and paused at the intersection. Mufflers chugged threats. I peered through the hedge: Jerry Zanger's Mercury.

'Bastards," Skip hissed.

The long car slithered by without changing speed, its red taillights menacing eyes until the car turned a corner and gunned out of sight.

We crawled from the hedge and jogged down Willowyn Terrace past Our Lady Queen of Heaven to Lorrence Boulevard. The church crouched smaller in the dark than in daylight.

"Zanger prob'ly knows where you live," I said, breathing hard again when we reached the bottom of the hill.

"So what? I'll drag him to my house and beat the shit out of him."

On Lorrence Boulevard we stayed close to the walkways that led to porches. The closer to Jessup Avenue, the more I feared walking home alone. I'd have to run like crazy.

"What the *hell? Oh Jesus Christ!*"

Skip's fright slapped me out of myself.

Halfway down Jessup an ambulance flashed red lights, police cars pulsed blues. At his house. Something inside me tripped, stumbled; my legs weakened. Shadows and silhouettes wavered in front of Skip's house.

Actions and voices swirled around us in a matter of seconds. A policeman blocked Skip's path to the porch: "Who're you?"

"Skip Malloy, I *live* here, you stupid—" He put his hands on the policeman's chest.

The first officer and another policeman smacked their hands on Skip's shoulders. "Wait here, son."

Skip's voice shook: "I've gotta go *in.*" He began to shove his way between them.

"Skip, stay *there!* You don't wanna see it." The speaker was Liz. A tall young man walked beside her from the house, both escorted by a third policeman. Another man—Mr. Arvidson, I realized—walked next to the tall man.

"What *hap*pened?" Skip pleaded.

A man and woman approached us from behind: my mother and father.

Skip cried, "Did he *kill* her?"

He did not expect Dad's answer.

8

Streets

After midnight Monday:

Skip and I walked. Streets we had walked and bicycled when we were younger, on our way to school or to the Little League field where we had played catch, hit grounders. Streets of houses dark, the only light from streetlights above macadam pavement scraped with sand. Streets where we knew names of people who lived behind those darkened windows, streets where we didn't know anyone.

"Arvidson," Skip said as we walked a dark street; only a streetlight shone at the distant corner. "He heard the yelling and the first shot. Ordered his wife to call the cops and he came right over. Walks in the front door, hears the next shot, and Marty and Lizzie—They come in the back door. They were gonna take my mom outta the house, take her back to Ocean City. They see her dead on the bedroom floor. Marty—he saw the old man had a gun, he tried to grab, it goes off, and everything goes straight to hell…Not that it wasn't hell already.

"Damn cops still won't let me in the house," he added, not for the first time since we'd left my house and begun our walk.

My mother had asked where we were going. Dad told her "Let them go, Grace. They'll be all right." Dad trusted us, not that Mom didn't, but Dad realized Skip and I couldn't sit in the house; it would be impossible for us to sleep, at least not right away. Maybe not for a long time.

"Be careful," Mom had impressed upon us.

No cars in sight on Willowyn Terrace, only a faint glow behind an upstairs window of a piano teacher's house across from St. Thomas'. Everybody in town probably knew what had happened…maybe not everything but enough to give them stuff to gossip about. Like Marty Bannon walking in on the argument between Mr. and Mrs. Malloy just when Mr. Malloy shot her. She never had a chance. Then he turned the gun on Marty. Marty had to defend himself, they fought for it, and that's when the gun went off. Mr. Malloy was dead before they took him out of the house.

"I just wanna get my goddamn clothes…Stupid cops still don't want me to see anything," Skip complained now. He wasn't crying. He sounded in control, as if he was explaining how he solved an algebra problem. "What the hell…I've seen plenty."

So had I. The sound of the cop's voice—private, secretive--when he had advised my parents, "We've got more work to do here, Mr. and Mrs. Harper. Take the boys home with you. We'll take the young lady and Mr. Bannon to the station and start the questioning. Mr. and Mrs. Arvidson, too. We'll get in touch with you soon's we're ready and know who's going to take care of Skip for the time being."

Something had been sucked out of me. I couldn't get it back. The houses like rigid and dark wooden blocks we passed didn't know a damn thing about what had happened. They were blind and helpless.

I listened for cars and footsteps behind us, the low rumble of Jerry Zanger's Mercury. The only noise on the street came from our steady footsteps. We were alone on the streets…

We walked a side street in the north end of town. Skip didn't look at houses, he didn't look at sidewalk cracks and crevices or at tree limbs that nearly touched our heads, he didn't peer at the black sky and pin-like stars when we came to an open space. He just kept walking.

He said, "Cops asked me a bunch 'a stuff…how things were before we went to the dance…I shoulda stayed home…*Fuckin' shit!*"

He stopped, rubbed the corners of his eyes, shook his head and then squinted as if sunlight glared back at him. No sunlight, of course; no moonlight. Only swaths of black sky above the trees. Next to us slabbed a stone wall hip high, the ragged stones sparkly silver in streetlight glow. The lawn that sloped to the wall looked like unmoving black water. Taking deep breaths, Skip stared at the wall. He mumbled something about needing new glasses, then—"Sonova *bitch*!"— attacked the wall as if it was an enemy. He kicked it, right foot, left foot, right, left, "Sonova *bitch*!" over and over, and then he made fists and pummeled the uneven top slabs, "You *fuck*!" over and over, until his arms stiffened and his hands became claws he shook as if they were wet with water. Now they were wet with blood.

"Oh Christ, what am I gonna do? What the hell…They wouldn't let me in to see'em… not even let me in my own goddamn *house*…Ah Harper, what am I gonna *do*?"

—————

"Let me see your hands," my mother said to Skip at the bottom of the stairs after we walked into the house. She wore slippers and her terrycloth robe, her hair held back in bobby pins. She winced when Skip held up his hands to her. "Come into the kitchen, we'll wash them."

The clock on the wall near the cellar door read three thirty. The white-ish yellow light of the ceiling reflected fuzzy impressions of the wallpaper's pink and blue flowers.

"Is Dad awake?" I asked.

"He'll be down in a minute. We heard you come in."

I didn't feel young anymore. I was sure Skip didn't feel young, either. Something I couldn't define had been yanked from our guts. Skip had retaliated by pounding and kicking a stone wall. He had cried out to me in search of an answer I did not know. I could only give him my arms.

I watched my mother tend Skip. Under cool water she smoothed a wash cloth over the bruises, scratches, and cuts on the heels of Skip's hands and fingers. He hissed, muttered "Oh damn," and closed his eyes and turned his head away from her and the water. She applied a wand of Mercurochrome to the wounds. She had done the same for me when I had come in with little wounds, completing these motherly tasks with a kiss to the hand or arm I had scraped or cut. "There…all better," she had reassured me and kissed my cheek or forehead.

"How did you *do* this?" she asked Skip, dabbing his fingers dry with a paper towel.

He smirked and squinted at my mother, his lower eyelids still puffy. I wondered if he could clearly see our faces and the kitchen cabinets, table, and chairs. "Stone wall got in my way," he said.

She shook her head, tsk-tsked. Then she opened her arms and embraced us longer than I remembered her ever hugging me or Skip.

"Your sister Liz called. She and Marty and your Aunt Ceil are at a hotel in Forgeville. They'll be here in the morning." As if to reassure him even more, my mother held his hands in hers. "Liz is doing the best she can to get you a new set of glasses," she added.

"I wanna get my stuff from the house," he said.

"You may not be able—"

He yanked away from my mother. "Goddamn it! I wanna go *now*. I've gotta get what belongs to me, for Chrissake."

If my father had not stood in the kitchen-dining room archway like a policeman, Skip would have darted through. He almost did. He bumped my father's chest but then took one step back. Dad kept his arms at his side.

"Let me through, Mr. Harper."

"Not now. You'll be able to get them soon."

Skip laid his forehead on my father's chest. He sniffed, rubbed his cheek with the back of his right hand. "Sonova bitch," he wept. "Sonova bitch…"

Dad's tan bathrobe was tied over 'shorty' pajamas. His legs below the knees looked like thin birch trees, his feet milk-white. Dad the ex-athlete suddenly became Dad the ordinary man I saw every morning.

Skip pulled away from Dad and challenged him: "It's *my house*, for God's sake."

My mother brought Skip's hands together in hers and said, "We'll see what we can do. It'll be all right."

"No it won't. It'll never be all right!" He wept again.

My mother held him.

———

"What I'd do for Scotch and Coke right now," Skip mumbled ten minutes later on the living room sofa. My mother had made it his bed since—

Since. That was time now. *Since* we came back from his house Saturday night. *Since* a Lorrence policeman told my parents about the shootings. *Since* Mom and Dad had broken that news to Skip and me. *Since* Skip and I had stayed in, except for walking around at night.

He took long deep breaths. Close to sleep.

I went up to my room.

What the hell am I supposed to do? Pray to You? I can't pray.

Father Hepplewhite and all my Sunday School teachers tried to teach met that prayer was a way to ask for Your help to solve problems. When I was little, Mom and Dad watched me say my prayers before I climbed into bed. Like a good boy I folded my hands and recited "The Lord's Prayer," the "Twenty-third Psalm," or "Now I lay me down to sleep..." I was just a kid. I accepted my parents' and teachers' and minister's directions. I thought they were right.

I'm not a kid now, and they're not always right.

Not that Mom and Dad are watching over me. They're in their room, behind closed doors. So am I. Don't look for me to get down on my knees and whisper a prayer. Not even to Nana. She's far away, almost a stranger. I can hear her in my memory, but she seems like someone I knew a long time ago.

You? You're like a shadow. Somebody I can't understand or trust. Heaven? A warm paradise? Forget it. Forget all of it.

So where are Mr. and Mrs. Malloy? In some damn waiting room?

I turned over in bed and closed my eyes, but all I thought about, all I saw, was a replay of the same lousy episode over and over.

Mom and Dad had overheard one of the cops explain that he had found Mrs. Malloy on the bedroom floor, Mr. Malloy on the hallway floor, the gun next to him, Marty Bannon standing over him empty-handed, and Liz bawling her eyes out on the sofa. Marty had said over and over again that all he had tried to do was grab the gun away from Mr. Malloy because he didn't want anyone else to get hurt.

Was Marty's statement true? Or did he kill Mr. Malloy in a rage for what Mr. Malloy had done to Liz? What was the truth?

Dad had asked if he could call a lawyer for Liz and Marty from inside the house. The officer gave permission.

"The attorney's on his way downtown," he had said to us when he came back outside. "I'll drive you home and then meet them at the police station."

Skip and I were slumped in the back seat of Dad's Plymouth. Mom wiped her eyes. Skip didn't cry; he shook his head and mumbled "Sonova bitch...goddamn sonova bitch," and snarled "Ya seen enough? I'll sell tickets!" to people on the Jessup Avenue sidewalk watching us go by, his shouts muffled by the window he had not rolled down. I was relieved Mom and Dad had let him spout off what he needed to.

Willowyn Terrace had loomed awake but empty of cars and people, the only signs of life the blurry grayish-white flicker of a TV screen through a window of a house a block away from ours. The inside front door of our house was open when we pulled into the driveway, the living room in a dull yellow glow from a table lamp, Mom and Dad's upstairs bedroom in soft ceiling light. They had given no thought to their possessions, only to Skip and me.

I closed my eyes. I didn't sleep, or maybe I did but it wasn't real sleep. It felt like skin being pulled off my arms and legs. What was left wasn't warm, wasn't cold. Just my flesh and bones and my heart pumping blood. The flesh, bones, and heart all belonged to me, but they didn't say or do anything to make me feel better. In fact, when I opened my eyes and saw gray sky beyond the window and five minutes to six on my bureau clock, I felt the same damn way I had felt when I'd laid down a couple hours before. Probably worse.

I got out of bed, went to the bathroom, closed the door, and puked and cried my guts out into the toilet bowl.

9

Breakfast and Booze

Tuesday morning Skip took a ten-minute shower, the bathroom door closed. I heard him talking to himself. I couldn't understand the words; the sounds resembled questions and curses. Probably at his father. I had never heard him say an unkind word about his mother.

What would my life would be like without Mom and Dad? I wondered. My stomach curled tightly as barbed wire at the question. I couldn't imagine living in our house by myself, walking room to room and not seeing or hearing Mom or Dad anywhere. The more I thought about this, it seemed my bedroom walls pulled farther away from my bed, the ceiling higher than it was when I'd first woken up. It was like I was a victim of a weird dream in a science-fiction movie. I gripped the sheet on both sides of me.

I'd probably go live with Granddad. We had a good relationship, but what it would be like to live with him every day? What would we talk about? What freedom would I have? Would Granddad be more strict with me than Mom and Dad were? Would he tell me I had to still be an acolyte? We'd argue about that.

The bathroom door handle clicked.

Skip laid one knee on the middle cushion of the living room sofa and looked out the front windows. "Lizzie and Aunt Ceil are here."

"Not Marty?" I asked.

Skip had dressed in clothes I had loaned him: jeans, a tan pullover, white sweat socks. He wore the same scuffed brown loafers he had worn Saturday night.

"Hi, folks! I'm Ceil Kinsale. Thank you very much for inviting us here." She and Liz stepped into the living room, shook hands with Mom and Dad, and hugged Skip. "And you must be David. Nice to meet you, David."

Liz and Skip's aunt, the younger sister of their mother, was the antithesis of Helen Malloy. Ceil Kinsale reminded me of a pop singer I had seen on TV—blond-tinted hair styled short and curled around her ears, her broad smile wowing the audience. However, Ceil Kinsale was no youthful pop singer. Wrinkles lined her cheeks, her voice a heavy smoker's, like sand scratched against a tin bucket. She held a cigarette between the first two fingers of her left hand. After she shook hands with my parents, she turned head to the side and coughed into her right hand. "Terrible habit, but what're you gonna do?"

"I don't know how to thank you," Liz said to my parents. She put her arms around Skip and me. "David…" A hint of lilac perfume from under her ears, and her arms felt warm. She hugged us, let go, and dabbed her eyes with tissues she gripped in her right hand. The white sleeveless blouse she wore ruffled above the waist of her navy blue skirt. Below her shoulder the lower seam of the blouse was damp. Behind the seam stretched the white band of her bra, her skin pink above and below the band. "Oh here," she said, and pulled a case for glasses from her purse and handed it to Skip. "Try them on. Let's see how they look on you."

He looked older in the black frames and thick lenses.

"Thanks. They'll do," he said to Liz. "How's Marty? Where is he?"

"Okay…" She let the word hang in the air. "The police are going to release him to his parents later today. Mr. Arvidson corroborated what Marty and I told them, so…"

Liz then thanked Dad for recommending a lawyer for Marty. "That gentleman didn't know us at all, but he was very kind."

"Nothing left unsaid, to the police or the lawyer?" Dad wondered.

Liz closed her eyes and shook her head. She let out a deep breath, as if she had just finished running a marathon. "I don't know what we're going to do now." She drew a tissue from the pocket of her skirt and dabbed her eyes.

I asked myself, Did Marty hide anything from Liz, Arvidson, and the police, or did he tell the truth? Did he shoot Mr. Malloy on purpose because Mr. Malloy had taken advantage of Liz? I looked at Liz, her face and eyes, and tried to see what had happened to her and what she had seen at her house last Saturday night. I saw only the surface of her face and eyes, nothing beyond her fair skin and green eyes.

My mother put her arm around her. "Right now we're all going to sit and have a nice breakfast," she offered, and led us to the dining room where the table was set for six. I stood next to Skip.

"Not me. I don't feel like eating," he said before we sat down.

Liz paused on her way to the other side of the table. "You have to eat. You may not think so but you'll feel better afterwards," she said.

"I don't wanna do a goddamn thing 'cept get my stuff out've the goddamn house and get out've here." He didn't move from his place next to me. He waited for the next person to challenge him.

Ceil Kinsale stood behind the chair next to Liz. Aunt Ceil's short-sleeve cream-colored sweater hung loosely on her shoulders and across her breasts, which reminded me of thin mounds. She looked at her cigarette, chuckled, and then, waving the half-smoked tube, asked my father, "While we're waiting, can I trouble you for an ash tray?"

He brought her one from the living room desk.

She held the ash tray in one hand, rubbed the cigarette out, and cleared her throat. "Like Lizzie said, dear nephew, you'll feel better after you eat."

Skip sneered at his aunt: "Don't tell me what to do. How the hell would you know what'll make me feel better? Your father ever shoot your mother?" He shoved his chair into my hip, strode through the living room, and pushed open the front screen door.

Liz's face reddened. "Skip, for God's sake!"

"God's sake? You kidding? Where the hell was He Saturday night? Not at our house, for damn sure!"

The screen door slammed shut. The sound reverberated against the door jamb before it trembled to quiet.

Ceil Kinsale's fists clenched the knobs on the back of her chair. "Jesus, Mary, and Joseph!" It took her more than five seconds to unclench her fingers.

"Want me to go after him?" I asked Liz.

"I know where he's going," she said. She rummaged in her purse for something she clutched in her fist.

"I'll go with you," I said.

Skip sprinted down Willowyn Terrace past St. Thomas Church. We heard specks of his shouts—"goddamnit..." "away from me!" "...me alone!" as if someone had closed a door on him, opened it, then slammed it in his face. He ran as fast as he had Saturday night after the fight; he was charged up with where he wanted to go.

I jogged. Liz ran, her legs restricted by her skirt, her breaths short. She caught up with me at 'the Queen' at the bottom of the hill.

Breathing heavily, hands on hips, she managed, "My poor brother..."

A half block away Skip jogged down Lorrence Boulevard. He didn't slow to a walk until he reached Jessup Avenue. He strode deliberately, his mind focused on one place, one house, until he stood in front of the screened-in porch. No police car parked at the curb or in the driveway. No neighbors— the Arvidsons included—on porches. Still, through nerves on skin beneath my shirt, I felt people's eyes prick on me and on Liz and Skip. It had been three days since the "shootings—" the Philadelphia newspapers and television newscasts term for the tragedies.

Skip inhaled and exhaled long breaths. He did not regard us when we reached him. He seemed to study his house and held out his hand to Lizzie. "You got a key?"

She opened her right hand to show him the house key.

"Unlock the goddamn door."

It would be trespassing if I went in, I thought. But Skip was my best friend, and I felt a kind of love for Liz. I followed them through the front porch into the house.

They went upstairs. I stayed down. The hallway that led to the Mr. and Mrs. Malloy's bedroom lay empty, the carpet and wood clean of stains, the bedroom door closed. My imagination flashed scenes I turned away from. The screen of the bulky TV console was a black square, no smiley faces, no action, no music. Pope Pius XII looked at no one, not even at me. To him the house was a blank nothing; or, maybe it was a place he didn't want to look upon anymore. Maybe the entire house existed in a quiet that wasn't real. But that was a lie. Sure, nothing was disturbed. No fists clenched, no bruises, no bodies on the floor. Furniture, lamps— everything in order: a house where the people who had lived in it were now dead.

Coming back down the stairs, Skip and Liz's footsteps sounded like strangers in the house they had once lived in. Each of them carried one suitcase.

He gave her the house key before we left the porch. She turned the key in the lock, the sound of metal upon metal smooth, final.

The Arvidson porch and chairs empty, the open front door the only sign of life in that house.

Down at one corner, cars passed east and west on Lorrence Boulevard; at the other corner, east and west on Crosstown Avenue. The high school three blocks away on Crosstown… Six more weeks until classes begin, I thought to myself.

Time had moved like a yo-yo since…

———

Skip and I sat at the kitchen table, specks of scrambled eggs and crumbs of toast on our plates pushed to the side. Pulp of oranges clung to our juice glasses.

The family and Marty would stay at the Forgeville Inn, a recently opened hotel one mile from the Forgeville State College campus. Skip would have his own room. My mother and father had offered to have them stay with us but, as Liz had explained, "We thank you, really, but I think we'd do better staying in Forgeville. A little more privacy there. You understand…"

Skip spoke to me out of the corner of his mouth. "Come and visit. There's room at the Inn but no holy family."

My father, Liz, and Ceil Kinsale walked past us toward the back door.

Liz included Skip and me when she explained the reason for them wanting to talk in the backyard. "Complicated legal stuff. I'll talk to you about it later." She put her hands on Skip's shoulders and leaned in to kiss him on the cheek.

He shrugged away from his sister but urged her, "If you're gonna talk about me, I need to be in on it."

"You will be, I promise," Liz said.

Dad closed the back door. His and Ceil's voices drifted to silence as the three of them walked to the lilacs at the end of the yard.

It seemed to me that Skip wanted no one to touch him.

————

Gray sky through leaves and branches. Nothing moved: not in the house, not outside. Nothing moved anywhere.

After Liz, Skip, and their aunt had gone to the Forgeville Inn, and after Mom and Dad had gone to work (Both had permission to come in late), I stretched out on the sofa. Clouds hung heavy. They moved slowly across the sun like enormous dark mountains.

I closed my eyes… couldn't sleep…not that I really wanted to. Behind my eyes I saw a yellow-white light, nothing else. No breeze touched my skin. Nothing touched me except warm air. I was in a still-life.

Did life mean flesh and blood on a bedroom floor and too much other stuff I couldn't get rid of, I asked myself. Did life mean no life at all?

The telephone rang. I didn't answer it. Even if the call had been from Skip, I didn't want to talk. I didn't want to talk to anyone.

Nine times, then silence.

But not everything was silent.

"Did he kill her."

In my head I still heard "See You Later, Alligator," the song on the auditorium PA system when Jerry Zanger and his creeps had pushed and pummeled Skip. I still saw Skip shoved around the inside of that circle, still felt my head and shoulder slam into some creep's stomach when Skip and I bulled our way through the line and ran like hell down Long Avenue. I still heard him retch out his gut on the ground of the railroad embankment.

A knock at the front door jarred me. Skip?.

It wasn't. Tan Bermuda shorts, red polo shirt, red Phillies cap—Jack MacAdams. "What the hell happened at Malloy's?"

I didn't invite MacAdams in. He sat down on the top porch steps. I didn't sit down with him. The conniving way he had asked the question…I didn't trust him. I leaned against the porch railing beside the steps. He jounced his left leg like a pump.

He had to look up at me when he asked, "So what do you know? Anything?"

I only told MacAdams that Mr. and Mrs. Malloy were dead.

I wanted to protect Skip, Liz, and their mother. Last night Mom and Dad had taken me aside and explained that the best thing I could do now for Skip was be a friend. "In the truest sense of that word, David," Dad had said. He bit his lower lip and looked at me in a way I had seen him look at my mother when he thought I wasn't watching. After he turned away, he shook his head and put his right hand up to his face.

I didn't tell MacAdams that the police had found chairs overturned in the kitchen and the cardboard patch over the hole in the living room wall kicked in. I didn't tell him that Mrs. Malloy's body had two bullet holes around her heart, or that one shot had killed Mr. Malloy. I didn't want to tell Jack MacAdams anything.

"No kidding…I know that…But holy shit...Double murder must be a first for Lorrence." He held back a laugh. He lifted the bill of his red Phillies cap and tugged it lower on his forehead. His left leg pumped up and down.

"Everybody knows about it," MacAdams went on, sounding like a greedy gossip. "My dad went downtown to buy a paper…said everybody was talking about it." He hinted a smile and then seemed to take it back. "You seen Malloy?"

"Not since last night," I said, not regretting the lie. Then: "Whyn't you go to Hell! Get out've here!" I pushed Jack MacAdams off the porch step, watched him regain his footing and flip me the finger.

"Same to you," I said, and retaliated with the same gesture before he turned his back and walked away.

I slammed the inside front door behind me.

The pantry off the kitchen was a storeroom: food, baking supplies, cleaning materials, soda, and liquor. Boxes of three brands of cereal, including Cheerios, corn flakes, and Rice Krispies. Cans of beef stew, stewed tomatoes, corn, peas, green beans, and gravy; tuna fish, deviled ham, peanut butter, jelly; flour, sugar, baking powder, powdered sugar; window cleaner, toilet cleaner and waxed paper. All of these items categorized and aligned in neat rows perched or huddled on shelves. A mop, a broom, and a dust pan and brush leaned against the wall in a corner beside a small window that looked out to the backyard.

Not only had Dad arranged and categorized these groceries, beverages, and household cleaners and utensils. Under his bedroom bureau he kept his slippers a couple inches apart from his casual shoes; his casual shoes apart from dress shoes. Patterned neckties hung on four winged hooks bracketed to one side of his closet; solid color neckties onto four other winged hooks next to the patterned. Socks, shirts, trousers, underwear—you name it, my father organized it. Practically everything he owned had its proper place.

Even wine, liquor, and soda on the kitchen pantry floor: wine, bourbon, gin, vodka, soda. No Scotch.

So what? There was bourbon. Something new to try.

To see the pantry at night we had to pull a string attached to a thin chain attached to a globe-shaped light in the middle of the ceiling. This afternoon I didn't need to pull the string.

What I wanted was time and a bottle of my choice. Mom and Dad wouldn't be home until five thirty. Jack MacAdams wouldn't be back. Skip was at the Forgeville Inn. I was by myself. I had time. Plenty of it.

I carried a bottle of ginger ale and the bottle of bourbon to the kitchen table. A highball, Dad had called this mix of ginger ale and bourbon, a drink requested mostly by men—from church, from the bank, and from his and Mom's high school class during reunion planning meetings. The women usually asked for wine or tea.

From a cabinet I took down a medium-size drinking glass and then dropped in a handful of ice cubes. The ice made a pleasant rattle in the glass. I mixed the highball the way I had seen Dad make his: an inch and a half of bourbon and two to three inches of ginger ale stirred with a spoon.

First sip: kind of shiny, like sunlight on Halcyon Lake.

Second sip: I closed my eyes the way some of Mom and Dad's friends did when they took a drink; the way members of the congregation did after they took communion wine from the chalice. The way I did after I sipped cream sherry from the bottle in the Sacristy cabinet. The bourbon felt like a tangy cold-hot cord into my stomach after the third swallow, and after that an all-warm feeling that shot tiny seeds to nerve points on my skin, even to my scalp.

The ginger ale and bourbon bottles on the table looked like statues. *Still life*, I observed to myself. *Statues. Let's make things move.*

I tossed the rest of the drink into the sink, dropped three more ice cubes into the glass and poured in three seconds worth of bourbon.

What now? I tilted the glass to my mouth and drank. The bourbon burned more than the scotch and Coke Skip had mixed at Halcyon. The heat spread from my stomach up through my face to my head.

"Here's to you, Skip," I said aloud, raised my glass toward the ceiling, and swallowed another sip. "Something we can try sometime."

Well now, I announced in my imaginary sarcastic voice to no one in particular. *Well, let's tour the downstairs of the Harper house. Here's the dining room…table cleared now, no tell-tale breakfast crumbs. Empty chairs, including the one Nana used to sit in…*

No parents now, no Skip, no Liz. Just the plain old table with a bowl of artificial something-or-other flowers Mom puts in the center…Plain old chairs…The window seat on the right, telephone there, Mom's philodendrons that crawl over the edge and reach practically to the floor…She's gonna have to trim'em or else they'll get sucked up in the vacuum cleaner.

I stand now at the archway between the dining room and living room…Mom's pencil lines on the pillar to my left, ladies and gentlemen…measuring my height year to year…Taller than Dad now, have been for a couple years…wonder if he's gonna play in the Old Timers game, or if what happened'll change his mind…

Skip at the Inn. Here's to ya' again, Skip. You're gonna have to try this stuff sometime, maybe before you move away…a going-away drink. Here's to ya'…

How much left…a swallow, maybe two. Let's make it one.

Jeez, even my ears are warm…

Hey Skip, is there room at the Inn? Mary and Joseph there yet or they on the way? Probably stuck in Philly, cops won't let a donkey on the Ben Franklin Bridge. Might have to take a ferry across the river, then have Mary ride and Joseph lead the donkey the rest of the way…Hey, nice ass you got there, buddy!

I strolled back through the dining room, my head warm, *whole body's warm, tingly…Jeez, I only drank one…two?*

Ladies and gentlemen, I am now under the archway…I am now drinking bourbon on ice. Tastes good, like a bourbon on ice should. Maybe better.

I have now passed through the archway and am standing in the living room.

Table model TV in the corner to my right, Dad's chair here to my left…likes to read there, watch TV…Westerns and police shows. Gunsmoke, Dragnet. Just the facts, ma'am. I'm David Harper. This is my partner Skip Malloy. Give us the facts.

The fact is this drink is making my stomach feel like it's moving back'n forth. But it's good, no question about it…

Sofa and coffee table under the front windows, the sofa where Mom reads… sometimes knits when she's watching TV. Mom likes Perry Como Shomomo, music shows like that. Stuff puts me to sleep…

And now the front desk, where Dad writes checks for—

Who's that coming up the front sidewalk? Granddad? Holy—Gotta get ridda this stuff!

I gulped the rest of the bourbon, beat it to the kitchen, and tossed the ice in the kitchen sink. I heard the front screen door clack shut.

"Anybody home?"

I closed the pantry door all the way, bottles aligned neatly in their proper place…*Jeez, I hope so.*

My head swirled woozy when I bent over, then stood up fast. Maybe too fast.

Outside the pantry door I scanned table, chairs, and cabinets. *Everything in place. Nothing moving, just my stomach…*

"David, you home?"

I heaved a deep breath. I managed "In the kitchen, Granddad."

I ambled toward the living room, the back of my head tingly *like my hair's coming loose.* Dressed in typical Granddad style, he stood between the coffee table and the archway. One lens of his clip-on sun shades peeked at me like a round green eye from his shirt pocket.

"How are ya', Davy? Thought I'd come by, see how you're doing." He took two steps toward me. "Are you all right? How's your friend Skip doing?"

Easy…easy…Don't stand too close.

Six feet away from Granddad I couldn't remember the last time I had hugged him. Had I ever put my arms around him? Maybe. Maybe when I was very young and didn't understand the deeper meaning of the gesture.

"Okay," I managed. "Skip and his sister 're at the Forgeville Inn…"

Jesus, if my stomach would stop sliding around, and if my head would just cool off…

I breathed in another deep breath and let it out slowly.

"You sure you're feeling all right, Davy? You look a little piqued."

My whole head tingled, my feet fuzzy, I wanted to laugh and cry at the same time. Not much to laugh about, lots of stuff to cry about, what the hell…

"Maybe you oughta lie down, Davy. Here, let me feel your head."

I shrugged, mumbled "Not doing much, Granddad."

That's when the palm of his hand on my forehead felt big as my baseball glove. That's when he looked me in the eye and asked, "Davy, have you been *drinking*?"

"I cannot tell a lie, Granddad," I replied and burst out laughing.

"Here's some hot tea. Drink it slow."

"You're not gonna tell Mom and Dad, are you?"

"Drink your tea. We'll worry about that later."

I was lying on my back on the sofa. After I had scrambled upstairs and puked my guts out in the toilet. After I had swabbed my face with a cold wash cloth. After I had brushed my teeth to wash the taste and smell of vomit out of my mouth. After I told myself I'd never pull anything like this again. Ever.

"What time is it?" I wondered.

He pulled out his pocket watch from a pocket below his belt. "Two thirty," he said. He thumbed the watch down into the pocket. "Have some more tea, then close your eyes and try to take a nap. You'll feel better."

I took the first half of his advice. He set the half-drunk cup of tea on the coffee table.

"I never thought I'd see you like this." He made a click inside his mouth. "What'd you do it for, huh?"

"You gonna tell Mom and Dad?"

"That the only thing you're afraid of, Davy?"

Granddad did not inform my parents of my escapade, and I didn't fall asleep, at least not before they came home. Did I want a toasted grilled cheese, bacon and tomato sandwich for dinner? No thanks. I gave my mother the excuse that I wasn't feeling good, hadn't slept very much the past few nights. Granddad, who had stayed for my mother's favorite quick dinner, advised me, "Better get a good night's sleep, Davy."

My bedroom door closed, I fell asleep, but not before I tried to picture exactly where I had placed the bottles of bourbon and ginger ale, and not before I replayed Granddad's question "What'd you do it for, huh?"

"For kicks. I wanted to. See what it feels like," I had replied, being sure to add, "I'm not gonna wind up like Mr. Malloy. I'll be all right."

And not before I remembered the bourbon sliding into my stomach and the blurred fuzziness in my head, and how I felt like crying and laughing at the same time.

And not before I imagined Mrs. Malloy's body, her dress draped above her pale knees, on the bedroom floor, Mr. Malloy's body, mouth open, in the hallway, and Marty facing the first policeman on the scene.

And Skip weeping *What am I gonna do, Harper?*

10

Touch

Wednesday morning.

"We're early," my mother remarked. "Let's wait a few minutes."

My parents and I stood in the humid shade of sycamores and scarlet maples next to Our Lady Queen of Heaven Church.

Twenty hours after my bourbon adventure. Head clear, stomach calm; my mind swirled around Skip and Liz, their parents, and the funeral service: What would the service be like? What would happen tomorrow? How would the rest of the summer be? Too many unknown answers. Too much to think about.

Cars: four-door black and dark blue sedans, three with Pennsylvania license plates, parked like somber attendants on Lorrence Boulevard in front of the church. The grills of Buicks and Oldsmobiles reminded me of mouths that frowned at everything in front of them.

I saw no one yet from Lorrence High School, not even the principal who had reprimanded me as "a little boy" after the incidents with Skip's oafy bullies, walk toward the church. Not even teachers. Would anyone from our class come to support Skip? It was the right thing to do, even though they didn't get along with him.

Lorraine? Wyles I expected she would come to support Liz. I looked for Lorraine, didn't see her. I understood why she might stay away.

"Where're we gonna sit?" I asked my parents.

"As close to the family as we can," Mom said. She smiled sadly as if the tragedy had kept her awake at night. It had. I had heard her sniffles and choked cries behind their bedroom door, and Dad's soft voice within my mother's cries.

"You've been here before, right?" I asked them.

"For weddings," Dad replied. "Don't worry. The Catholic service isn't that much different from ours."

We joined other mourners at the church's front entrance. Dad and I wore dark suits—his black, mine navy blue, the same ones we had worn to Nana's funeral. My arms felt sticky under the sleeves of the jacket. Mom was dressed in a navy blue suit and wore a black lace veil that covered her forehead and made her skin shadowy. I squinted from the sun glare on the flagstone steps. Nana's funeral had been on raw, drizzly spring day.

Mr. and Mrs. Arvidson approached from behind us. She dressed in navy blue like my mother's skirt and jacket, he in a gray-striped seer sucker suit as if he were going to dinner at the Lorrence Country Club. His mustache looked like a thin black crayon. He looked at me, nodded once, and then looked away.

A low rumble from Lorrence Avenue turned me toward the street. Jerry Zanger—his elbow out the window and aimed in my direction—chugged by in his low-slung Mercury. Its engine gunned, rowled like a middle-finger salute. I ran down the steps two at a time to the sidewalk.

"David! Don't you dare!"

Dad's command stopped me. People around me frowned at the black car that my vision followed until it was out of sight. They turned, uttered "...not very polite" and "awfully loud" and walked up the steps to the church entrance. I was the last to follow them.

"What'd you think you were going to do?" my father demanded.

"That was Jerry Zanger. I wanna smash his head."

"Let it go."

"I wanted to get in the first punch," I replied. Dad didn't smile, not even a hint of one.

We walked entered the church.

"Good morning," an usher greeted us matter of factly as we stepped into the foyer. It felt strange to enter a church on a Wednesday morning.

Candlelight: a wavy, darkened candlelight from the altar and from in front of statues of saints that faced both sides of the congregation: on the left the Virgin Mary with her arms at her sides, her palms open; on the right a man carrying a child on his back. *St. Christopher*, I realized, and remembered the medal strung one side of Skip's bedroom mirror.

Another saint's statue tucked in an alcove along the wall on our right: the statue stood on a pedestal above a small altar; in the back of the church another statue seemed to give its blessing near a baptismal font. The interior of Our Lady Queen of Heaven seemed like a museum. A weird idea, maybe impolite, at my best friend's mother and father's funeral. *Better shape up*, I warned myself.

I counted that we sat six rows from the vestibule.

Organ music piped from the balcony above us. I didn't recognize the melody.

No "Hound Dog" today...

My father whispered, "David, turn around."

Pews filled with men stocky and serious, women stocky and tearful. Women in face-hiding, broad-brimmed hats; men in suit coats unbuttoned over paunchy stomachs: Skip's aunts and uncles.

What did they know about the shootings? Where were Skip, Liz, Marty, and cigarette-cough-crazy Aunt Ceil?

My question was answered in part when Ceil Kinsale and Marty Bannon, her arm through his, walked by us and sat in the front pew. They immediately knelt and bowed their heads.

Now a woman in the balcony began to sing "Ave Maria." I tried to determine what some of the Latin words meant in English but I gave up. I hadn't taken Latin, neither had Skip. Latin was for really smart kids like Jack MacAdams. Skip and I weren't in that group.

My mother bowed her head. Except for Mom, the other women in front of us dabbed their eyes with handkerchiefs and tissues.

The congregation whispered, cleared their throats, scraped their feet. I wanted to see who was here, but I didn't want them to stare back at me.

The soloist finished "Ave Maria." Her voice shook as she sang the last words.

Then, like a stab in the back, the killing scene inside Skip's house flashed inside me again. Mr. Malloy smacked, punched Mrs. Malloy, knocked her down, called her obscene names…She crawled into the hallway…Malloy came after her with a gun, Marty grappled with him—

"Stand up, David," Dad said. He put his arm around my shoulder, something he had often done the past few days. I didn't pull away from him. His touch was reassuring.

The outer front doors had closed. Inside the vestibule the priest, Father Bradeen (He drove a black Oldsmobile around town), four acolytes (They looked more like junior high kids than high school types), Skip wearing sunglasses and a black suit, Liz in a black dress and—I counted—altogether twelve pallbearers (husky men who looked uncomfortable in their duty and stiff in dark suits) escorted two closed coffins.

Father Bradeen uttered prayers. He spoke rapidly in Latin, his voice like an unwinding spring. The congregation responded. My parents and I didn't. I was an acolyte used to offering responses; it felt odd not to speak, like being a new kid in school and not understanding what I was supposed to say or do.

Reciting another prayer, the priest walked around the coffins and sprinkled holy water on them, a ritual Father Hepplewhite had not done to Nana's coffin. I wondered if Bradeen had downed a shot or two of bourbon after breakfast.

Maybe I should pray, too, I thought, but I didn't want to kneel when no one else was kneeling. What could I think about Mr. and Mrs. Malloy that was nice? They had accepted me at dinner, they had always asked how Mom and Dad were, and they always told me to come back again.

I addressed someone who had not given me answers: *Why didn't You help Mrs. Malloy, Liz, and Skip? You could have done something. You should have.*

The organ pumped the processional, a hymn that sounded both joyful and sad. "Kyrie eleison," the congregation sang, "Kyrie eleison." I remembered seeing "Kyrie Eleison" in the *Book of Common Prayer*, remembered reciting it during Communion. It sounded all right in Latin. I didn't sing it now—(*Sing along with Father Bradeen, everybody!*). I watched.

Four acolytes—a crucifer, two candle bearers, and the altar boy— slowly walked up the center aisle. I recognized the crucifer, an eighth grader who lived down the street from Granddad, but I didn't know the younger candle-bearers. The altar boy was a kid who rode around town with Father Bradeen in the Oldsmobile. Skip had once told me the kid wanted to be a priest. Dressed in black cassocks and white cottas the acolytes, their faces tight, reminded me of young, crew-cut monks. Had they known Mr. and Mrs. Malloy? They had to know about—

Dad murmured to my mother. She nodded. I wasn't sure what he said, but it sounded like "Poor Liz and Skip." I did not turn to look at Dad. If he was crying, I didn't want to see it.

I watched my best friend. He had removed his sunglasses; his eyes were tearless behind the new thick lenses. He stared straight ahead as if he didn't want to look at anyone. I thought he glanced at me, but maybe what I really saw was a flicker of light on his lenses or a trick my own eyes played on me. I wanted him to see me, wanted to have some contact with him. Then he was past my parents and me. His lips still moved in the "Kyrie Eleison."

Did he believe what Marty and Liz had told the police?

We faced the front of the church again. *Umpire and players,* as I looked at Father Bradeen and the acolytes. *Now then: rules of the game: one base on an overthrow, two bases off the altar, all you can get if the acolytes have to chase it around the Sanctuary.*

You're off again, Harper, my conscience reminded me. **You're thinking strange things in church. And as you know, it's happened before.**

Can't help it. The jokes are just there. Can't get rid of them.

Be careful. God knows what you're thinking. So does Nana.

What does God really know?

I looked down at my folded hands. *Nana, do you know what's going through my head? Did you know I puked my guts out the other night?*

We sat. Dad's arm touched mine. His touch took me away from questions I didn't know answers to. He gave me a hint of a smile, then looked away at Father Bradeen as the priest began to read in that springy voice. I tried to concentrate on Bradeen's slicked down, black hair combed straight back from his forehead; how he held out his hands like Jesus. He spoke in English this time. His lesson focused on being baptized again into living a new life. He talked about how Jesus raised Lazarus from the dead—figures I had colored, not always staying within the lines, in a Sunday School work-book.

I couldn't concentrate, not that I tried to concentrate. I looked at the back of Skip's head. Behind my eyes I visualized his parents in separate coffins: Mrs. Malloy's worried, frightened face, and Mr. Malloy's pinkish-red neck above a white collar, his pinkish face and the purple-red bruise-like bullet hole in his stomach. I couldn't help what I saw in my imagination. No matter how much I struggled, I couldn't put any of it away from me.

Father Bradeen kissed the book.

Once more I wondered how the pages tasted. Dry as a Communion wafer? *Had Bradeen ever kissed a nun? Really kissed her and tried to make out with her?*

How many steps did he take walking back to the altar? Five. How many candles were lit on the altar? Six. How many more days until football sign-ups? 25. Until school? 38.

Father Bradeen and the congregation recited another prayer and response. I thought about Robin Roberts. Would the Phillies give him enough runs and support to win? Would his legs stay strong?

Get your mind back on the service, Harper. Remember why you're here. Your best friend is just a few rows in front of you.

Skip bowed his head.

I felt numb, empty, angry. I wanted to go for a long ride or a long swim. I didn't care what God thought of me. I didn't care if He was angry about how much I drank or how much I wanted to smash Jerry Zanger and his cronies and everybody else who had hurt Skip. I'd make them regret everything they had ever done to hurt him.

An acolyte brought something to Father Bradeen from a room behind the altar. It looked like a metal football attached to a chain. When Bradeen began to swing it over the altar, I realized the football-shaped thing contained incense. The chain clicked as he released the incense over the chalice and the wafers and then toward both sides of the Sanctuary.

"Sanctuary!" Quasimodo cried out in my head.

The incense's bitter scent drifted toward us as Bradeen released the incense over and around the caskets... *Good luck? Have a nice time wherever you're going?*

Father Bradeen next addressed the incense to Skip's family as if he was anointing them. What Skip would Skip do after all this was over? He could come and live with us, I thought. Would Mom and Dad invite him? Maybe he'd want to move away, live with Liz in a town where no one else knew them or knew what had happened to their mother and father? What would it be like to start over again?

The incense smelled like bitter licorice. Its aroma made me hungry. "Famished," Granddad used to say before meals. "So famished I could eat a horse. Time to feed the inner man."

As if in response to the incense, Ceil Kinsale coughed into her hand.

We knelt. Mom and Dad folded their hands and closed their eyes. Maybe I should pray, too. For Mr. and Mrs. Malloy. Where the heck were they now? Heaven or Hell? If there really was a Heaven. If—

I bowed my head: *If You're there, God, there are people I'd like You to—*

A chime-like bell rang near the altar. I opened my eyes and looked toward the altar. Father Bradeen genuflected. When his right knee touched the carpet I heard the same chime-bell again.

Dinner bell...Let's eat!

Laugh or cry: I didn't know what to do.

I pulled in on myself. I bit down on my lower lip and looked straight ahead at the junior acolyte. Hands folded, face staring directly across to the Epistle side of the Sanctuary, what was running through his head? Baseball cards? Girls?

"We won't take Communion," my father said in a low voice to me. "Only the people who are Catholic."

A strange rule, I thought, but didn't argue the point.

Six rows in front of us, Aunt Ceil, Marty, and Liz walked to Father Bradeen to receive Communion. Skip remained in the pew. Not for his father I could understand, but not even for his mother? Ceil Kinsale, Liz, and Marty kept their eyes to themselves when they returned to the front pew. Skip stared straight ahead toward the altar.

I tried to pray. *Please watch over Skip and Liz and Mrs. Malloy, wherever she is.* I couldn't go any further. The sights and sounds from that Saturday night crawled like spiders into my head again. I tried to watch people take Communion from Father Bradeen. They knelt at the railing, accepted the wafer on their tongue, and then return to their seats. Were those wafers dry as the ones I had eaten? Did all churches buy Communion wafers from the same supply store? *Nick's Wine and Wafers: All Denominations. Check our summer specials. Bourbon and scotch on sale.*

Watch it, Harper.

Once more I pulled in. I studied the wooden crucifix above the altar. How could one man's death mean we all—if we were good—would go to Heaven?

Father Bradeen prepared to offer another round of wafers. *No wine here.*

I made a quick scan of the congregation: pews filled end-to-end, people kneeling, waiting like a slumped-over line-up. Melinda and Janice Taggart in navy blue dresses. Janice sniffed, and dabbed her eyes with a tissue; Melinda looked at her hands in her lap. Skip had a few friends here, but no Jack MacAdams, no Guy Ross. The Arvidsons, though, sat heads bowed.

My parents and I knelt again. At St. Thomas' we always said a prayer of thanksgiving after Communion. I felt I should give thanks for something. Be thankful for Mom, Dad, and Granddad. Pray something more for Skip, Liz, Mr. Malloy, and Marty too. What was in my head was jumbled like trash. I couldn't find—

At that moment I felt a strange calm yet frightening sensation: the touch of a hand on my right shoulder. I looked. No hand was there. Nothing. The sensation lay there for maybe five or six seconds, then lifted away.

I looked at Dad. His hands rested on the rim of the pew in front of us. Behind me was a woman whose face appeared suntanned. She wore gold earrings and was dressed all in black. She sat with her back against the pew's back rest, her head bowed. Her lips moved silently as she fingered rosary beads. She reminded me of a gypsy.

Another sensation settled over me. A peaceful wave spread across my shoulders and flowed down my arms into my hands; nothing like what the bourbon had given me but almost the same as the pleasant feeling I had experienced when Dad gave me a back rub.

Immediately I felt the touch of a hand again. A signal? A warning? It lay once more on my right shoulder. A lightness and calm and fear all through me. I had committed no crime, had only sampled Dad's bourbon. *Nothing terrible. I hadn't hurt anyone.*

We stood for the recessional hymn. The touch melted away. In its place a cool-warm liquid sensation flowed within me. It calmed me.

"Was that you?" I quietly asked Dad after the family, acolytes, Father Bradeen passed by us.

"What?"

"Did you put your hand on my shoulder?"

He looked puzzled. "No," he said.

"Did Mom?"

"No. How could she do that? Be quiet now until this is over."

Weak, without any strength at all, I felt as if blood had drained from me. My lips and the inside of my mouth tasted dry. I looked behind me again. The gypsy-looking woman still whispered over her rosary beads. Her hair was coal black except for a white, feather-shaped streak on one side.

The Malloy family accompanied the draped coffins out of the church. Ushers walked to the front pew and dismissed the congregation one row, left then right, at a time.

As my parents and I left our pew, I noticed the gypsy woman had suddenly disappeared. She was not in the pew behind us. I did not see her outside walking toward the priest's house; I didn't see her on Lorrence Boulevard or Willowyn Terrace. I did not see her behind the wheel of any car.

"Did you put your hand on my shoulder during the service?" I asked my mother.

She said no.

"Something touched me there," I said.

"Probably your imagination," she replied.

Nana, was it you?

Mr. and Mrs. Malloy were buried at St. Mary's Cemetery two miles from the church, on the southern edge of Lorrence. A statue of the Virgin Mary stood atop a granite arch over the entranceway. Her arms and hands welcomed visitors.

The gravesites lay fifty yards from where the entrance road forked to the right. Skip, Liz, and Marty stood together; relatives sat in chairs around the graves under a green canopy. My parents and I joined other mourners and stood behind the family. The Taggart twins, the Arvidsons, and the gypsy-looking woman were not there. Two coffins rested on metal supports above the empty graves.

The service lasted only fifteen minutes. The whish-whish of highway traffic disturbed Father Bradeen's prayers spoken in Latin. I really didn't care how Latin sounded or what it meant. I wanted answers to questions. Each question began with *Why*.

After final prayers Skip and his relatives shook hands with the mourners and expressed their thanks. Mom and Dad went before me. I didn't hear what they said. I fixed on the green mat around the graves and the brown mahogany coffins still above them. I waited for another touch of a hand.

Dad tapped me on the shoulder. "David?"

I stepped forward. "I'm sorry, Skip," I said to my best friend, but couldn't look him in the eye for very long.

"Thanks, man," he replied.

Marty gave me a firm handshake, and Aunt Ceil, whose hair and dress smelled of cigarettes, and Liz embraced me. I wanted to hold Liz longer than she let me. "Thank you, David. Please come to the reception?" she whispered before she slipped her hands from me.

As Dad drove out of the cemetery, I spotted Jerry Zanger in his Mercury angled to one side of the entrance.

Who's that kid?" Dad asked.

I told him.

"Is he the one who—?"

"Yes."

Part III: SEARCH

11

Comfort

I walked into the Forgeville Inn reception room. I saw myself as an intruder, someone not recognized by the men in dark suits and loosened neckties: *Who's that kid? Why's he here?* I was conspicuous but also I was someone to whom the women in dark dresses and gabbing like starlings gave little attention.

I spotted Liz. She clutched tissues in her hand and shook her head as she talked with Ceil Kinsale and a girl in a black suit with her back to me.

No one smiled.

The black-suited girl stood. It took me a couple seconds to recognize Lorraine Wyles. *While away the hours with Wyles*...Right now she didn't give the impression she could make out in the back seat of a car or on a bed or anywhere. She dabbed her eyes with a tissue, then walked to a bar where soda, beer, wine and liquor were served. The man tending bar poured a glass of wine and handed it to her. When she offered to pay him, he shook his head and waved his hand back and forth.

Marty Bannon separated himself from a group of men and walked toward me. He took long strides and nodded as he extended his hand to me. "David, thanks for coming," his handshake strong and tight, the way he had probably gripped Mr. Malloy and tried to wrestle the gun from his hand: *"Give it to me!"* He looked behind me. "Your mom and dad with you?" he asked.

I said that they might come later. The inside of my mouth felt like dry paper.

Marty squinted, but sunlight was not shining in our part of the room. He blinked when he asked me, "Soda? Whuddia like? Coke? Root beer? Ginger ale?"

Scotch and Coke, or bourbon and ginger ale, my playful self nearly told him, just to watch his reaction. I settled for root beer.

He brought two bottles of root beer from the bar and handed me both bottles. "One for you, one for Skip. He's up in room two-twelve, second floor. He didn't feel like coming down here. Can't say as I blame him." He turned away, but over his shoulder he said, "Go on up. He'll be glad to see you."

I knocked twice at Room 212 and called out, "Skip, it's me." From inside I could hear a disc jockey's patter. I gave another quick knock-knock. He opened the door.

"No room at the Inn. Mary and Joe left already," he mumbled and rubbed his eyes. In khaki shorts, navy blue polo shirt, and bare feet, he looked ready more for the Ocean City boardwalk than for the aftermath of a funeral. He slumped down on the bed on his back, hands clasped under his head.

I showed him the root beers.

"Got something better," Skip retrieved two bottles of beer from the toilet tank. He said he had robbed the reception room cooler next to the bar and sneaked the bottles upstairs squeezed between his left arm and suit coat. He flashed a 'church key' now—"Came prepared," to uncap his treats.

"Cheers," he said, and took a long swig and then belched. "Ahh...Sorry I'm uncouth...Do I give a shit?"

"I saw Lorraine Wyles downstairs with Liz," I said. "She's drinking wine."

"Nice. The old man'd be proud of her."

Skip's face blurred sarcasm and anger, anger strong enough to hit someone.

From the radio on the bedside night-table the Four Aces sang "Take my hand, I'm a stranger in paradise..."

I skimmed the room: bed, bureau, one window giving a view of a field, a desk with an attached mirror, desk chair, a painting of a desert at sunset, bathroom, and an alcove with a horizontal metal bar to hang clothes.

Skip switched off the radio and blew air from his mouth. "Christ, Harper, donchya have anything better to do than come here? You must be hurtin' for somethin' to do."

I remembered something Dad had told me the morning Liz and Aunt Ceil arrived at the house. He and I were alone in the living room before Skip came downstairs. As gently as he had ever spoken to me, he had said, "Let him talk about whatever he wants. You don't have to say much. Just listen, and let him know he can count on you."

"You okay?" I asked Skip.

"What the hell's it look like? I ain't doin' much. My head's scrambled. Everything's like a jigsaw puzzle dumped on the floor. I'm supposed to pick up the pieces and put'em together and I don't know where to start. That make sense to you?"

Was it you, Nana…?

"I'll help you."

He squeezed his eyes shut and immediately opened them. "My head…I see the old man, I see my mom. They're laughin', next minute yellin' their heads off at each other, and then Mom goes out and takes care of her garden and the old man takes off or else he plops himself in front of the TV and swears at the Phillies. Bottle of Ballantine in hand…Ask the man for Ballantine!" He raised his bottle in salute. "My whole life's been a goddamn roller coaster."

"That why you didn't take Communion?"

"What the hell'd you do, Harper? Keep score on who went up and who stayed put? Put in the pew? *Pew, pew*! I had my reasons. I told Lizzie and Marty and my crazy aunt I wasn't going to. My business. Not theirs, and right now not yours or anybody else's." He puffed air from his mouth and said, "You're lucky the way you have it at your house, Harper."

"My parents argue once in a while but not like your mom and dad."

"Ha! I won't have to hear'em bitch anymore, for damn sure."

He lifted the bottle of beer as if he intended to bruise his mouth or force the beer into it. The bottle's lip clicked against his front teeth. He swigged three swallows, held the bottle in both hands on his belt buckle, and blew air from between his lips. "Bastard," he mumbled.

"*Who?*" It was a foolish question but I had slipped into my own puzzle of a touch on my shoulder and could not explain that experience to him.

"The old man, that's who, numbnuts. Who'd you think? Hitler, Mussolini, McCarthy?" He turned, faced me, pointed the bottle at me. "Anybody else you wanna add to the list? The old man, stupid. My own *sister's* father. The guy who played grab ass with her and that Lorraine, that's who, in the garage the night of Lizzie's party. You and me and Lizzie and my mother, we're cleaning up while my old man's in the garage tryin' to get into Lorraine Wyles' pants. Jeezus Christ, Harper! And probably every girl he could get his grubby hands on. She never said a word about it, not till after that dance. She told Lizzie and me and Marty.

"I should've cut the old man's little prick off. Prick off, jerk off, knock off…Marty took care of that, didn't he." My friend turned back and faced the wall as if shoved there, the bottle cradled against his chest. His voice had risen with each action, risen and fallen with each repetition until he pounded his fist against the wall, twice, three, four, five times, each harder than before until strength and hope left him. Muffled by the bedcovers, he cried "Mom…"

Minutes? A half hour? Longer? I wasn't sure how long Skip cried and how long it took him to stop. Like the angry names and hurled accusations, his sounds and shoulders rose and fell until his breaths drifted slowly into sleep. I stepped to the bed and looked down at his face; his eyes closed, mouth open.

I stepped away.

"Whu!" Skip swerved onto his back. He flailed with his left arm as if to ward off an attacker. Beer spilled from the bottle onto the bedcover.

"Whoa, man! Calm down! I'll take care of it," I said.

We toweled off the top bedcover and stuffed the bottle between the mattress and bedspring. Skip went to the bathroom, blew his nose on toilet paper, and flushed the wad down the toilet. He ran water in the bathroom sink, wiped a washcloth over his face, washed his hands and dried his face and hands on a towel folded on the metal bar above the toilet.

I leaned against the wall at one corner of the window, the curtains bunched at my back.

"Bad dream," he said, and lay down on the bed again. "Big black truck outside the house. No lettering on the side or the driver's door. The engine's running. Nobody else around, just me by myself looking out the front door. I'm still a kid. Can't even see a driver but I know...I knew the truck's there to take me away." He gave a short laugh. "Then I woke up."

"You were pushing somebody or some thing away."

"Don't know who, don't much care right now."

The touch of a hand on my shoulder...Was it You?

"What's goin' on at that thing they call a reception?" he asked. "Bunch of women yacking their heads off? Probably about me and the old man and Mom. Women yack yack yack, men get blitzed. The second national pastime."

His sarcasm was back. I felt confident about knowing what to say to him.

"You wanna go out somewhere?"

"You kidding? No goddamn reception, that's for sure."

Too many people he didn't want to talk to. Too many questions, too many tears. He had heard enough questions, seen enough tears. I wouldn't add another question.

"I'm tired of shaking hands and having people hug me. Lizzie probably feels the same way."

Behind my eyes I imagined Mr. Malloy hug and touch his daughter. I saw Liz pull away and fix her father with a stare as if he had slashed her open and cut out her heart.

"How's she doing?"

He realized what I meant. He looked at the floor between us and then at the fields and sky beyond the window. "We stayed up last night and talked—Lizzie, Marty, and me. She told me some stuff she'd never told me before."

He spoke without anger, without desire for revenge. After she had moved to Ocean City, Liz had still felt her father's presence beside her, behind her, everywhere. His hands all over her when she thought about her mother and Skip. She would shiver, bow her head, close her eyes and strained to will those hands away. Around people, she would excuse herself until she was ready to return.

"That's how she met Marty," Skip said. "Working at the restaurant, bunch of the waitresses, cooks, bus boys, and friends closed the place one night and had a party. End of school bash. Lizzie went out to the boardwalk, just stood outside…When she came back in, Marty was waiting for her. Guess she likes him. He's a couple years older than her. Saving up cash to go to college. The guy's a pain in the ass sometimes but I guess Lizzie likes him. "

What's she think when Marty puts his arms around her? I asked myself.

"Lorrence cops gave her and Marty the third degree about why they came to the house," Skip continued. "Was it really to take my mother to Ocean City, or was it to get revenge on the old man? They asked Marty 'When you took the gun away from Malloy, is that when you shot him?' Lizzie kept explaining no, no. Marty wasn't able to get the gun from the old man. They had their hands on the gun—both of'em— when it went off. Marty didn't point the gun barrel at my father. It was just turned that way when it went off. Just that way. Right at his stomach."

I guess I had my answer.

"Arvidson there, too," Skip continued. "He saw the fight, he corroborated everything Liz and Marty told the cops and the lawyer. He and Marty tried to stop the bleeding but the old man, he was a gusher. All blood'n beer.

"And my mom…She's on the goddamn bedroom floor like he forgot her. Sonova bitch, sonova *bitch!*"

I heard Skip's words, but at the same time I remembered the presence of a hand on my shoulder and the feeling of peaceful water flowing through me.

Like an afterthought, Skip said, "I saw Zanger at the cemetery. Gave him the finger. Bastard..."

"Whud he do?"

"Just nodded."

"Something weird happened to me during the service." I had said it quickly, before I had the chance to take it back, keep it secret.

"What're you talking about?"

I described the sensation and my parents' explanation of it.

Skip lifted his glasses and rubbed the corners of his eyes with his thumb and forefinger. "That's weird. You making this up?" his voice as cautious as I had ever heard it.

"I'm not kidding."

I looked out the window again. An empty field. Beyond the field, construction of a long brick building on the Forgeville State College campus. Workers, two cement mixers small as toys from this distance at the work site.

Maybe I shouldn't have mentioned anything about the touch. Maybe talking about it made it only a story; a lie. But the touch had been neither a story nor a lie.

"Talk to your good Father Hepplewhite, even Bradeen. They got connections to whoever's upstairs. Good luck with that, but I don't think anybody's home up there now."

"I doubt it, too. But...you ever see a woman who looks like a gypsy in your church? Black hair, a white streak in it?"

"Like a *gypsy*?"

"That's what she looked like. I never saw her before."

"I dunno, Harper. The more you tell me...You sure you didn't have a hangover?" he asked. He made a pfttt sound with his lips.

"So you never saw this woman like that in church or around town?"

"We don't got no gypsies in our church, numbnuts. Damned if I've seen any in good ol' Lorrence." He clasped his hands behind his head and closed his eyes.

"You don't believe me, do you."

"I don't know what the hell I believe anymore. Yours sounds like a good story, though."

He didn't open his eyes.

I watched him breathe, the rise and fall of his chest. I wanted to be for Skip what Dad had told me: a friend "in the truest sense of the word." Maybe I could be, maybe not. I had a goal. Beat the shit out of Ross and MacAdams and Zanger and anybody else who had mocked and bullied and beaten up my best friend. I could take them on one at a time. Get in the first punch.

Nothing more to do here. Skip slept, safe for the moment. I quietly closed the door behind me.

The empty stairwell reminded me of one at the high school when classes were in session. My footsteps thunked down the concrete stairs. *No Sanctuary*...I squared up against two choices: going home or riding off somewhere. I nixed home...Somewhere else, sure, even some place I had seen before. Today I'd view it in a new way.

When I opened the stairwell doors to the hallway outside the reception room, the low and serious voices of the guests covered me like thin towels. The voices diminished when Liz Malloy and Lorraine Wyles walked to me.

Lorraine waited behind Liz when Liz took my hand. She didn't say a word. She kissed me on the cheek and walked away, her head bowed, Lorraine's hand on her arm.

———————

The side door to Our Lady Queen of Heaven's office and Sunday School classrooms was unlocked. I pushed it open, clicked it closed behind me. Where I stood at one end of a hallway the air smelled like rooms that hadn't had windows opened in a long time.

I didn't want to stay down there.

I walked the length of the hall to a flight of wide concrete stairs. The vestibule my parents and I had entered that morning lay above me. I tip-toed up the stairs, pressing down on the upper part of my soles so that my footsteps sounded soft and blunted.

The hand on my shoulder had felt human...like flesh and bone...

No one else in the vestibule. I pushed open one of the outside entrance doors an inch. No one approached the church. I closed that door and opened the inside door on the right and entered the church.

Quiet. "Quiet as a church," Granddad had sometimes kidded. Without a smile he had said it about his and Nana's bedroom the night she died.

Two candles flickered on the altar. Like a larger-than-life casket the altar seemed farther away from me then than it had been that morning when people had knelt in prayer in the pews. Maybe a lot of people brought things closer to you. The pews were empty.

I walked up the middle aisle. Six rows back from the front pew. *There. We had sat there. And the gypsy-looking lady sat behind me, her lips moving silently as she slipped the rosary beads through her fingers.*

Who are you? Where are you?

I stood next to the pew where she had fingered her rosary beads as if they could transmit power to her. I hadn't seen that gypsy woman come in, hadn't noticed her behind me until after I had felt the hand touch my shoulder. I looked at the backrest of the pew where she had prayed and the pew's backrest where Mom, Dad, and I had sat. I strained to see, *find something* that proved the woman had been there; that proved she had not been someone in my imagination. I searched the floor for rosary beads. None. I even sniffed the air for some perfumy trace of her. None. Only aromas of wood, paper, and cloth. Not even incense drifted in the air anymore. No one but me in the church.

I walked out.

I walked the Schwinn down the sidewalk to Lorrence Boulevard. A gray, white, and blue bus lumbered up the hill toward the railroad.

Like a fort on the hill overlooking the church presided the rectory, a two-story house with a wide porch and four pillars supporting the porch roof. The rectory's windows looked like wide dark eyes. From where I stood the second story didn't fit properly above the main floor. The second floor seemed to push down upon the first. No one stood on the porch; no one walked up the sidewalk to the porch stairs. Like the inside of the church, the outside of the rectory was empty.

Locked up. Trespassers forbidden.

Ten minutes later, walking into my house was like re-entering a classroom and feeling as if I did something wrong, everyone staring, snickering at me. Everyone turned out to be only my mother and father and Granddad in our living room. I knew damn well I hadn't done anything wrong. Catholic Church rules were wrong. Jerry Zanger was a lousy son of a bitch, so was Guy Ross, so was Jack MacAdams and Mr. Malloy.

"Where did you go?" "What did you do?" "Are you all right?" "How's Skip doing?"

I answered the questions. After the interrogation I ignored my parents and Granddad. I made myself a beef bologna and sliced tomato sandwich, poured a glass of iced tea, and transported my snacks to my bedroom.

No more questions. No more suspicious eyes on me.

No beer, Granddad. No hard stuff. Just iced tea…

I closed the door. Listened to the radio—"Mystery Train" on a Philadelphia station, Elvis Presley's voice and the band's guitar, bass, and drums mourned love and hope and carried them toward a dark and final place.

I must have fallen asleep early that night. Beyond the window the sky loomed gray-black. My radio on, a newscaster reported the Secretary of State had met with President Eisenhower in Palm Springs, chance of thundershowers throughout the Delaware Valley tomorrow. The illumined hands on the bureau clock read five minutes after eleven.

I slipped out of bed, cracked open the door an inch, and listened for Mom and Dad's voices. Nothing from downstairs, nothing from their bedroom across the hall. Not even a strand of light beneath their door.

So far, so good.

I tip-toed down the stairs, stayed on the balls of my feet to the kitchen. The pantry door was ajar enough for me to go in sideways. I yanked the cord of the pantry light. Old friends Corn Flakes, Raisin Bran, and Cheerios; five pound bags of sugar and flour. Broom, dust pan, and floor mop propped in a corner. Blackberry wine, something called pinot grigio, something labeled merlot. Bottles of gin and bourbon. Dad's collection in order.

I pulled the pantry door about three-quarters closed. Just in case I heard creaks or footsteps on the stairs.

What the hell. Make myself comfortable on the floor, my confident imagination persuaded me. Time for night-cap.. Eeny, meeny miney, mo. Catch a tiger by the toe. If he hollers…Bourbon it is.

I unscrewed the cap. *Good ol' bourbon…Smells thick, kind of bitter, right up my nose.* I tipped the bottle to my lips and let the sip slide across my tongue and down my throat.

Don't be a chicken, Harper. Be a man. Take a man-size swig!

Seconds later I felt the bourbon slide into my stomach. Warm. A burning but not a burning that hurt.

I took a longer sip and swallowed it right away. I imagined the warm stuff as it floated down my esophagus, down, down. A little pond of bourbon in my gut, mixing and stinging with the sandwich or what was left of it. Nothing painful.

What the hell you doin', Harper? my conscience sounded off. **Get away from that stuff. Don't you know what it can do to you?**

Sure, but don't worry your little head about it.. Wanna find out for myself what it's like. About time I try the stuff, anyway. Not bad so far. A little warm, not enough to hurt me.

I drank another swig, another, and then another.

Stuff feels hot. No wonder people get drunk on it…

No creaks or steps from the stairs. Nothing moving in the house. Still life again.

I stood, the uncapped bottle in one hand, both feet on the pantry floor. *Leaned back against the shelves…Don't knock anything down. So far, so good. Warm fuzzy head, dry mouth. A little sway from side to side inside my head but not dizzy. Arms and legs tingly, but I'm fine, I'm fine.. Not gonna keel over like some stupid comedians on TV or the movies…Do this more often, build up strength.*

One more.

I then screwed the cap back, set the bottle exactly where I had found it and went back to my room.

Safe! He's safe at home, ladies and gentlemen.

You know what I did downstairs. You're not happy with me, I guess. I was trying things out, testing myself. I feel okay…I'll be fine.

You're almighty, You know everything. That's what Hepplewhite preaches, that's what my Sunday School teachers told me. So, Mr. Almighty, since You know about everything, what happened to me in church?

Nana, was it you? What the hell's going on?

Sorry about my language. Somebody better give me an answer soon.

12

Storm Season

Southern New Jersey's July summer erupted into thunderstorm season. Afternoon skies spread endless haze. Humidity wrapped around my neck and shoulders and pushed against me on Halcyon's tee.

I lolled on that platform three days after the funeral. Jack MacAdams and Guy Ross stretched out like teen movie idols on the boards at a cautious distance. MacAdams' smile conveyed apology for prying questions about Skip's parents and offered a half-hearted wish for renewed friendship between us. I wasn't ready for his friendship. Ross's familiar swagger proved he knew about me telling MacAdams "Go to Hell!" I didn't give a damn if they talked or didn't talk to me. I wanted to be left alone.

"What's Alfred E. gonna do?" Ross asked me out of the corner of his mouth, his question more accusing than sincere.

"Fuck you, Ross," I said matter-of-factly.

He pulled himself up on one elbow. I didn't change my position, which was the same as his. We stared each other down, my attention to him a silent challenge: *make one move, you sonova bitch, and I'll pound the shit out of you.*

MacAdams directed a remark to Ross, part of which I didn't hear but which sounded a warning to his friend. What I did hear MacAdams tell Ross was "Wait: some other time."

Ross sniffed and moved his mouth as if to choose his words carefully. "Oh, I humbly apologize. Harper, to you and everyone here on this tee"—

he stood up and extended his right and left arms to everyone else on the platform—"I humbly and *sincerely* apologize."

MacAdams pursued the subject with something between a smile and a sneer. "Doesn't Malloy feel like coming here?"

The question wasn't worth a response. I gave none.

Ross laid down again and turned onto his back and closed his eyes against the sun. Drowsily he said, "That fool's gotta be spooked. He'll never make it through school this year. Everybody asking him about what happened? He should get the hell outta town."

"Who's he gonna live with?" MacAdams asked.

"Not *me*," Ross laughed." I mean, I'll be honest: I do not like the boy. Never have. Just one've those things, I guess. You get along with him, Harper. Maybe Malloy can move in with you."

I said nothing.

"I *still* think that sonova bitch pushed me down the fire escape that time in seventh grade. Claims he didn't, I know he did. I *know* it. I can still feel his hand push me."

Maybe Skip had lied. Maybe he had told me the truth. I didn't care. The truth of that incident didn't matter to me. I wanted the truth of something else.

"Nobody helped him," I mumbled.

Ross and MacAdams snickered. Maybe they had heard me, maybe not. Did I care? No.

"Goddamn right Alfred E. needs help," Ross said. "What happened to his parents was the worst. I'm not the man for the job, though."

He saw me look at him in a way I had never looked at him before.

"Sorry, Harper. I'm sorry for what Malloy's going through, but I wish the bastard'd just go away."

Before my brain flashed a retaliatory plan, I lunged at Ross and pinned him to the tee's wet boards. I lifted and pounded his shoulders and head, lifted and pounded Guy Ross into the wood. I screamed into his face as I snapped his head down and up on the boards like a coconut: "Shut up, you bastard...you *shit*...you *lousy shit*!"

"Get the hell *offa* me!"

MacAdams grabbed my arms and swerved me off of Ross's flailing body. "Damn, take it *easy*, Harper! He didn't mean it. You're one crazy kid."

I yanked away from MacAdams and crouched wrestler-like in front of him and Ross. Ross didn't flinch as he pushed himself up from the boards. He rubbed his neck and narrowed his eyes in wait for my next move.

"Sonsa' bitches, you better hope you never go through what happened to Skip! *Bastards!*"

I plunged into the water, swam to the beach, grabbed my towel, and swung onto my bike. Lake water slid and dripped from my body; my mouth felt dry as a communion wafer. If my parents weren't home, I'd grab another shot or two of bourbon. Maybe more.

———

The following morning I stood next to Skip, Liz, and Marty as they sold housewares, appliances, and furniture displayed on the front lawn of the house where they used to live; what they didn't sell, a crew of three men loaded into a moving truck with Pennsylvania license plates in the driveway. The truck and family's destination? Mount Howard, a small town on the southern edge of the Pennsylvania coal region. Liz and Skip would live with Ceil Kinsale.

The air in the front yard felt close and damp, the sky a pale, hazy white. The forecast was for temperatures in the low 90s with equal humidity. Cicadas buzzed their tight rise-and-fall signal in the maple and oak trees along Jessup Avenue.

I felt strange to watch a sister and her brother and boyfriend as they sold the TV, washing machine, refrigerator, tools, the kitchen table and chairs, lamps, and a rug "on the cheap," as Marty characterized the goods' prices. I had shared meals at that table, seen those lamps, sat in one of those chairs, and walked on that dining room rug. I couldn't picture those things in another house. I thought that maybe everything from the house should be hauled to the Lorrence dump, where it would decay or become ashes in a controlled burn. As my father had said to me the night before, "They should get rid of every single thing in that place. No one will want to buy a damn thing from where somebody was murdered."

One man and woman—They looked like a husband and wife in their fifties—bought the table and chairs, and a woman Liz recalled from Our Lady Queen of Heaven bought the picture of Pope Pius XII. "I have just the place for it," she said, giving Liz the five-dollar asking price and then sliding the painting into the back seat of her car.

Marty grinned. "She'll probably hang it in her bathroom. She could talk over Church policy with him while she's doing her business."

I recalled the woman who looked like a gypsy. I had not seen her since the funeral service. I wondered where she was today, where she lived. She wouldn't be allowed to live at the rectory where Father Bradeen lived. So where was she?

The quick light-hearted mood of Marty's remark changed when the movers carried a mattress and box spring, a throw rug, and a box of tools from the house and into the truck. All of the items so small, I thought, as the crew maneuvered them into the truck's gaping dark mouth and against the walls.

Looking at truck's contents, Liz turned away and bent toward the screened porch. "I can't watch this," she said.

Marty followed her. They entered the front door and moved out of view. We heard her sob.

"She's had it worse than me," Skip murmured next to me. "I just wanna get the hell out've here."

Liz then called out, "Don't *do* that, you know I don't like it."

We heard Marty's voice say something that sounded like an apology.

"What's going on?" I wondered to Skip.

He shook his head as if he didn't want to talk about it.

The final item sold was Mr. Malloy's Ford. A father and son from Forgeville gave Skip a check for $500 for the car. Skip stuffed the check in his jeans pocket and gave the Ford's keys to the son and wished him "Happy motoring." Skip didn't look at the vehicle as it angled out of the driveway onto Jessup Avenue. I did. As if some unexplained force directed me—like the touch on my shoulder?—I watched the black Ford move gradually down Jessup and turn onto Lorrence Boulevard.

Skip mumbled, "I didn't want the damn thing anyway."

A minute later one of the movers, removing his work gloves, called over to Skip, "One more bed frame, and that's about it."

Skip gave him an "OK" wave. "Who's gonna wanna buy this place?" he wondered. "Might as well tear it down."

I retreated to my room again after supper that night. A thunderstorm murmured in the distance through the evening. Beyond my windows rain washed from the roof and gurgled down the drain pipe.

I tugged Granddad's boxes from my closet and studied the photographs of Nana and Granddad and my mother again. I read names and dates on the bottoms and backs, studied the stiff, stern-looking man and woman in high collars and high-ankled shoes, the unsmiling girl posed with her parents. Sepia and black and white photographs. Scenes of life— still life, in a way, but not pieces of a puzzle that needed to be placed in a kind of order. Maybe Granddad had given them to me so that I could simply look at them and remember them.

Nana, you probably know what happened at Skip's house and about the touch? Did you do it? Do you know what's going on in my life?

I felt stuck inside questions without answers. Maybe it was stupid to keep wondering what the answers were. Maybe I wasn't meant to know the answers.

Rain slackened, thunder grumbled. I stashed the photographs in their boxes and left the boxes stacked on the floor under the bureau.

From downstairs, the pantry beckoned me but not before I listened for Mom and Dad's voices and the TV (nothing); not before I checked for light (none) beneath my parents' bedroom door. Not before I tiptoed down the stairs, careful to step on the mats to avoid the creeks of the wood stairs, and to tiptoe through the living room and dining room to the kitchen. I didn't turn on the kitchen light; if they checked on me, there'd be no tell-tale light. Through the shadowed kitchen I saw the pantry door three-quarter closed. I slipped between the kitchen table and the wall of cabinets, pulled open the pantry door, reached up, found the cord, and pulled.

Light. Suspicious silence.

I looked over my shoulder at the kitchen: no suspicious bodies. I listened. Waited. Waited until it was safe to unscrew the cap from the bottle of bourbon and take my first sip of the night. Not a lot. I wasn't going to cause trouble. I wouldn't hurt anyone. I'd be all right.

I stayed there. Long enough for the thunderstorm to circle back, for lightning to flare on the kitchen walls, and for thunder to boom like rocks and boulders tumbling down a hillside.

Long enough to swig the bourbon. Many times. Time enough to feel it settle in my gut. To wonder how many times Ralph Malloy had ever tipped it.

To wonder about the touch on my shoulder. Warm, good, but frightening. That gypsy-looking woman behind me didn't know me, she couldn't have reached me. Was I being punished because I couldn't understand God and Heaven?

Hi, we've never met, but I've heard a lot about You...

Time enough for me to picture Guy Ross's startled and teeth-clenched face as I slammed his head down, down, down on the tee's boards. The sonova *bitch! MacAdams too!* Time enough for my head to feel wavy and warm after I screwed the cap back on, my legs and feet rubbery and weak when I stood up.

I made sure to pull the cord to darken the pantry. Made sure to slide my right hand along the counter to guide me through the kitchen. Made sure I didn't bump any dining room chairs or Dad's desk chair in the living room, where he wrote checks to pay rent, insurance, car payments on the Plymouth...How long before he traded in that car?

Lightning blurred the window at the bottom of the stairs. At least ten seconds passed before thunder rumbled. The storm probably on its way to the shore.

The stairs: *This'll be good.* Left hand on the banister post. Brace, first step up, second, third—right hand sliding along the wallpaper— fourth, fifth, sixth. The landing: turn left, climb one, two—

A burst of light on the hallway ceiling.

Whoa, not good.

"Where were you? What were you doing?" Dad demanded, hands on hips. He wore only undershorts the color of the bourbon label.

"Downstairs." I turned my face away from him as I walked toward my bedroom door. My feet felt like fuzzy, swollen slippers.

"What were you *doing*? David? What—What's that—Is that liquor on your breath?" He grabbed my shoulder and turned me to face him. "I can smell it! Tell me the truth."

He steered me into my bedroom and flicked on the light. He did not close the door. He planted both his hands on my shoulders and sat me on the bed. "I don't care if you squint or blink or if we wake your mother. You're gonna remember this. How many drinks?"

"I dunno. A few. Two or three."

"Why?" I was surprised he didn't raise his voice. His tone was level, like Joe Friday on *Dragnet*.

"I dunno…I just felt like it."

"Felt like it. How'd you like it now if I made you drink more of that stuff? You think you'd like it? Huh?"

"Not much."

"Damn right you wouldn't. Let's go!" He squeezed my arm and urged me up from the bed.

I pulled away from his grip. "No!"

"Come on. You wanted it. I'll give you some more! I'll pour it and watch you drink to your heart's content. You think you're old enough. Come on, big boy!"

"I don't want to."

"What's the matter? You a sissy now?"

"What's going on?"

My mother leaned against one side of the doorway. Except for her face, arms, and the pink straps of her nightgown, her body was hidden by the enameled molding.

Dad ignored her. He didn't ignore me at all when he made the accusation: "David's been drinking." He then pulled at my arm again and ordered me, "Downstairs."

"I don't feel good. I'm gonna throw up."

"Too bad."

"Phil, take him to the bathroom," my mother said.

"Not yet. I want him to sit here and feel it come all the way up, *then* he can walk to the bathroom. That is, if he doesn't fall down." I recognized what lay behind his eyes: I had damaged his trust in me.

———————

"Be smart, Harper," I told myself the next night. Act as if nothing unusual happened last night."

Mom and Dad had invited Skip, Liz, Ceil Kinsale, and Marty Bannon for a going-away dinner before they drove to Mount Howard, Pennsylvania, 125 miles northwest of Lorrence. Skip would begin his sophomore year at Mount Howard High School. "I want him to try out for football," Marty mentioned during dinner. "Might toughen him up." He had squeezed Skip's left bicep. "Yep. You need some muscle there, my man."

Skip had curled his left arm. "I can always carry the water bucket if I don't make the team."

We had laughed. So had Skip. He seemed to have broken out of his funk.

Later, Skip and I on the back steps, my narration of the one-man liquor pantry raid and subsequent detection probably shoved him back into the funk.

"Sounds like booze got the best of you. Serves you right, you dumb shit. What the hell you tryin' to prove? Didn't you learn anything from my old man?"

"Yeah, I learned he was a sonova bitch."

"Sounds about right. So, you gonna follow in his footsteps? Might as well learn from the best, right?"

Skip was right. I was a dumb shit. But I wouldn't be a dumb shit for the rest of my life. I might break the three commandments my parents had made me promise to abide by. On my honor I will do my best and all that stuff: never drink liquor until I'm 21; try hard to make Honor Roll; talk to them—Mom and Dad—if I've got something on my mind.

Yeah, sure, right away. I didn't admit to them I had felt proud of my brief success. Something I had never done before but might try again. Before the next raid I'd wait until it was safe. Until Mom and Dad weren't home. Test myself. See how far I could go and get away with it. Break the promise.

"I haven't touched the stuff since," Skip said. "Do yourself a favor, numbnuts: stay away from it."

"You think I'm gonna become a drunk?"

He didn't answer me.

Dinner dishes, glassware and silverware clicked in the kitchen. Things touched you, then slipped away. Nana, the hand on my shoulder, now Skip. That's how life was. I'd have to start over, use the rest of the summer to sort things out by myself. Miracles? Forget it. Heaven? No proof. The gypsy woman? Did she vanish into thin air? What the hell was the truth? People lived, people died and were buried. That's how things were. That was the truth.

My mother opened the back door. "I spoke to Liz and Marty about this, and they said it was all right with them. How would you and Skip like to spend this weekend down the Shore?"

13

Ocean City

The weather-shingled cottage my parents rented for a three-day weekend sat adjacent to a corner grocery and two blocks from the southern end of the boardwalk. "We'll have to carry chairs and blankets and picnic things to the beach," my mother announced. "Mother Nature's supposed to be nice to us…Being here will be a nice change for all of us."

Granddad joined us, too. When we had crossed the Egg Harbor Bridge Friday morning, smelled the salt air, and caught sight of the bluish-green Atlantic, he commented "This ol' body's not in good beach condition. I'll sit on the boardwalk and watch."

"Us" did not include Liz and Marty; they would finish their summer jobs at the boardwalk restaurants, then make the trip to Mount Howard in Marty's Chevy Bel Air.

Before Skip and I tried out our independence, my mother's advice to us revealed more leniency than restriction: "Dad and I know you'll want to be on your own," You both have your allowances" (Skip's from Liz). "If you want to eat dinner by yourselves someplace on the boardwalk, fine; on the other hand, you're welcome to join us here. It's up to you. Just be careful, and come back tonight at a decent hour. And when you do," she smiled, "take off your shoes and tip-toe quietly."

Skip thanked her immediately. Seconds late with my thanks, I felt the push-pull of guilt meshed with rebellion that had gripped my shoulders when Skip had tabbed me "a dumb shit."

Already I had begun to consider where and how I could test myself.

At the beach:

Skip, Dad, and I tossed three-way spirals to each other along the warm sand. Dad moved lightly on bare feet as he faded back, as he pretended to evade imaginary defenders. He seemed to move like the popular Phil Harper, Lorrence High School athlete who had scored the winning touchdown against Forgeville on Thanksgiving 1928. The grinning, shoulder-padded 18 year-old on the wrinkled LHS yearbook page: He was my father. Since childhood I had feared his stern features and voice. A few nights ago I had disappointed him and Mom. Now they had awarded me another chance to be a trustworthy son. Dad had made a late-night deal with the cottage owner, one of his bank's customers, to rent our weekend retreat Friday through Sunday. I loved Dad for that but not just for that gesture. In those moments on the beach that afternoon, when he dove into high waves and swam out and, acknowledging my mother's call to "come in where it's safer," when he pushed back through the surf, stood up and shook water from his hair—"Ahh, feels good!"—, I loved him as if he was not just my father but a man who had touched me in ways I had not expected.

"You can still throw that high spiral, Phil!" Granddad congratulated Dad as we hauled our chairs and blankets back to the cottage.

"I've got players that make me look good."

"What about that Old Timers game, Dad? You gonna sign up?" I asked.

He chuckled, "I'm still thinking about it."

"You should, Mr. Harper," said Skip. "I'd pay to see you play."

On the boardwalk:

That night Skip and I feasted on cheeseburgers and shakes at a burger-and-hot dog shack, a hang-out for high school and college students. The only grown-ups a chin-whiskered woman at the cash register and a full-bellied man who shared the grill with a Trenton State T-shirted boy.

Because of what I had seen and experienced the past week, I felt older than fifteen. No specific age older but certainly older than their voices sounded. They were planning their night ahead: Meet me at the Chatterbox. You got wheels? Somers Point. We'll get served there, I know it. The persuasive rhythms of their voices reminded me of sounds at a dance at Sunrise Auditorium.

What Skip was thinking then? Of splashing through shallow waves to catch a pass Dad had lofted a pass to him? Of hearing Dad call out "Good catch!" after he had snagged the leather? Had Ralph Malloy ever tossed a football or baseball to his son? Had Ralph Malloy ever called out "Good catch!"

"Harper, you in there?" Skip snapped his fingers in front of my face as we walked out of the shack onto the boardwalk. "You got your mind on some girl's legs? Where we goin' from here?"

At the movie:

$.75 apiece to see *Shane*, a western Dad had taken me to when it had first come out. Shane, a loner, had wanted to give up his gunfighter reputation. Bullies, though, picked fights with him, first with fists, later with guns. I envisioned MacAdams, Ross, and Zanger as the bullies in the saloon. The one-time gunfighter wasn't a coward. He fought back. In the final shoot-out Shane killed the hired-gun Wilson. Outnumbered by henchmen, he was wounded, and rode off not into the sunset but into the night. Maybe he'd die. Maybe not. Dad and I had believed Shane would find a place to live in the mountains where he would hunt, fish, and grow vegetables: the kind of life Shane's friend Joe Starrett had worked for. Tonight, I still thought Shane was a hero who'd never die.

But Shane wasn't real. He was a fictional character. In the real world, people good and bad died. Fact of life.

What went through Skip's head during that final gunfight again? He didn't get up and leave; he stayed in his seat, stared straight ahead at the screen. When the gunfight was over, he swallowed and took a deep breath.

Outside again, we walked the boards.

At mini-golf:

Two junior high-age-looking girls whispered and giggled and played ahead of us. They spied on our skills. I matched Skip in holes-in-one—one apiece—and in pars and birdies. I matched him in shots around corners, through tubes, over and under bridges, and under windmill wheels. After 18 holes our scorecards showed us even at 42. That left the Free Hole-in-One test: up a ramp, through the middle of three tubes to send the ball down a chute to sound a buzzer and ring the bells.

I missed.

So did Skip.

The girls covered their mouths, giggled, and hunched away.

"Face it, Harper," Skip complained on the boards after the game. "Girls look at you, they think you're worth a shot. They see me, they laugh and walk away."

"They're jerks. They don't really know you. They don't see you the way my mom and dad and Granddad do."

Before we fell asleep that first night, he said, "I thought it'd be okay here. Not knowing anybody except Lizzie and your family. You're the only ones here who know what happened…The whole goddamn mess. Now I've gotta start over where I don't know anybody. You're the only friend I've got, Harper."

My throat tightened. "I'll come up there when I can." But how, when?.

"Zanger—at least he came to the cemetery. The Back-ups, they came to the funeral. Ross and MacAdams…Screw'em."

"That time on the fire escape, back in seventh grade: Did you push Ross?"

It took five seconds for Skip to answer. "I think he tripped on something," Skip muttered.

With Lizzie:

We saw her first with Mom, Dad, and Granddad Saturday night at Jetty Place, the restaurant where she waited tables. In a black uniform trimmed with a white lace collar, her blond hair pulled back and pinned in a bun, she made a show of "Good evening! May I help you?" and brought us extra rolls, served us our meals, including free refills of iced tea. After my parents and Granddad went back to the cottage, the restaurant staff let Lizzie off an hour early.

Now she had changed out of her uniform into khaki Bermuda shorts, brown sandals, and short-sleeved blue and white Villanova University sweatshirt Marty had given her. She walked the boards with Skip and me. Under and out from boardwalk lights, her face passed from bold light into shadows, as if she was two people in one body: the chatty Lizzie Malloy from before her birthday party, who had kissed me on the cheek that May afternoon, and who hugged me that night before all hell broke loose; the serious, anxious Liz who glanced right and left on the boardwalk in anticipation of someone who would harm her.

Tonight the different Liz Malloy.

Had she heard from Lorraine?

"Marty wanted to see you two," she explained, "but he has to work late…put in overtime."

"Good," Skip said out of the corner of his mouth. "Something about that guy…I dunno. He gets to me."

"Come on, Skip. Marty's nice. Nicer than a lot of the other guys I've met here. All they wanna do is drink and man-handle you. I've had enough of that," she said. She shivered, flexed her arms to signal she wanted more space between Skip and me now, and looked straight ahead as if she dared people in front of her to get in her way. Then, "Marty's nice to you," she said to her brother, "so be nice to him."

"If I have to. Long as he doesn't give me orders on how to live my life."

I walked with my best friend and his sister. I heard what they said to each other. I would remember it. Tonight the words drifted out of my head to the boardwalk crowd, out to the waves that spilled onto the beach. I wanted to be with Liz and Skip. I didn't want to be part of the clusters of kids and adults around us. I heard their voices too, but their words meant nothing, stuff to discard into trash receptacles along the railing above the beach. Only Liz and Skip were important to me.

The whoosh and spill of black waves set off an alarm in my head: *Go somewhere. Leave the parents and friends behind. Do what you want. Be alone. You can always come back if you need to.*

But the notion of being alone was like sucking in my breath on a winter night. I retreated into myself. The inadvertent touch of Skip's and Liz's arms on mine signaled I was safe with them, not ready to be on my own. I was still a kid but didn't want to be still a kid.

The by-chance touches of my friends' arms roused another touch in me. In a handful of seconds, I saw myself in frustration pick up a stone, fling it through St. Thomas' stained-glass window of Jesus the good shepherd. Pieces of pasture, sheep wool, and Jesus' cloth robe scattered to the ground. In this fantasy I spied the gypsy-looking woman standing at the edge of the St. Thomas front lawn. Her dark eyes accused me of a sacrilegious act. Without speaking, she conveyed to me that I would be hauled in front of and punished by the entire congregation: *Get rid of that kid! He's no good!*

When I approached the gypsy woman, she vanished.

The fantasy ended. I became a small figure in front of the church. I looked again at the stained-glass window. The hole was gone, the window complete as before I threw the stone.

I gathered a fistful of pebbles and flung them to the ground. The only answer to my question was nothing. No voice, no other touch, *Nothing.*

"You talking to yourself, Harper?" wondered Skip.

"Huh? No."

"I heard you, too," said Liz. She put her arm around my waist. "It's all right. I talk to myself now, too." The feeling of her arm and hip made me want to hold her, hold her close. How would she react if I held her close? Would she push me away, or would she stay in my arms, hold me close to her? Did Marty hold her close?

"Do you answer yourself?" her brother asked.

She laughed. "Sometimes I do."

"Weird. Do I know you? You really my sister?"

Liz linked her left arm around Skip's waist. "Always have been, always will be." She pulled Skip and me close to her so that our hips bumped hers. Liz, our cushion.

An outside wooden stairway provided rickety access to her apartment. Liz introduced us to Linda, one of her apartment mates, whose brown hair crunched in curlers. She waved hello, goodbye, apologized for her anti-social behavior, and exited down a hallway to her bedroom.

Lizzie poured three iced teas and led us through a kitchen door to a balcony. The view treated us to a long driveway below to several garages for other apartments. With one foot Liz pushed two aluminum beach chairs to us and saved a third for herself.

"Nice view." Skip toasted the panorama of garage roofs, rear apartment walls, and more outside stairways.

"Home away from," Liz offered.

For a minute, maybe two, no one said anything. Maybe we didn't need to. The absence of conversation expressed what we were thinking. When Liz asked, "How're you doing, David? Any girlfriend in your life?" it was a relief to me to hear her voice, to have something other than people who bled to talk about.

"Not really," I replied, thinking of Janice, thinking of Liz's lips on my cheek outside the Forgeville Inn reception room.

"Nobody special?"

Skip answered for me. He named Janice Taggart, a twin.

"A twin, huh? Identical?"

"Easy to tell them apart," Skip said. "You can talk to Janice. She's okay. Melinda? Forget it."

Liz gave me sisterly advice: "Be a gentleman at all times to the Taggart twins. Girls appreciate good manners in a young man."

She seemed older tonight, older than any other time I had ever be around her. When she slid her eyes away from me and Skip, she seemed to go off to a place only she knew. I wondered what that place was, and when I imagined what it was and where it was, I didn't want to see it. I just wanted to hold her and feel her close to me.

"Harper always does all the right things," my best friend commented. He punctuated his statement with an exaggerated clearing of the throat. "Does Marty? He better."

"Marty's a gentleman." Liz spoke it softly, as if she wanted it to be a quiet compliment. She was the different Liz again. "I wouldn't—Never mind. David, just be a good friend." She put her hand on my arm. Her hand felt chilled from her iced tea glass. I didn't care. I liked the feel of her hand on my arm.

We didn't talk much longer. Liz explained the rest of her and Marty's summer schedule, adding, "Both of us need money for school. No school, though, for either one of us for a while." Marty would work on a crew at his father's Mt. Howard lumber yard, Liz as a clerk in the business's office. "Life has a way of taking your dreams away."

She hugged Skip and me and thanked us for coming to see her. She kissed us both, and as she had done one night in April she held me seconds longer than she had held her brother. Liz let go before I did.

Before we went into the cottage, Skip and I stretched our legs from the front steps. Above the glow of streetlights, stars shown like points of needles. Front porch conversation from boarding houses and apartments drifted out to us, the words indistinguishable but sounding private. An Ocean City police cruiser passed in front of us at normal speed toward the center of town.

"I heard what you did to Ross," Skip began.

"How'd you find out?"

"MacAdams called me. You believe it? We had a good talk. He's okay, I think."

"I still don't trust him."

"He might be useful to society someday. Ross, I don't think so. Thanks for beating the shit out of him."

"I enjoyed it."

I asked about Lorraine Wyles.

"What about her?" Skip replied.

"She going out with anybody?"

"I dunno, I don't care."

"Just wonderin', that's all."

"I don't wanna talk about this stuff."

What would have been the right words of comfort and confidence to say to my best friend? And why did 'While away the hour with Wyles' keep creeping into my head like a dirty secret? What did that stuff make me? Was I really any different from the man who had broken the trust of his daughter and her friend?

"I been thinking about what happened to you at church," Skip said. "The hand on your shoulder."

"That's what it felt like."

He sounded like a lawyer interrogating a witness when he asked me, "You sure it wasn't somebody near you? That gypsy-looking woman?"

"Pretty sure."

"Nobody walked by and touched your shoulder?"

"Nobody. It happened before the last hymn. I knelt down, that's when I felt it. My parents didn't do it, neither did the gypsy woman."

"How'd you know she didn't?"

"She was sitting back in her seat and doing stuff with her rosary beads. She couldn't've leaned that far forward. I'd've seen her."

"Who was she?"

"How the hell should *I* know. I never saw her in church, never saw her before in my whole life."

He dropped his lawyer act when he said, "You're not much help, Harper. You sure she was there when you left? She wasn't a ghost?"

"No. Do ghosts wear perfume? But she smelled sweet, and she had black hair except for a weird looking patch of white on one side. I'm gonna look for her again after I get home."

Skip bit his lower lip. "Don't know any gypsies. Maybe I'll ask—"

He caught himself. I knew what he had almost said. He made a noise through his lips. "Stupid, Malloy. They're dead."

I flashed the pained look on Dad's face that awful night as he answered Skip's question: *"Did he kill her?"*

Crickets sounded signals beneath us. The front door of the house across the street hung open, downstairs windows glowed pale orange. No laughter from there, no conversation, not even voices and music.

"It's strange," Skip said quietly. "I had this gut feeling it was gonna happen. Not that exact night, but it was coming. The old man…Couple nights before, he came at my mother. He was gonna hit her, but she grabbed a knife and pointed it at him, told him if he took one more step she'd use it."

"You saw it happen?"

"No. She told me the day after. That's when she called Lizzie and asked her to come home and bring her down here." He cleared his throat and became silent for a while.

I should have said something but all I did was sit there.

"Be thankful what you got at home, Harper."

Skip looked over his shoulder through the screened-in porch, then down at the sidewalk in front of us. The lenses of his glasses flashed headlights from a passing car.

"Thanks for a good weekend," he said, his voice still tight.

————

"I want to talk to you," I told Mom and Dad Monday evening, the night after we came home from Ocean City; the night after Skip and his family had gone to Pennsylvania.

"What about?" Dad answered.

We had finished dinner. Dad stacked plates and utensils on the sink counter.

I glanced across the kitchen to the pantry door, partially open. If I leaned in my chair, I could see the neat rows of wine, liquor, and soda on the floor under the lowest shelf. I did not lean. I sat as casually as I could at my place at the table. Dad sat across from me, Mom to my right, their faces and arms sunburned. Through the open window above the sink we heard a blue jay's angry squawk.

"Not about what I did before we went to Ocean City," I said. "Something else: what I felt on my shoulder at Mr. and Mrs. Malloy's funeral. You didn't believe me."

"What did it feel like?" my mother asked.

I reminded them it was the touch of hand and the strange and peaceful feeling that went through me afterwards. "You told me I'd imagined it."

"You probably did," Dad said.

"I'm not lying, Dad!"

They looked at each other as if they didn't know what to say or do.

"Did someone inadvertently touch you?" my mother asked.

I described the gypsy woman who had sat far back in the pew behind us. "She was doing stuff with her rosary beads. It couldn't've been her."

Dad stood, ran water in the sink, and rinsed the dinner plates. "I don't know…I think you were so upset about things you only thought someone touched you."

"I didn't just think it. I felt it, twice."

"Then what?"

"It went away. I was afraid and I felt strange but all right. What do you think it was?"

My mother gave me a half smile, shook her head, and quietly said, "I don't know. I think you were just so caught up in your emotions. We've been through a lot."

I wanted an explanation I could understand and accept. I believed in my emotions and truth. I couldn't accept my mother and father's doubt.

14

"Dog Days"

So Granddad called them: hot, muggy days of early August when a normally friendly dog might turn on you, snap at you and bite you for no reason.

I liked working up a sweat in 'the dog days'. I created my own version of football prep. I biked around town every day, pumped fast and hard to strengthen my legs for runs, blocks, and tackles. If I made the team. If.

Dad approved my regimen. Home from work one afternoon, he stood in front of the porch and watched me churn the block from St. Thomas' to our house. He tapped a folded newspaper against his leg as I angled into our driveway, and then he pursed his lips and nodded as if he realized something previously unknown to him. "Working hard?"

He turned his attention to the front lawn. Maybe he still held a grudge against me for drinking, but he walked alongside me while I guided the bike to the front steps. He gripped the rear fender and helped me lift my personal mode of transportation onto the porch.

"What position will you try out for?"

"I dunno. Probably half-back or end."

He nodded again. He didn't smile. He studied me. "You might be a little short for an end, you need to be tall to catch those passes, but you're right for a half-back. Keep taking these rides," he said nodding toward the bike and tapping the front fender with the paper, "get your legs in shape, you'll make some good runs."

He walked onto the porch.

"You made some good runs when you played, didn't you," I said.

"Me? Yeah." He looked down at the spindles of the porch railing while he pushed his foot against the rung of the rocking chair he had sat in during the Fourth of July parade. The chair tilted forward and back, forward and back. "I was just a little guy, but I made a few touchdowns." He tapped me twice on the arm again with the newspaper. "You've got a couple inches on me already. You get right in there. Show the coaches you've got something."

"I wish you'd've signed up for the Old Timers game, Dad. It would've been fun."

He nodded and bit the right corner of his lower lip. "Yeah, it would have. I had other things on my mind, though. We all did."

He went inside; the front screen door clicked behind him. I heard him call out "Anybody home?", his usual greeting when he didn't see my mother in the living room. I heard their voices together deep in the house.

I stayed on the porch steps. I squeezed the bike's tires and checked the tightness of the spokes. The bottle of bourbon still rested on the pantry floor. I had looked at the bottle more than five seconds a couple days ago. Only looked at it. Nothing more. I hadn't touched bourbon since the night Dad met me in the hallway. I had made a promise to Mom and Dad. After the weekend in Ocean City, I planned on sneaking a swig. Just one swig. But after Dad had talked football with me, I felt proud I hadn't broken that promise. I didn't want to let him and Mom down.

I'd ride tomorrow, the day after that, and the day after that. I'd put somebody on their ass for sure.

Sometimes I rode to Halcyon Lake. I swam, swigged root beer, pedaled home. MacAdams and Ross dove and swam around the tee like porpoises putting on a show. They reveled in the laughter and applause from three or four sunbathers. I maintained distance from the human-marine life.

Shirley Brackett was absent from Halcyon. She, her younger sister, and their mother spent August at the family's beach house in Cape May; Mr. Brackett stayed in Lorrence to take care of funerals. I didn't miss Shirley now; there were other girls to look at and daydream about. Even Back-ups Melinda and Janice Taggart, suntanned and smiling when they called out "Hi, David," didn't seem mousy anymore, especially Janice. Freckles across the tops of her breasts were like bracelets, the space between her breasts a narrow valley. I might ask her to go to the movies after the school year began. Maybe after I played in a few jayvee games, gave some hits, and gained some yards and popularity. *Hey, you see that block Harper made? Some hit, man!* If I made the team. If.

I wanted bruises, symbols that would rid my system of bloody bodies and unanswered questions.

One afternoon I pedaled my Schwinn out to the farm where the little boy who rode on the tractor lived. The boy had smiled as he helped the man steer, his father's arms around him. I slowed as I passed the property. The barn door leaned open halfway, laundry hung on a line between the back porch and a post in the yard. I saw no little boy, only men and women picking beans and tomatoes in the field.

I braked, skidded to a stop on the shoulder, checked traffic both ways, and turned around and pedaled back to Lorrence. I missed that little kid. Maybe he was still having fun somewhere, I hoped.

Another afternoon I rolled toward a certain house on Pine Lane, on purpose, a narrow, fifty-yard-long avenue of small, tired-looking houses with small, tired yards. There, second house on the left: the house where Jerry Zanger lived. A tin trash can, its lid hanging off one side, stood on the back porch. Peels of white paint lay like open scabs on the street side of the house. Zanger (I assumed the dungareed pant legs were his) worked under the chassis of the maroon Mercury, one door open, one closed, its grill aimed at the garage. I almost intentionally ran over Zanger's shins when I swerved into the graveled driveway; at the last moment I decided against it. I braked to a stop, swung off my bike, and let it lean against my right hip.

The dungareed legs moved, boot heels dug traction on the gravel. Zanger, monkey wrench in his left hand, emerged.

He squinted up at me. "Yeah? You want somethin'?"

"Nothing," I said but didn't push off and ride away.

"So you gonna just stand there? Go ahead for all I care." He pushed with his hands and dug in his boots again to slide back under the car.

I wanted to hurl words that would berate Jerry Zanger and force him apologize for the bullied beating he and his buddies had doled out on Skip. I wanted to make Jerry Zanger feel the pain and terror Skip had experienced that night.

"I saw you go by the church the day of the funeral."

"So? Good for you. Anything else on your mind, Harper?"

"Why'd you drive by? Why'd you go to the cemetery?"

His palms on the ground, he pushed himself up and stood in front of me. A shadow of black whiskers splotched his cheeks and chin. I smelled oil and grease and sweat from his body. He hefted the wrench in his right hand. "Why you wanna know?"

"Why'd you pick on him and mess him up?"

"Jeezus, you're dumb. He was a wise ass, that's why."

"And you're not much, either, Zanger. You needed a buncha jerks to help you do your dirty work."

"Don't push it, Harper. We're just clownin' around. The madder Malloy got, the more fun it was till you barged in." Zanger sniffed. "Ride your little bike somewhere else. Get the hell out've here."

My hands on the handle grips, I took two steps away and then I spun, stepped forward, and faced him. "What're you gonna do, Zanger? Slam me with the wrench? Go ahead. Prove you're a fuckin' idiot." I breathed hard. Zanger didn't move. " Skip Malloy doesn't have a home anymore. You and his father took it away from him. He had to move away," the only accusation I could think of.

I could have decked him right there. I had challenged and defeated Guy Ross, hadn't I?

Jerry Zanger stared at me. I couldn't tell if he was happy or sorry that Skip had left town. He shook his left hand clutching the wrench. "Doesn't make any difference," his voice lower, maybe reconciled to the situation between us. He turned toward the Mercury's rear fender and then squinted at me. "Now it's your turn to move away. Get your ass out've here." He slid back under the car.

I rode away, past houses where scooters lay on sidewalks and tricycles angled toward porch steps.

What had I accomplished? I wondered as I rode past houses that seemed to close in on me. Had I defeated my best friend's enemy? Would Jerry Zanger prowl for me in the Mercury? Would he and his jerk-off buddies plan to ambush me some night?

I thought of the hired gun Wilson terrorizing the homesteaders in *Shane*. Zanger wasn't like Wilson. Zanger wouldn't kill but he would bully someone he thought weaker than himself. Maybe I was physically weaker than Zanger but I had held my ground.

I turned onto Taylor Avenue, a steep climb toward the Sunrise Auditorium neighborhood. I fantasized me punching Zanger in the stomach, knocking the wind out of him. I saw him clutch his stomach, then I landed a right hook to the jaw and a left to the chin like Shane did in a barroom brawl. Zanger fell on his hands and knees on the gravel behind the Mercury. He breathed hard, his lips bled. He said nothing. He didn't stand up.

I left him there, defeated.

But it was only in my imagination.

Minutes later I stopped at a large cottage style house painted pale yellow on Taylor Avenue, three long blocks away from Pine Lane. A weeping willow that resembled a fat woman dressed in a tent drooped in the Taggart front yard and blocked one side of the house.

Melinda and Janice, the Back-ups, sunned themselves in the side yard, portable radio between them. I eased down my kickstand and thought of sneaking up on them; instead I called out a normal "Hi," and tried to appear suave.

They both had one eye closed against the sun and peered at me with the other. Their "Hi's" were a beat apart and were not the only similarity about them. Melinda and Janice both wore shorts—Melinda's white, Janice's blue— and halter tops buttoned behind the neck—Melinda's white with green polka-dots, Janice's white with yellow polka-dots. Next to the radio vibrating Elvis Presley's "My Baby Left Me" lay a bottle of sun tan lotion.

"What're you doing?" Janice asked me turning down the volume.

I wanted to keep my football fitness plan private. I tried to sound casual. "Just riding around. Not much else to do." Little islands of freckles smeared her cheeks and the space between her throat and breasts.

I glanced toward the street. Had Zanger followed me? No Mercury prowled Taylor Avenue.

"How come you didn't stay on the tee the other day?" Janice asked. "It was fun. We got lots of sun…Hey!" she smiled. "I made a rhyme. Fun and sun."

"My twin sister's a genius," commented Melinda.

Janice challenged her: "I *did* make Honor Roll last year, remember? Twice!"

"Like I said, you're a genius." Melinda waved her thumb at Janice like a hitch-hiker. "She likes to brag about stuff. She even brags she was born ahead of me."

"It's true," Janice said. "Mom and Dad've told us: I came out first, you were second."

"So what." Melinda changed the subject. "I wish they'd have another dance at Sunrise Auditorium."

"Maybe before school starts," I said. I stuffed my hands in my jeans back pockets—a cool and confident pose, I thought.

"Have you heard from Skip Malloy?" Janice said, squinting up at me. She opened the bottle of lotion, shook white gobs onto her palms, rubbed her hands together, and smoothed the lotion up and down her arms and legs.

"Not yet," I said. I had hoped Skip would have called me the day after he had moved in with Liz and her aunt.

Janice bit her lip. "I hope he's all right." She sounded honestly concerned.

How would she react if I told her about the touch on my shoulder? That I'm crazy? Maybe I really had imagined it. Like Mom said, maybe I really had been caught up in the emotion of things.

"Did you see that gypsy-looking woman at the funeral?" I asked them.

"A gypsy?" Janice said. "No." She turned to Melinda. "Did you?"
Neither had Melinda.

"Why?" Janice asked me.

151

"She sat behind me. I'd never seen her before, either. I looked for her after the service but I guess she left right away."

"My Baby Left Me" faded out. The radio disc jockey chatted "Now all you out there, give a listen to 'Whispering Bells.'"

Melinda said, "I like this," and bobbed her head side to side to the melody and looked toward neighbors' yards, away from the conversation.

I wanted to say more about Skip. "It was really nice you both were there at the funeral service. It meant a lot to him you were there."

Melinda mentioned the service was sad. "People still gossip about the shootings," she added and made a face as if she smelled a foul odor. "We're over here on the other side of town, way over here from you and Skip, but it's all people talk about around here. I wish they'd shut up or talk about something else."

Janice rubbed the heel of her left leg back and forth on the blanket. "Skip's a nice guy, deep down," she said. "A little obnoxious but a lot of people are. He was a lot nicer than some of the stuck-up guys at school."

I scouted the street again and then made the excuse that I had to go home and take care of some chores. I would avoid back-tracking past Jerry Zanger's house.

"See you later," I said and pedaled away.

"See you later," they called out, Janice a beat behind Melissa. It was Janice's voice I remembered that night when I went to bed.

———————

After dinner one evening I swung on the Schwinn and rode to the high school football field off of Promenade Avenue. My confidence soared. Bleachers, field, and track lay empty as if asleep before a major event. Lorrence High School no church, of course, more a strangely silent fort, *quiet as...*

I leaned the bike against the chain-link fence behind the last row of bleachers. I squeezed between the fence and gate posts and jogged down concrete steps to the track. Before I began my work-out, I scouted Promenade Avenue: no maroon Mercury, no Zanger and his cohorts.

I scraped the soles of my sneakers on the cinders and then began to run, a slow jog at first, skirting puddles behind the end zone closest to the gym, a steadier pace as I kicked into the second lap.

In my imaginary play-by-play voice, I reported, *Halfback David Harper takes the hand-off and scoots right, breaks one tackle, straight-arms another, and turns the corner at the forty-five, the fifty...There's no one who's going to catch him, ladies and gentlemen. Harper is going all the way for a--touchdown! And Lorrence High School takes an early lead in this one, six to nothing.*

What a beautiful run that was by David Harper, ladies and gentlemen!

It wouldn't happen, I figured, as I coasted into a third lap. I'd see more of the game from the bench than I would on the field. First time out for football...Second string jayvee, that'd be my speed. Anyway, I'd see some action. Girls—maybe Janice Taggart—liked guys who put themselves on the line, took their share of hits and bruises. Mom, Dad, and Granddad would be proud of me. I'd be in good shape, not as great as Hal Chauncey but what the hell...Little more muscle...I'd get there.

At the start of the fourth lap, parallel to the Lorrence bleachers, I reversed direction and sprinted onto the field. Ten, twenty, thirty, forty...I churned *(Harper all the way again, ladies and gentlemen, his second touchdown of the afternoon!)*, my head up, lungs heaving, legs pumping two strides behind where I actually was, my eyes on the goal line that seemed a hundred yards away.

Fifty, forty, thirty-five...

At the thirty I darted right to avoid imaginary defenders.

Harper again this time...He's got one man on him but he dances out of reach--Boy, that's a move we haven't seen before! Here comes the safety, but Harper feints left, right, left again...He's at the twenty, the ten, and he's done it again, ladies and gentlemen! Touchdown Harper! That makes it twenty to nothing. Quite a show tonight by this young halfback David Harper.

"Made it this time, Skip! I didn't give up."

On my way home I braked to a stop in front of Our Lady Queen of Heaven's rectory. Lights shone on the porch and behind curtains in two upstairs rectory windows. At the church, candles blurred wavy light behind stained-glass figures. Whoever those saints were, they looked ghostly. No signs of life behind the church and rectory windows. None.

15

"Truce"

Lorrence High School varsity football coach Sal Costello stood hands on hips in front of his office door and blew into a silver whistle attached to a black and orange cord around his neck. The call shrieked through the boys' locker room and jerked our heads in Coach Costello's direction.

"Listen up, gentlemen: Physicals first. After physicals, returning varsity and jayvees line up outside my office. Everybody else, incoming freshmen included, take ten around the track. Start spinning your wheels now."

After I ran my laps and took a physical, in which I weighed in at 150 lbs. and stood a gigantic 5' 8". I joined first-year sign-ups and incoming freshmen outside in the chilled, hazy morning air. We lobbed passes and ran a mix of one-on-one and two-on-one short passes, buttonhooks, and long passes. Assistant Coach Erskine strolled over to scout us. On one long pattern I outran my defender, jumped, finger-tipped and held on to the ball. I was too far away to see his reaction to my catch.

After patterns, Coach Erskine directed us to report to the Boys Gym. He would check us in. As I waited in line at the check-in tables under a basketball hoop, another assistant patted me on the back and said, "Nice catch out there."

"Thanks," I replied. *Maybe the bike rides and sprints were paying off. Maybe I'd see some jayvee action.*

I had not walked away from proving myself to Jerry Zanger. I was determined not to walk away from another challenge.

"Name?"

Coach Erskine also taught Sophomore English. He looked like a college professor type: white-flecked brown mustache, brown wavy hair graying at the temples. Either side of him sat two varsity players in white practice jerseys. Earlier this summer I had seen them lay next to their girlfriends on Halcyon Lake's tee. Now, their eyes doubted my athletic potential: *Benchwarmer.*

"What position, Harper?" Coach Erskine asked.

"End or running back."

He studied me the way my algebra teacher did last year when he handed back a quiz on which I had scored less than 70. "Harper…Your dad Phil Harper? Did he play football here years ago?"

"Yeah…He was a quarterback."

"I saw his picture in an old yearbook. Well, maybe not so old," he grinned. "Anyway, you gonna follow in his footsteps?"

"I'll try."

"Good. We need guys like you to give it a shot. Be here tomorrow morning at seven thirty for sprints and laps. Running shorts, T-shirt, good pair of sneaks. Consider today your last day of freedom for the next four months, Harper. Enjoy it. Tomorrow you belong to the team."

Already I felt I belonged.

When I got home, Jack MacAdams, in dungarees and blue and red University of Pennsylvania T-shirt, was sitting on the porch steps.

What the hell you doing here?

"Whud'you want?" I said in accusation.

"Nothin'. Just checkin' in. Where were ya'?" He ignored my sarcasm.

I told him I had signed up for jayvee football.

"No shit!" he smiled, as if the news sparked a scheme. "What position? What'd they make you do?"

I explained the try-out process. We would begin first practice tomorrow morning, seven thirty sharp.

"You doing anything right now? How much coin you got?" he asked, dismissing the rest of my news. "We'll grab some burgers, then hit Halcyon. Get your bathing suit. I'll ride your bike, you jog."

I didn't want to go with him. I didn't want him to ride my bike, didn't want to jog along with him. I hadn't forgotten his greedy, gossipy questions about the shootings at the Malloys'. MacAdams' next remark made me reconsider his plan.

"I'm sorry about Ross being a jerk. He gets that way sometimes."

"A lotta times. Too many."

"Come on, whud'ya say?"

Strange, threatening, to hang around again with Jack MacAdams. Could I trust him? Skip didn't. Maybe I shouldn't, either.

I walked, jogged, and worked up a sweat all the way down to Hobe's. MacAdams and I ordered cheeseburgers, fries, and root beers at the counter, then carried our root beers to the last available booth. Odors of grilled bacon and onions streamed through two saloon-type swinging doors behind us. Across the aisle from us two kids who looked about twelve were playing pinball, their hips and shoulders jerking the silver balls toward high scores.

Guy Ross? Nowhere in sight.

MacAdams tipped his root beer to his mouth, then plunked the bottle on the table. "So, any news from Alfred E.?"

"Cut that shit," I warned him.

"Sorry. Old habit." He shifted his shoulders right and left. "I called him before he moved away. Told him you beat the crap outta Ross." He paused, tapped the thumb and pinkie finger of his right hand on the table between us as if he was playing two keys of a piano. "I don't know...I feel sorry for Malloy, but there was always something about him...Sometimes I wanted to slam his face into a wall."

"What'd he ever do to you?"

"Nothing. He just got on my nerves."

"So's that the only reason you didn't show at the funeral?"

Jack MacAdams had no answer.

I did. "You're not the only guy who wanted to slam somebody's face into a wall. The only time Skip hurt somebody was when they picked on him. He fought back. Leave him alone. He's my friend."

Cheeseburgers delivered, I bit into mine right away. MacAdams poured salt and doused catsup onto his fries. He fired a couple of them into his mouth before he ate the first chunk of his cheeseburger.

"Damn!" groaned one of the pinball kids. "One more game. You got another quarter?"

"No," replied his buddy. "Let's go."

MacAdams extended his hand to me. "Truce?"

"I guess."

We shook hands.

MacAdams plunked two more fries into his mouth.

"You know something? I gotta hand it to you: the way you stood up for Malloy that day. The way you pounded on Ross—I never saw you fight like that before, man. Never."

Compliments or lies? Truth or a set-up for a trap?

He patted me on the back. "Hey," he said, "let's get over to Halcyon, finish your work-out there."

Halcyon Lake gleamed in the sunlight with streaks of yellow and deep green. Beach and tee smeared with sunbathers and swimmers. The Taggart twins lounged on the boards wet with lake water, damp with sweat. Melinda in a two-piece lime green bathing suit, Janice in a two-piece white.

"Race you to the tee," Jack challenged me.

Two steps and a dive ahead of me, his body submerged in the water as I waded in. His hand reached down to me when my hand touched the tee.

In those seconds I didn't feel equal to him.

"Big Dave, my man, how's it hangin'?" Guy Ross extended his hand to me but at the last second yanked it above his shoulder, my reciprocal hand left empty. He laughed at his practical joke. "Glad you could join me and my friends out here, Dave, on this fine sunny day."

In the middle of Ross's smile the chipped front tooth pointed like the tip of an arrowhead to his lower lip. He stood between MacAdams and me and put his arms around our shoulders and half-walked, half-pushed us to the other side. Under my feet the tee swayed like an overloaded boat. Janice Taggart leaned to her sister, cupped her hand beside Melinda's ear. The

Back-ups squinted at MacAdams, Ross, and me as if they waited to see what would happen next.

Ross patted me on the back and gripped my right shoulder. He proclaimed, "I want everyone here to know I have nothing but respect for Dave Harper. I'm willing to let bygones be bygones. And just to show all of you that I speak in good faith—"

"Show us your good faith, Ross!"

"Oh please, not here!" a girl's voice begged.

Ross addressed his audience: "Ignore the ignorant. I stand here in front of all of you and God and Dave Harper. I want you to see that I offer him my hand."

I took it.

His arm like a chain, he swung me like a toy over the tee's edge into the lake. The greenish-brown water muffled shouts and laughter, but the noise slid away when I hoisted myself back onto the planks. The Taggart twins watched; neither laughed.

MacAdams patted his hand over his heart. "Harper, I swear to God I didn't know he was gonna do it. Swear to God…"

"The hell you didn't!"

"He's right," Ross added. "I'd say we're about equal now, wouldn't you, Harper?"

"I don't think so."

"What do you mean? Try me," Ross took one step closer to me. The heat from his skin pricked mine.

I dared him: "Race you to the spillway." I nodded toward the wide dark mouth under the bridge over a hundred yards away. My challenge in the open, I couldn't take it back.

Ross reciprocated: "Right now?"

"Right now."

I sliced the water a split second ahead of Ross. Coming up, I shook water off my face, blinked it out of my eyes, and pulled for the spillway. I tried to focus on cars crossing the bridge, the sunlight bouncing off windshields, but Ross churned behind me. He had challenged me before in sneak-outs for midnight bike rides. This time I could prove to him and everyone else that I was no Mommy and Daddy's boy; I could beat him, beat the hell out of him in this swim.

Halfway to the spillway I heard the shriek of the lifeguard's whistle.

"Guess they see us!" Ross shouted parallel to me. "Go for the ladders!"

I put my head down and swam. My shoulders stiffened. I wanted to slow my pace, tread water, regain strength. My power subsided. Ross slipped ahead of me.

Water puddled over my eyes. Through its blur I saw back of Ross's head, his black trunks, and splashes from his kicks. In my imagination I saw his face, his tooth-chipped grin. I strained to pull faster through his wake, but I moved my head right to left, right to left like some stupid toy. I was fading, losing speed. I tried to gulp air; instead I gulped lake water and spat it out.

The lifeguard's whistle screamed once, twice, three times. I was tempted to quit, tread water until I caught a second wind and finish this race. Then I remembered those faces on the tee, the ones who had laughed at me as I sailed through the air, the ones who had heard me dare Guy Ross. I gulped more air.

He was five yards in front of me now, maybe twenty yards from the spillway's oval, gaping mouth. I couldn't remember how deep the water was in front of the lip. The current there was deceiving enough to suck anyone under, propel them over the edge and down to the concrete channel. I flashed broken glass...Ross and me holding on to the wooden ladders on either side of the mouth.

Ross yelled to me over his shoulder. My gasps and strokes blocked his words. He flipped onto his back and thumbed over his head at people on the concrete platform above the spillway.

I pulled even with him.

"Go for it, man!" he shouted, flipped over again, and stroked toward the ladders.

Slowly, deliberately, I aimed for the ladder to the right of the concrete mouth. A string of onlookers cheered us from the bridge.

A siren wailed, closer, louder, and then it died.

We're done for, I thought. Barred forever from Halcyon. Grounded for life. What the hell was I trying to prove?

Three strokes ahead of me, Ross laughed. Exhausted and giddy, so did I.

"Go Harper!" Ross urged me.

I grunted as I stroked left arm right down through the water. Left. Right. Ten yards from the ladders I heaved a breath, then another.

The water chilled my chest, my legs dropped like anchors toward the mucky bottom. I strained to raise them and kick once more, again once more.

Jack MacAdams stood on the concrete platform, directly above the mouth of the spillway, others from the tee on both sides of him and gawking at us. "Come *on*! You're *there*!"

Two more strokes I came even with Ross. He kicked ahead, the ladder on the left of the spillway's mouth three strokes out of reach.

"Cramp, *cramp*!"

Ross plunged his right arm beneath the water and with his left tried to pull toward the ladder. He swayed like a buoy in the water. *"Help!"* he yelled, and gulped air.

Halcyon's usually calm water swirled in front of the spillway. Ross drifted like a dingy toward the mouth. "Help!" his cry more frantic than seconds before.

"Get him!" "Help him!" the crowd shouted.

A tingly calm covered me like a blanket across my neck and shoulders and down my arms. I heard no special voice, felt no special touch. Only a cool calm that kicked me toward Guy Ross.

I pulled in behind him, braced my hands on his back and shoulders, pushed him away from the spillway. I pumped my legs as current shoved against them. With the strength I had left I pushed Ross toward the gravel embankment beside the concrete support for the bridge and platform. Then I braced myself on my hands and knees on the sandy bottom. Ross crawled like a dog onto the gravel. He stood, bent over, huffed and blew air, his hands on his knees.

I leaned over beside him.

MacAdams stood in front of us. "You guys all right? Holy shit, that was some show!"

Ross shook his head. He put his hand on my shoulder. Breathing hard, he said, "Thanks, man...thought I was going over."

"We have visitors," MacAdams said nodding at the tee crowd, Janice and Melinda among them, ran toward us. Beyond all of them a policeman stepped out of a cruiser, and a three-man rescue squad strode from an ambulance, its engine running, its body shaking like an impatient guard, parked in front of the cruiser.

16

Between

"What the hell you tryin' to do *now*, numbnuts? You crazy?"

I had taken Skip's call in my parents' bedroom: privacy. From over a hundred miles away his sarcastic accusation cheered and reassured me.

"Stick to football," he advised.

"That's what my coach told me."

Silence, though not uncomfortable.

I asked him how he had learned about the incident.

"Your mom called, said you took some stupid dare and ended up a hero."

"It wasn't stupid, and I don't feel like a hero."

"Ah, you're just being modest. So what happened to Ross and MacAdams? They going to be tried for attempted manslaughter?"

I explained the dare to swim Halcyon to the spillway was mine. Afterwards, Ross's parents and Mom and Dad had lectured us about the danger of swimming close to the dam. Mr. and Mrs. Ross had thanked me for saving their son's life. "They offered me a hundred bucks for saving him."

"Whud you do?"

"Didn't take it. I didn't think it was right."

"You *are* a numbnut, Harper. I'd've held out for two thousand minimum. What about the boy himself?"

"He thanked me."

"He ain't your best friend now, is he?"

"No way."

Another silence. We then talked football and school.

Like me, Skip was selected for jayvee running back and line. On the field he wore a helmet with a plastic visor to shield his glasses. The practices were tough.

He wasn't looking forward to starting school; being a new kid again, not knowing anybody, questions he'd have to answer: Where you from? How come you moved up here? "What the hell do I tell'em? My old man was a drunk? He shot my mom? Not something I wanna go through but I guess I'll have to."

"The guys on the team ask you anything?"

"I told'em my parents moved to Germany for a year. Company my old man works for told him he had to go. I didn't want to. I'm staying with my sister and aunt." He paused. "So what else's going on with you besides tryin' out for the swim team? You practicing the breast stroke? You gotta work on that, you know."

I told him Janice and Melinda had called to ask how I was doing. So had Mr. and Mrs. MacAdams. Granddad had patted me on the shoulder, brought me copies of the latest *Sport* and *Sports Illustrated*, and told me "You did something really special. Nana would be real proud of you."

I didn't tell Skip about the cool, calm feeling that had covered me in front of the spillway's dark mouth. I had wanted to tell Granddad about it, too, and ask him what he thought had caused it, but I had held back. Barriers: me sampling Dad's liquor, being caught, insults from Ross and MacAdams. Granddad, I figured, would have the same explanation for the touch Mom and Dad had given me: my imagination had worked overtime.

Yeah, sure. Bullshit.

And no sign of that gypsy woman anywhere.

"How's Lizzie?" I said.

Skip didn't answer at first. I thought the line had gone dead. The sound of his sigh proved that wrong. "She's all right." The tone of his voice indicated otherwise.

"What's she—?"

"She's okay," he said, then changed the subject. "You haven't raided the pantry anymore, have you?"

I waited three beats before I replied with the truth.

"Harper, you dumb shit. What'd you do that for?"

Another truth: "Felt like it." I didn't tell Skip that it had happened two days before. Home from practice, Mom and Dad not yet home, I had downed one sip. Just one. Then one became two, two became three. No more. I had brushed my teeth and gargled afterwards.

"Did it work?"

A third truth, but my head concentrated on Liz Malloy, someone more important than bourbon and football. I could experience bourbon and football. I could not see and talk with Liz Malloy.

A thunderstorm rumbled in a smoky gray sky beyond my bedroom window. The same storm poured rain onto Connie Mack Stadium, where the Phillies and Dodgers waited out a rain-delay, the Phils uncharacteristically up 6 - 2 in the third inning.

What's out there? I asked, not God, not Nana. Just anyone or anything special. Just someone who might be listening.

Ross almost had gone over. I didn't feel anything on my shoulder but I had felt that "tingly calm" when I had saved him.

Did something help me or did I save him all by myself?

Lightning shimmered behind the clouds. I wanted answers I could understand, reasons I could not only see but feel and touch.

Every muscle in my body ached from laps and blocks and tackles at practice. Flat on my bed, I hurt if I moved an inch. I knew from the way coaches had used me—subbing for a starting running back, subbing for a first-string receiver—I probably wouldn't 't make the jayvee starting eleven. I hoped I would get to play, see some action, give somebody hell. Coach Erskine had complimented my speed but added, grabbing my biceps, "Where're your muscles?"

Standing beside him, Coach Costello had chuckled, "Oh yeah, he swam them off. Better make up your mind, Harper. Swimming or football?"

"I'm not quitting," I told them.

"This kid a varsity prospect?" Coach Costello, fingering the whistle attached to a cord around his neck, had asked his assistant.

"He's not there yet, but I think he will be someday."

But I hurt. I hurt from football *and* swimming. I hurt from letting down Mom and Dad again.

They had caught me with bourbon-breath in the kitchen one afternoon after he and Mom had come home from work. Dad tore into me. "What's the hell's the matter with you? You want to end up like Ralph Malloy?" Like a judge, he laid down the law. "You broke your promise, so here's what you'll do: no more Halcyon Lake; no more gallivanting around on your bike; no more—"

"What about football?" I had challenged him.

"You go to practice, you come right home. Nothing else."

"You gonna tell Coach Erskine?"

"That's up to you. We thought about it but decided not to. If you're honest with him it might help your conscience. Your mother and I leave that up to you.

"The *same* goes for when school starts," he continued. "School, practice, home. No dances, no nothing." He pointed his right index finger at the space between us. "Not until you show some good common sense and understand what a promise means."

My mother studied me. She didn't have to say one word for me to know her feelings about what I had done. Sadness, disappointment, worry, and *Why?* showed in her face and eyes.

After Mom had detected liquor on my breath, her mouth quivered, she shook her head and turned away. She didn't cry.

I had lost a friend.

Toward the end of this interrogation, Dad's eyes and voice had changed from judge to counselor. "Why are you doing this? What is going on with you? Do you *like* this stuff?" He tapped the bourbon bottle in his hand. "You saw what happened to Ralph Malloy. Didn't that make an impression on you?"

"I'm not gonna be like him."

It wasn't that I loved the taste of it, I had explained. The bourbon burned going down, sure; it made me feel sleepy, even whoozy. But it didn't make me feel strong or better than anybody else. I thought it might but it didn't. It didn't even make me feel happy. "I just wanted to *try* it."

"So you tried it. Now what?"

"I don't know."

"You damn well better figure it out soon, or else you can forget about privileges in this house."

Lightning flashed again now and colored clouds a strange yellowish-gray. Distant thunder rumbled the dark air. The storm had slid off to the east. Heavy dark gray clouds bulked the sky when I left my room, came down the stairs, and pushed open the front door.

"David? Where're you going?" my mother demanded when she heard the front screen door clack shut. And Dad reminded me, "We told you not to go anywhere."

I didn't stop. "I'm just going for a run, that's all."

They didn't try to stop me. I wouldn't have obeyed them anyway.

I jogged past neighbors who chatted on porches. Tree limbs and branches swayed in the wind, lightning shimmered clouds, and thunder still rumbled as the storm had pulled away to the east. The air smelled clean.

Were You there? Even though I didn't feel it, did You touch me, keep us from going over?

What were MacAdams and Ross planning now? Some new game to fool their next victim? I was their equal now. I wouldn't be their victim again. They weren't my friends. Skip was my only friend. I could trust him.

Within sight of the railroad, I wondered if passenger trains ran from Philadelphia to Mount Howard. Granddad would know.

I jogged home. Lightning brightened clouds. Thunder seemed only a rumor. St. Thomas Church stood in shadowy streetlight, larger than it appeared in daylight. Candlelight glowed inside at the bottom of the front stained-glass window of Christ the shepherd tending His flock. I looked left and right. No one else in sight. I walked up the lawn, stood in the shadow of the church, and looked at the image again.

What was it? Where is she?

Nothing happened. Only the distant rumble of thunder and the smatter of new rain on leaves.

Forget it. You never answer me. I might as well quit talking to You.

Home, my mother and father said nothing to me. I went up to my room. I opened my windows wider to let in fresh air. The tires of cars hissed on the street. I watched the rain tap bushes and leaves.

———————

I served at Eight o'clock Communion the following Sunday.

I didn't trip over my feet, I gave Father Hepplewhite an accurate count of congregation present (22), and I didn't spill the cruets of water and wine. I heard no invisible voices, I felt no spiritual touch on my shoulders.

In the Sacristy afterwards, 'the good Father' raised his bushy eyebrows and asked, "Getting a little nervous about going back to school, David?"

It would have been easy to tell him about the touch and the gypsy woman, but he seemed tired, his forehead damp, his breathing husky. Besides, he probably would have said, *Well, that certainly is amazing, David, but are you sure it wasn't your imagination?*

I ignored the stained glass image of Jesus and His sheep when I walked home.

That evening on Granddad's back steps I tapped the toes and heels of my sneakers on the concrete.

"Maybe you should take drum lessons," Granddad chuckled, and scratched the back of his neck. His thin, gray hair was long around his ears. "That high school band of yours could use another drummer."

"I'll stick with football."

School would start in a couple days. I was edgy about classes, football, and all the questions I had no answers for. All that, plus I thought he was probably upset at me for sneaking Dad's stock. Would he believe I had squared things with Mom and Dad?

Twilight edged between the trees and houses a minute earlier each evening now. Kids at play slouched into houses sooner than they wanted. Back doors slammed hard behind them.

"Any news from your friend Skip?" he asked.

"Nothing." I didn't tell Granddad why Skip was upset with me.

"Give him time. He's got a lot to think about."

I said I had looked at the photographs he had given me.

"Keep'em as long as you want," he said. "They'll be yours anyway someday."

I knew what that meant. I didn't want to talk anymore about that, either. I retied the laces of both sneakers, even though the strings weren't loose. It just felt good to have my hands busy and the laces tight.

"Granddad, if I tell you something, promise you won't think I'm stupid?"

"I never have, I don't think I ever would. What's the story?"

"Did anything ever happen to you that you couldn't explain?"

"Yes indeed: your mother marrying your father."

He winked. We had a good laugh.

"I mean something *really* strange...something you felt afraid and good about at the same time."

He sat forward, elbows on his knees. "What is it?" he said.

I explained what had happened to me in the church and when I had saved Guy Ross.

When I finished he sighed, pursed his lips, and was silent. Then he shook his head as if he was trying to understand it. The lines at the corners of his mouth deepened as he smiled. "I know what I'd *like* that touch to be, David."

"I thought about that, too. The thing is, Mom and Dad said it was all my imagination. I told them it wasn't. I'm sure. I haven't told them about what I felt in the water. They wouldn't believe me, anyway. I wanna know what's going on."

"Maybe you're not supposed to know for sure. Maybe you never will."

"That doesn't make sense."

Granddad brushed his hands across the knees of his trousers. "Like I said, you might never know for sure, but you have to believe what you felt was something special."

I couldn't accept Granddad's answer; it sounded too much like a story with no definite ending. I wanted a definite answer I could believe in.

I asked him if he had ever seen a gypsy woman in town.

He hadn't. He rubbed his hand across the bottom of his chin. "What's she got to do with all this?"

I explained what she looked like, where and when I had seen her, and that I had looked for her near the church. "I can't find out what I want to know," I said. "Maybe I oughta forget about this stuff."

We watched the sky shade from deep twilight to dark.

"Do you ever dream of Nana?" I asked.

He spoke slowly and scratched the back of his neck again. "I do. Just the other night I did. We were dancing. Nana and I liked to dance. She was a little more light on her feet than I was, but I did the best I could."

"How'd you feel when you woke up?"

"I miss her. Always do. But it was nice to hold her for a while."

"I hope Skip doesn't dream," I said.

17

Sophomore

Strange starting school without Skip this year, I thought to myself on the first day. I had walked down Jessup Avenue as if he and I would meet. A For Sale sign stabbed the front yard. The sign reminded me of a lopsided cross.

How much was the house going for now? Who'd buy a house where two people had been shot and killed? *"That's the Malloy house where the husband shot his wife,"* my sarcastic self imagined. *"Then some other guy came in and shot Malloy. Self-defense, I heard, but you never know.*

That's right, buddy, you don't know. Not unless you were right there with Marty Bannon.

I looked across the street. The Arvidsons' cream and bronze '55 Pontiac shone like a prize in their driveway…

Skip and I were still best friends but now best friends who wouldn't see each other, probably for a long time. We wouldn't walk together to the high school. We wouldn't eat lunch together, wouldn't joke about our teachers' idiosyncrasies, and wouldn't stay for dinner at each other's houses.

How much was the house going for now? Who'd buy a house where two people had been shot and killed?

I looked across the street. The Arvidsons' cream and bronze '55 Pontiac shone like a prize in their driveway.

Being a high school sophomore didn't give me status and privilege.

At assemblies our class sat in the auditorium rear. For pep rallies we scrunched one section closer (Big deal!) to the juniors, who lorded over bleachers next to the seniors.

However, there were benefits: upperclassmen didn't demand we carry their books to class or haul lunch trays to their cafeteria tables. Sophomore boys didn't get de-pantsed in the locker room and shoved into the hallway to be squealed, screamed, and laughed at (the way Skip had been) by gawking girls. Sophomore girls didn't suffer their bras and panties tossed into the showers. No more ritual initiations for us.

Janice Taggart and I were assigned different home rooms but we shared the same English and Biology classes; Melinda and I the same cafeteria study hall. She and I faced each other but were assigned different tables. On the first day of classes studious Melinda sat down, opened a textbook and notebook right away. She annoyed me the way she pursed her lips as she read and took notes, the way she sighed, sat back and closed her eyes before she read again and penciled lines in text books. So sophisticated, so intellectual. Older than she had acted at the summer dances. She acted oblivious to me now. That was all right. I didn't care.

My study hall habits were more casual than Melinda's intense routine. I took my good old time opening textbooks. My priorities included Coach Erskine's play charts, my routes on T-43 Quickie, T-23 Crisscross, and my position and role as Safety on the Receiving Team. No bruises yet, but my confidence bolstered as I studied the charts and imagined my runs for first downs and blocks of defensive backs taller and heavier than me. I was jayvee, sure, but I was a member of the team.

"Hear anything from Malloy?" Ross asked me at lunch in the cafeteria that first day. He stood at the end of the table. The tone of his question straddled sincerity and sarcasm. He waited for my approval for him to the other four sophomores at the table. I withheld. MacAdams gave a nod of consent. Ross plunked down his tray arranged with two hot dogs and three chocolate milks.

I avoided his question. While part of me felt weak and guilty for sitting at the same table with MacAdams and Ross, I had decided to sit with them because they were familiar to me. Maybe they realized I wouldn't be their punching bag anymore; maybe they knew I would punch back.

I bit into my second hot dog, relish and mustard seeping over the top edges of the roll.

Ross smirked. "Been swimming lately, Harper?" he continued, sarcastic laughs his reception.

"I'm staying in shape a different way: football. Try it," I said, knowing my opponent didn't play any sport.

"Maybe I will," he replied.

I didn't hate Guy Ross; I just didn't want him as an enemy.

At football practice I tried to "give'em hell," as Skip had urged me. I pushed myself in calisthenics, threw myself into the blocks and runs of T 43 Quickie, T 23 Crisscross, and all the other plays Coach Erskine had jv's memorize. "Dig, Harper, dig!" Coach Erskine hollered. "Stay with your man!" Sometimes I imagined my man was Ross, sometimes Jerry Zanger. I dug in, I rushed and hit, blocked and hit. My face ate dirt but I stood up proud of my smears and early bruises: my badges.

––––––––––

"You have a letter from Skip," my mother said one afternoon in early October when I walked in from practice. She nodded to the envelope on the living room desk.

I grabbed the letter and took it and my books to my room.

233 South Kenton Street
Mount Howard, Pa.
September 30, 1956

Dear Numbnuts,

Hey, how's it hangin'! Long time no hear from me, thought I'd let you know what's going on.

Hope your behaving yourself and setting a good example for your parents. Don't let temptation get the best of you.

Aunt Chainsmoker and Liz haven't shipped me off to a juvenile home. They decided I should live with them as long as I want. Marty put in his two cents worth, so here I am until they kick me out.

I guess I'm doing OK. Sometimes I wake up and can't get back to sleep. Most times I feel OK, try not to think a lot of stuff, you know how it is.

Here's my schedule: English, Geometry, Biology, Western Civ, Art, Wood Shop, and Gym. Teachers here give too much homework, a lot more than we had in Lorrence. I got a book report due Friday in English, supposed to read a bunch of short stories but haven't found any I like yet. For Western Civ I have to make a time-line from the Greeks to 1955 (Think I should include the Fizz Kids losing the World Series in 1950?). My average in Geometry is 76, Bio 81. In Wood Shop I'm working on a couple end tables for Aunt Ceil. She still smokes like a chimney.

That's about it. I'd like to come back to Lorrence, just for a visit. Don't know about that yet. We had a lot of good times. I was looking forward to us graduating together, but the old man shit on that. Liz and Aunt Ceil say I'm better off up here in the boondocks of Mount Howard than Lorrence. Marty thinks so, guess they're right.

Your allowed to come here anytime. I checked with Liz and Aunt Ceil, they said OK.

You got to buy your own bus or train ticket but I'll let you stay here free.

Your friend,
Skip

I answered his letter right away. I didn't mention his few mistakes in grammar, but I explained my schedule, including study hall every day in the cafeteria after lunch, football practice (first game next week, doubtful I'd see much action), and the GS (girl situation): "I eat lunch with Janice. There's something pretty cool about her…" and "You won't believe this,

Melinda and Janice don't hang around much with Shirley these days. Don't know why, could care less. Chauncey gives her a squeeze and smooches her after he walks her to class."

I didn't ask about Lorraine Wyles. I wanted to avoid names and situations from last spring and summer.

I ended by reporting I couldn't come up for a visit till after football season, "but let me know when you might come down this way."

––––––––

Homework, football, dances: autumn's rituals.

In my first JV game I had six carries. Total yardage gained that cloudy afternoon--29 yards. I wasn't sure what Coach Erskine thought of my efforts. When I jogged back to the sidelines, he folded his arms across his chest, scraped the ground with his cleats, and studied the action on the field. After the game Granddad, who had watched and cheered from the bleachers, reasoned that 29 yards gained was better than 19 lost.

"See what you can do about bringing up that C in Geometry," Dad said when he saw my report card for the first marking period. My other grades were higher, including A's in Gym and World History.

My mother gave me good news: "Dad and I think we can trust you again. Don't let us down. You can go to the Saturday night dances."

I thanked them. I remembered what Skip had advised about "behaving myself."

I didn't want to let Mom and Dad or anyone else down. How long could I do it? As long as I could.

The dances were sponsored by Student Council and held in the gym every Saturday night. Fifty cents admission, a dime for a Milky Way, a dime for soda.

I slow-danced with Janice, her cheeks warm, my fingertips knowing the hooks of her bra strap, and the back of her blouse damp from jitterbugging with Melinda. Janice and I didn't talk when we slow danced. Our arms around each other, our chests against each other, and our hands together was enough music for us.

Oak leaves curled crusty brown, maple leaves yellow. I scuffed through them and crunched acorns on the way to school and on the way home from practice. Stained glass windows of Our Lady Queen of Heaven and St. Thomas' had not changed, not that I expected they would: still-life figures with no heart, no blood.

No letter from Skip.

I performed acolyte duties because they were expected of me and because I was afraid not to do them.

"Make us mindful of the needs of others," Father Hepplewhite prayed during eight o'clock Holy Communion Sunday mornings. Hearing that, I thought of Dad writing checks for rent, insurance, and the car. I thought of Nana and Granddad.

I thought of Skip.

"Basketball try-outs are next week," I wrote in another letter to him toward the end of football season. "I don't think I'm good enough. Maybe I'll concentrate on the books instead of sports."

I omitted another reason: too much on my mind. Heavy homework load, how far I could go with Janice, and something else. In Biology one morning I dissected a frog. The scalpel in my hand, I imagined Mrs. Malloy's body slumped on the floor, the fatal wounds in her chest.

When I glanced at Guy Ross in the cafeteria lunch line one day, I envisioned him drifting toward the spillway. I pressed both hands on the cafeteria chair and moved the chair closer to the table where Janice was sitting. The memory of a hand on my shoulder and a soothing, peaceful feeling passed in seconds.

We played Kenner's Point at home our last jayvee game of the season. "KP," was a refinery town twenty miles away along the Delaware River. Our foe played smash-mouth football, their jayvee squad no exception. By the end of the first half we had not moved the ball beyond our 45-yard line. Kenner's Point, meanwhile, had racked up three touchdowns plus two extra points, while their linemen and blockers had doled out punishments of dislocated fingers, cut lips, a chipped tooth, and a broken ankle. I was lucky. When I attempted to block a punt, I ran into an offensive back who head-butted my stomach and knocked the wind out of me. Half-time score: Kenner's Point 20, Lorrence 0.

As we jogged onto the field for the second half, I spied Mom, Dad, and Granddad bundled in overcoats in the bleachers. Mom and Granddad waved to me. Dad didn't. He stood up and yelled, "Come on, Lorrence! You gotta *do* somethin'!"

We didn't do much. All we could do against KP's defensive line that snarled and growled and stabbed our faces and eyes whenever they got a chance, was plow our way to their twenty. No farther.

I played most of the second half. I ran the ball, punted the ball, even intercepted one of KP quarterback's passes. I leaped in front of the intended receiver, clutched the ball, and scooted for our sideline, the only open area. My teammates and Coach Erskine stomped, yelled "Come *on*, Harper! Turn the corner!"

I turned the corner at our 45 and scrambled as far as the 50. There, two Kenner's Point safeties hurtled me into my teammates and bench. Grunting, I landed on my back. My teammates' legs from ankles to knees around me like grass-smeared field growth, the two KP safeties huffed, hissed, and sprayed like plow horses in my face; for good measure they were kind enough to press their hands like vices on both sides of my helmet and knock my head once, twice, into the dirt.

At the whistle, my teammates and the refs stepped in, yanked the tacklers off of me, and awarded Kenner's Point a 15-yard penalty for unsportsman-like conduct. The penalty didn't matter, nor did my interception. We didn't score. We lost.

Our coaches told us we had nothing to be ashamed of about this game or about our entire season. Three wins, four losses wasn't the best of records, but we had played hard every game, we could hold our heads up high. The coaches were proud of us. Varsity coach Costello, clipboard in hand, said, "You lost to a better team, but you gave it all you had. Next year, you take it to'em on their home turf."

Coach Erskine patted me on my shoulder pads. "Good catch, Harper," he said and shook my hand. "Stay in shape for next season. We'll need you." He then patted me on the back, his hand a memory of other touches.

"I'll need you, too, Harper," Coach Costello added, fingering the silver whistle in front of his chest. "We'll get you lined up to run some routes and catch some passes before practice officially starts next summer."

My personal jayvee football record: 76 yards gained, 14 tackles, 1 interception. Better than nothing. Could have been worse.

That night I was sitting up in bed and reading Act II of *The Merchant of Venice* when Dad knocked on the door. "I just wanted to tell you again played well today. You did the best you could."

"Thanks," I said.

"Get a good night's sleep."

I heard his footsteps pad down the stairs.

Did Mom and Dad really trust me? Or were they waiting for me to slip up again? I knew that he and Mom loved me. In a way, I was alone in the house. The only kid. I had to keep their respect. I had to do things that were right for me, even if Mom and Dad didn't agree with my decisions.

I closed the copy of *The Merchant of Venice*. I wrote another letter to Skip. I asked him if he could visit us Thanksgiving weekend.

He didn't answer.

The Monday night before Thanksgiving I dialed Pennsylvania Information, asked for the telephone number of Ceil Kinsale, gave the operator the address, and then placed the call myself.

"What's up, numbnuts?" Skip said after he took the phone from Aunt Ceil.

"Not much. How about you?"

We talked a steady diet of high school life: homework, grades, football season, and girls. He liked a girl named Cori, who was in his homeroom and English and Biology classes. "Haven't asked her out yet, but I think she's my friend. She doesn't write me off like the Lorrence crowd use to. You still sweet on Back-up Janice?"

"We slow dance a lot. That's about it."

"Don't slow down too much, Harper."

I asked him about Thanksgiving weekend.

"Afraid not. Aunt Ceil doesn't wanna drive that far, she's scared it might snow. Marty can't get time off, either, he's gotta work at his dad's lumber yard. So, no dice."

Before I fell asleep that night, I had the feeling that the distance between Skip and me was growing greater than the number of miles between Lorrence and Mount Howard.

Staying home Saturday after Thanksgiving had all the thrills of dull punishment. Doing homework hard labor. Watching Penn State trounce Penn by four touchdowns self-inflicted boredom. No Saturday night dance because of the holiday weekend self-denial of pleasure.

At the phone in my parents' bedroom I took a deep breath and dialed the Taggarts' number.

A laughing voice answered "Hello?"

"Janice?"

"No, Melinda. Is this David?"

"Yes."

"Oh jeez! I was just going to call you. Janice and I're wondering if you want to come over and watch a couple horror movies. My parents say it's all right." She snickered, and then said, "They heard you were a suspicious character but we said you're a good kid. So, can you come over?"

I told Mom and Dad where I was going, didn't wait for a response.

Janice met me at the front door. In black and red plaid skirt and gray crew-neck sweater she looked more a college co-ed than a high school sophomore. Her parents had gone out to a dinner and card party and wouldn't be home until midnight.

"Mel and I vouched for your good character," she chuckled, and pulled me in to the family room where her sister, the TV, and cheeseburgers awaited us. "Come on, *The Wolf Man*'s about to start. Have you seen it? I swear, I love horror movies, this one's my favorite."

"Just in case you didn't understand her, she likes this movie," Melinda added.

"Shut up. Not you, David. Her: cheeseburger juice dripping from her mouth. You are *so uncouth*, Melinda."

"Uncouth?" sneered her sister. "Where'd you get that word? What're you trying to do, sound intelligent or something? Eat your food, you brat."

We watched *The Wolf Man, Dracula*, and jitterbugged and slow-danced to some 45s on the portable record player Melinda brought down from their bedroom. We consumed root beer, pretzels and potato chips, and prepared for *Frankenstein*. The wall clock in the Taggart dining room chimed ten.

Melinda snapped off the lamp in the corner behind us. A silvery glow from the TV screen made the room a hazy cave. Melinda's and Janice's faces shone pale, their eyes dark. Like sci-fi creatures, I thought.

Melinda snuggled beside me and lay her head on my shoulder the way Janice did. I was a king with two wives.

Janice put her hand on my thigh and squeezed.

"Here comes the lightning," she whispered as Dr. Frankenstein controlled the table that lifted the monster to the open ceiling.

"Shh," whispered Melinda. She nestled closer to me. "Dr. Frankenstein's creating life."

My mind ran wild with 'what if's.' Embarrassed, I shifted back to the right a little, then back to the left to hide evidence of what was happening to me.

They must know, I thought. All the times Janice and I've danced together, she's gotta know.

Janice kept her hand on my thigh and stared at the TV.

So did I. My ears heard the spoken words, my eyes saw the monster come alive, but my mind was a rollercoaster of emotion. *Stay cool*, I told myself.

"Forget it. I'm going upstairs," said Melinda.

She promptly left the room. Her footsteps thumped the stairs.

"Don't worry. She's in a mood," Janice whispered.

Dr. Frankenstein's creation sat with a little girl at the edge of a pond.

I closed my eyes and slowly, gently, pushed against Janice. As if she read my mind she stretched out beside me. Her face lost its alien color in the TV's shine, her cheeks now soft, her freckles faint fingerprints. She closed her eyes and opened her lips. I kissed her, the first time I had seriously, truly, kissed a girl, and I was sucked into everything that happened next. She slid her tongue into my mouth. I slid mine into hers. French-kissing ticklish, the tips of our tongues touching like little fish kissing. After a while she breathed heavier. I moved my hand to the front of her sweater, her breasts soft-hard, mysterious. I didn't know how good I was at kissing or touching—I did what I had daydreamed of doing with Shirley Brackett. I must have been more than good because Janice didn't pull away, only came up for air and flicked strands of hair away from her face. She kept her eyes closed.

Mad townspeople demanded death for the monster.

Janice and I picked up where we left off. Our mouths locked in synch, my hand explored the curve of her breast again. I wanted to know more about this mystery, how it would look and feel in my hand, but when I tried to slide my hand under Janice's sweater she murmured "Uh-uh."

We French-kissed again. I gathered courage again to slip my hand under her sweater. She squeezed closer to me; her body locked my hand between us. I pressed closer to her, and when I did we began a rhythm that ended with a pulsed release I had only experienced in fantasies and dreams.

Shades of gold and white swirled behind my eyes, I didn't know what to do or what to say. I was embarrassed, afraid of what Janice might think of me, but I wanted to have it all again right away. I felt experienced, older. Did Janice share the same feelings?

The room came back: the glow from the TV, the shouts and torches of the crowd pursuing the monster. Janice's breath on my neck was like a warm pillow.

What if…?

She sat up slowly, brushed her hair away from her forehead again, and gave me a half smile of embarrassment, uncertainty…

What should—

"I'm sorry if—" I began.

"No, no. It's all right. I didn't…It's all right."

"I never…"

"Me neither," she said, catching herself in a laugh at the last second. She looked at me as if she wanted to ask a question. "It just—I just wanted to see what it felt like."

I didn't tell her about the stickiness inside my pants. Did she understand what had happened to me? Did she know about wet dreams? What was the right thing to say? "You're not mad, are you?"

"No…It was—I don't know…It was the first time I was ever that close to anyone. It was nice."

I put my arm around her, and she leaned against me again.

She asked, "You're not going to tell anybody about this, are you?"

"No."

"That includes my sister. I don't want her or anybody else to know about it. I like you, David. Very much," she whispered, tears in her eyes.

"I like you, too."

I held her close. She rested her head on my chest. I listened for a car in the driveway, for the click of Melinda's bedroom door, her footsteps on the stairs. I wanted to express more to Janice, say something special and romantic. That was what you were supposed to do when you liked someone very much. All I could think to do later when she walked me to the front door was hold her hand.

"I'll call you tomorrow," I said.

"Okay…No, call me as soon as you get home. I'll stay down here near the phone."

"See you later." I kissed her, her lips warm, her arms around me as welcoming as Liz Malloy's embrace.

"Goodnight." She hunched her shoulders and smiled. "Happy Thanksgiving."

In my bedroom I turned out the light, slid into bed, and pulled up the covers. What would it be like to lie in bed with Janice? I wanted her beside me again in my bed, us touching each other, nothing between us. "I'm thinking about you," she had said to me over the downstairs phone, her voice above a whisper. "What are you thinking about?"

"About you." I had wanted to say more but I didn't want to say the wrong thing. I didn't want spoil this new thing between us.

We were a couple now, like other couples at the high school were. Maybe they had experienced what Janice and I had experienced together tonight. We could have that closeness and rush again if we let ourselves go that far. Maybe not all the way. She probably wouldn't go that far, only far enough to know we loved each other.

"I like you, David," she had said once more.

"I like you, too."

"Goodnight."

18

Gifts

"Hope you didn't spend a lotta cash on me," Skip greeted me at the front door of Ceil Kinsale's house the weekend before Christmas. "I didn't spend much on you."

"You like toy trains?" I asked.

Same voice, same thick lenses, same sarcasm: My best friend was OK.

An inch or two taller, an inch or two broader in the shoulders. Maybe because the blue and black heavy flannel shirt snugged his chest. My parents and I stood in Ceil Kinsale's cozy living room, lighted Christmas candles in the windows. Skip stood taller than me now. Maybe stronger. Maybe he had settled in to his new life.

Mom and Dad and I put our presents beneath the living room Christmas tree. Our gifts bulked beside a thin scattering of other presents there that weekend before Christmas.

"Hi there, folks! Welcome to our cozy little home." Ceil Kinsale hugged my parents, took my mother's hand, and held her ever-present cigarette in her other hand. "By the way: I'm not sure if you passed the Kinsale Pub on the way, but I'm no kin to those folks. They're the rich Kinsales, I'm one of the just-making-ends-meet Kinsales."

She covered her mouth with the back of her cigarette hand and cleared her throat. Tiny lines v'd out from the corners of her eyes and mouth.

"Is Liz here?" I asked.

"Lizzie and Marty'll be home soon," Aunt Ceil acknowledged me and then turned to Mom and Dad: "Lizzie works now for Marty's Dad, you know…Bannon Lumber."

Skip chucked me on the shoulder and said, "Come on up. Show you my room."

We took the narrow steep stairs two at a time. At the top, when I turned to follow him down the hall, I overheard my mother say to Aunt Ceil, "I'm glad we could do this…We came through some flurries on the way…How's he doing? He seems really happy…"

Ceil Kinsale's cough blurred her response.

"NO KIBITZERS: ENTER AT YOUR OWN RISK." He had brought his old bedroom door sign. This space measured smaller than his previous one—the whole house felt smaller, more narrow than the brown-shingled bungalow still for sale. The stairway walls had pressed against my shoulders. The bedroom ceiling light was a globed eye spying down on me. Instead of the single bed he had in Lorrence, he slept "sometimes up top, sometimes down below" in the bunk bed hemmed against a wall. He patted the upper bunk mattress and said, "Next time you're here, you can have your choice."

Maroon and gray throw rug on the floor, the floor's brownish-black wood scuffed.

His old desk, a mirror above it; black loose-leaf notebook and two textbooks—Biology and English—on the desk; Philadelphia Eagles pennant and the 1956 team picture thumb-tacked beside the mirror. "Marty tried to get tickets for the last game of the season but it was sold out. Gotta wait till next year."

No picture of his parents. No picture of Liz or of himself. It seemed half of the bedroom belonged to him, the other half to someone else.

One window overlooked the backyard, snow-covered like the hills and low mountains we had passed north of Reading.

I had a flash of Lizzie and her mother arranging picnic tables for Lizzie's birthday party…*"I was sorry to hear about your poor grandmother…"*

The 45 RPM record player on an overturned wood crate between the bunk bed and the wall next to the window. A stack of 45s next to the record player.

"What've you got?" I asked.

"Not much. Bunch've old stuff. Haven't bought new stuff lately."

He slid a handful of 45's out of their sleeves, down the record player's spindle, and fingered the switch to On. "Wella one for the money, two for the show…"

"I don't have any blue suede shoes yet but maybe Santa'll bring me a pair," Skip said. He sat on the lower bunk. I took the desk chair. He moved his right foot and leg in rhythm to the song's guitar and bass rhythm and stared across the room to the empty wall opposite the bed. He seemed to drift off somewhere, stayed there until "Blue Suede Shoes" finished and another black disc slid down the spindle. Fats Domino greeted "Hello Josephine…How do you do!"

What was Skip thinking about as he moved his head and shoulders in time to the infectious, repetitious beat. He had seemed as happy as I had ever seen him when he greeted Mom, Dad, and me at the front door. He had shaken hands with Dad and me, had hugged Mom, and he had laid his arm conspiratorially across my shoulders, turned me away from the others, and whispered loudly in my ear, "How's it hangin', numbnuts?"

As he gazed at the wall his face expressed only questions. I had questions, too, but Skip's questions were more important than mine.

"So how's it going?" I said, to get him talking again.

"How's what going?"

"School, football…How'd you guys do?"

"So-so. Won five, lost a couple." He had played second string guard on offense and second string line-backer on defense. He had made some tackles, missed some tackles, and batted away a couple passes. "What the hell: I showed up for every goddamn practice and every goddamn game and kept my goddamn glasses on. Counts for something…"

School was school. He was still the new kid. He had gone through "initiation".

"What'd they try?"

On the third day of school three juniors in his gym class had assaulted him from behind, dragged him from the locker room, and tried to hang him by his belt from a metal hook in the hallway. "One of'em said, 'Initiation.' When they lifted me up, I kicked the shit out of two of'em and rammed the other against the wall. Then one of the coaches came by. I told him what happened. He told me to clean up, he'd take it from there. The three shit-heads got expelled for five days, I got famous."

Nothing since.

"Hello Josephine's" groove clicked once, the record player's arm swung wide, the next single dropped into place. Little Anthony and the Imperials Oo whad, oo wha'd their lead-in to "Why Do Fools Fall in Love?"

Skip lurched to the record player and jabbed the On-Off switch to Off. "Enough 'a that crap," he said.

"Any women in your life?"

"Cori," he said. "I can talk to her. She doesn't gossip. She's really nice."

He and Cori talked during study hall, Skip explained, mostly about homework. The study hall monitor didn't mind as long as they kept their voices down. Skip hadn't told her yet about last summer. He hadn't talked to anyone about except "you and my sister and Marty. Sometimes I don't wanna talk about it at all."

"Not much of a party going on here by the looks 'a things. You guys want lunch?"

Wearing a black skirt and a white sweater with a holly wreath broach pinned below her left shoulder, Liz stood in the doorway then took three steps forward and gave me a long hug. Sweet perfume and powder seemed nestled around her neck. I wasn't sure if I should hold her as tightly as she held me, but just as I had made up my mind, she stepped back and said, "Who wants subs? Marty's buying. Special pre-Christmas treat," she said. "Halves or wholes, hot or cold?"

"Hey, you slugs, get a load off. Come with me!" Marty Bannon ducked his head and hunched his shoulders as he came into Skip's room: "Give you character. Make men out've ya'. Plus, I'll give you the Mount Howard tour before we pick up the subs."

He backed out his Chevy Bel Air, Dad in the front passenger seat, Skip and I in the back. The rear floor mats were spotless, front dashboard and dials polished. Marty kept things clean.

Mount Howard High resembled a factory more than a school; the football scoreboard, press box, and chain-link fence around the field "all new since last summer," Marty reported. "This town likes sports."

"So does Lorrence," my father commented. "You played, didn't you?"

"Basketball. Center…Coulda played college ball but I didn't have the money. Still don't. I'll apply after I save enough. Don't wanna rely on Mommy and Daddy. Do this on my own. It'll work out."

I liked him for his determination and independence.

Houses beyond the center of town displayed Christmas wreaths on front doors, and strings of lights along the edges of some roofs. Chevys and Fords in the driveways. Marty pointed to a squarish, red brick house. On its roof a cardboard smiling Santa, sack slung over his shoulder, one hand on the chimney. "My mom and dad live right there," Marty said.

"That your boss on the roof?" Skip said, but he didn't smile or laugh after he asked the question.

"Doesn't look like him," Marty replied.

Snow flurries skidded the windshield as we approached the fire house and police station. Marty looked over at Dad and then in the rear view mirror at Skip and me and said, "I don't know what's gonna happen to this town." It was the weekend before Christmas, but little traffic meandered through the business area this early Sunday afternoon. A handful of cars were slotted in front of a diner, one police car at an angle in front of the city hall. Two stores showed front windows boarded over, 'Merry Christmas' printed in red paint on the boards.

"Most of the mines shut down after Korea," Marty said. "One's still operating, about twenty-fi' miles north. Then there's an army depot about fifty miles west. So the mine, the depot, lumber yard, and a few measly shops here—they keep the town going. Those places and the bars, like the one right here, next to Mazio's."

Marty nodded toward the right and pulled into a space in front of a brick-fronted building—"Mazio's Subs and Pizza" in gold lettering above red and green tinsel streamers inside the front window. Two men in navy pea jackets and work boots shouldered to Kinsale's Pub to the left of Mazio's.

"Bars here open on Sundays?" my father asked Marty.

"Every Sunday and holiday except Christmas and Easter." Marty gave a short laugh, patted my father on the shoulder twice and said, "Helps keep the local economy going, Phil. The owner gives Ceil a discount if he's in a good mood."

"You'd think those guys would wait till late afternoon to have a beer," Dad said.

"Any time's a good time to have a beer—or *more*, Phil. It's practically all these guys have in their lives when they're out of work. Get together with everybody else who's outta work."

Dad and Marty went in to Mazio's to order the subs.

A man wearing an unzipped parka pulled open the door to Kinsale's.

"Busy place," I said to Skip. "Wanna join'em?" not a serious invitation.

Skip sniffed. "You kidding?"

Maybe, maybe not. See what happens, I said to myself in an imaginary in-control- of-things wise guy voice.

Why'd Marty park in front of Kinsale's? Did he know I'd raided Dad's bourbon again? Did Dad tell him? Were they trying to teach me a lesson? I knew what was good for me. I didn't need another sermon on how to live or what to believe. I was testing things when I drank Dad's bourbon. So what? What the hell was so wrong about having a lousy beer or just a few sips of hard stuff? Wasn't going to kill me...wasn't like I was gonna wind up flat on my face, for God's sake.

What *the hell was God gonna do about it anyway? Tap me on the shoulder and say,* "**David Harper, you're in trouble. What are you going to do about it?**"

"Let's have a beer and talk it over, God. What'll You have?"

"You behaving yourself, Harper?" Skip asked.

I almost told him to shut up, mind his own business. But he wasn't Guy Ross or Jack MacAdams. "I'm all right...I'm hungry."

Back at Ceil Kinsale's house Liz greeted us by holding a sprig of mistletoe above our heads. "A kiss before lunch," she said as she kissed each of us on the cheek when we filed in to the kitchen. "Two kisses for you, David, because you're such a good friend." She didn't hug me this time. I missed her arms around me but liked her scent of her powder and perfume.

I thought right away of Janice, of the Saturday night after Thanksgiving, our slow dances together since then. I imagined Liz and Marty downstairs here on the sofa after Ceil went to bed. How far did Liz let him go? All the way? Did Liz think of her father when Marty put his arms around her?

Janice, the feel of her breasts in my hand, her sweater and bra the only separations between our skins. Daydreaming about Janice, I felt a familiar, pleasurable stiffening inside my pants.

As we began to eat, Ceil Kinsale raised a glass of beer to us, so did Marty. The rest of us reciprocated the toast with soda or coffee.

All through subs and soda I couldn't get sex out of my head—the feel of Janice's tongue on mine, the aching throb inside my pants, the need to have it all again right now. But that was impossible. Knowing I'd have to stand up soon, I tried to will my hard-on back to its normal size.

Forget conversation about Christmas shopping, the price of gifts and cards these days, and Christmas Eve Midnight Mass at the Catholic Church in Mount Howard (that was when my mother reminded me I was scheduled to be Father Hepplewhite's acolyte Christmas Eve). Try to forget feelings about Janice; about having a drink or two with the men walking into Kinsale's; and about Liz sitting across the table from me, Marty beside her, trying to convince Skip to sign up for either track or baseball next spring.

"I'm serious, man. You've got the build of a solid catcher or shot-putter."

"I'll think about it," Skip said, not eager to give it as much thought as Marty wanted him to.

I fixed on Marty's hands, the width of his palms and the length of his fingers. Hands strong enough to wrench a gun away from—

My mother pointed to a window that looked out into the backyard. "Look, it's starting to come down harder." Mom didn't like to travel in snow. Not because she thought Dad was a careless driver. She was afraid of skidding off the road, crashing into a telephone pole or tree or another vehicle. Dad had never been in an accident, but being over a hundred miles away from Lorrence, and seeing the possibility of driving home in a snowstorm, Mom feared the worst.

"Maybe we should open our presents now," Liz said.

"But I don't have a thing for you, Mr. and Mrs. Harper and David," said Ceil Kinsale. She cleared her throat. "I feel terrible, but I just haven't started my Christmas shopping yet. I'm so sorry."

My mother put her hand on Ceil's arm. "Don't worry. Seeing all of you again is a nice present."

The increased length inside my pants had changed to average, as it was when Liz had kissed me under mistletoe.

The lighted and tinseled tree looked tall and thin with only a handful of wrapped presents beneath it. A red and blue striped necktie for Dad from Liz and Marty; a gold tie clasp for Dad from Skip. A tan winter scarf for my mother. Brown leather gloves for me.

My parents' presents for Marty were work gloves and a woolen cap. Marty shook hands with Mom and Dad. "Just what I needed, Mr. and Mrs. Harper."

"Okay, Harper, here's yours. Some fat guy in a red suit told me to give it to you."

Skip was jolly again. The colorful lights on the tree flicked across the lenses of his glasses. He wasn't the Skip who had stared at his bedroom wall and who had nearly shoved his record player onto the floor when he had turned it off. Not the Skip who had asked me half-seriously if I'd been behaving myself. He was my best friend who had greeted us when we first arrived.

"Lizzie tied the ribbon. She's got ribbon skill," Skip said.

Inside the box lay a navy blue V-neck sweater with white and blue trim around the neck.

"That was Skip's choice, not mine, not Marty's," said Liz.

"Thanks," I said, and shook hands with my best friend.

He said and did the same for me, but after he first unwrapped socks and a tan corduroy shirt from my parents, and after he peeled off the paper and ribbon my mother had used to wrap my present to him: a blue, Oxford cloth buttoned-down shirt.

"Something to wear to church," I said grinning.

"When I go," he replied. Then he laughed, slapped me on the back, and offered his hand to me. "Thanks, man," he said.

His hand gripped mine stronger than my hand gripped his.

Snow, plus the smell of Ceil Kinsale's cigarette smoke embedded on our clothes, followed us to Lorrence. Dad kept both hands on the steering wheel. The only conversation we had until we got home concerned the wind-blown snow across the roads and the Ben Franklin Bridge. My mother sat up straight, her shoulders squared against the back of her seat as Dad stayed in the far right lane across the bridge. When we reached Lorrence, streetlights heightened sidewalk and street snow. Dad sighed, and flexed his fingers after taking them off the steering wheel.

I called Janice from Mom and Dad's bedroom. Door closed, lights off, we talked about the trip to Mount Howard, about Skip, and about Christmas. She and her family would spend Christmas Day with her mother's parents in New Brunswick, stay overnight, and come home the next day.

"We're staying here," I told her. "I have to go to church Christmas Eve, and then my grandfather'll come over Christmas Day."

"We don't go to church. I mean, we don't *belong* to a church. My mother used to take Melinda and me to the Presbyterian Church, but we don't go anymore. I have no idea what religion my Dad is."

After two beats I said, "Does your dad believe in God?"

"I don't know. We don't talk about religion." She paused, then, "Do you?"

"I'm waiting for proof."

"I think I am, too," Janice said.

"I wish I didn't have to go Christmas Eve. I want to stay home and sleep."

"Then why go?"

I explained I had to be an acolyte at St. Thomas'. I couldn't get out of it.

"An acolyte? What do you do?"

I described my duties. Janice listened. Something in her silence signaled she was curious about my routine during a communion service. "I'd like to see you do that sometime."

"I don't wanna do it but I have to. My mother signed me up when I was twelve. Tough to get out of it now without an argument. I've lost all the arguments so far."

"I bought you a present," she said, no further discussion of religious matters.

"What is it?"

"You'll find out."

Hungry again after we hung up, I came downstairs to the kitchen. Dad had made himself a highball, Mom a cup of hot tea.

I intended to make myself some soup and a sandwich. My mother's comment stopped me.

"They were standing in that little coat room off the kitchen. Marty wanted to put his arms around her, and Liz pushed him away. 'Don't *do* that,' she said, her exact words. 'I don't like it.' Marty wasn't trying to get fresh with her, he doesn't strike me as that kind of man. He likes Liz, and I think he just wanted to hug her."

"Did he say anything to her?"

"He said he was sorry, he just wanted to be gentle with her…She leaned against him for a few seconds and then stepped away."

"What'd you do then?" my father asked.

"They didn't see me. I backed away, waited a few minutes until they came back to the living room. Then I went to get our coats."

"I didn't notice anything unusual with either of them the time we were there," Dad said.

"I didn't either. I wasn't looking for it but that's what I saw. Poor kid…"

"More evidence of what her father did to her," Dad stated.

He sipped his drink and then held it in his right hand. "This is just among the three of us, David," he said. "You understand? Not even for Skip, unless he says something about it to you first."

"I know," I said.

It was no good to study for tomorrow's quiz on poetry vocabulary, no good to review notes for tomorrow's lab in Biology. School stood as far from me as next summer. Close, though not in a special order, were what to buy for Mom, Dad, Granddad, and Janice, what to do besides sleep during Christmas vacation, and what would happen to Liz. Stuck: that's what I was again. In a place where I couldn't help my best friend and his sister. A place where I had no proof for questions that had shadowed me since the previous summer.

The night before Christmas Eve Janice gave me a silver ID wrist chain, its clasp scripted with 'To David, Love, Janice.' In front of the Taggart Christmas tree, she looped the bracelet around my right wrist and clasped the two ends together. I didn't let on that I thought the bracelet looked girlish; that it wasn't something I would wear for fear of being called 'queer' or worse. In the minutes after she fitted the bracelet around my wrist, the more I looked at 'David' inscribed on the silver plate, the more I liked it, and the more I knew she would like my present to her.

And the more I was relieved her parents and Melinda were out doing last-minute shopping.

I gave her a silver friendship ring with tiny stars embedded in it.

She teared up when she asked, "Put it on my finger?"

I slipped it on the third finger of her left hand.

We didn't dance that night. We didn't listen to records. We laid on the sofa and kissed and held each other. Janice wore a cream-colored pleated blouse that made a sound like stockings rubbing together when I put my arms around her. I imagined her in her shorts and halter top from last summer, the pinkness of her legs from sunburn. Janice here close, her arms around me calm and safe. Liz over a hundred miles away. Would she ever feel safe again with Marty?

I pressed closer to Janice, as close as we were at Thanksgiving, cloth and uncertainty like fences between our clothes, the motion of our bodies the only words we wanted to say until we realized that if we went further it would be too far. Janice whispered, "David, I think about you and I love you, but we better not." She edged away from me. "It happened to you again, didn't it. I could feel it."

"What did it feel like?"

She pressed her forehead to my shirt and then she looked up at me. "Like...like spasms," and in her eyes and voice I knew she was not embarrassed. Neither was I.

"I've read about what happens when you get excited. It's strange but nice, isn't it?"

"What happens to you?"

She hunched her shoulders and she smiled. "It's tingly. Like goose bumps."

"Did it happen to you too?"

"Almost," she said sheepishly, and kissed me. "You're the first person I've talked with this way about sex…A little with my mother. She talked to Mel and me about the basic facts and getting our periods. That's all. Not about what you and I talk about. I'm glad we do."

"Me too." I put my hand on her breast. She covered my hand with her own. I pressed the palm of my hand and fingers against the soft-hard mound and fondled her as if her breast was a song. She moved her hand in rhythm to mine.

"I love you," I said.

She kissed me again. "I love *you*. Merry Christmas."

———————

Nothing new about St. Thomas Church Christmas Eve. The same yellow glow from the globed lights above the side aisles. The same yellow flames from candles carried by young acolytes and from the six candles on the altar. The same old carols and same old Christmas story: shepherds abiding in the fields, the message from the heavenly host, the star guiding the three kings to Bethlehem. Same story.

So, I drifted away from Mary and Joseph bedding down in the stable. I fantasized about Janice, her surprised look and tears when she saw the friendship ring tucked in the velvet box. Her face warm, her breathing heavy when we kissed and when I felt her breasts through her sweater and when our bodies rhythmed against each other. And here I was, dressed like a goody-good acolyte in my red cassock and white cotta and standing hands folded like a goody-good acolyte below the altar, and there was 'the doughy-faced good Father,' hands folded at his chest as he walked to the pulpit to deliver his Christmas Eve sermon.

Concentrate on your acolyte duties, David Harper, I imagined a voice saying from on high. **Or else.**

Duties, huh? Wait for 'the good Father' to finish his sermon? Give the offertory plates to the ushers? (Dad and Granddad two of them). Collect the plates after the choir's anthem? Carry the money-filled plates to the Sacristy, where Dad, Granddad, and two other ushers would take it to the parish hall office, count the money, and stash it in the safe?

And don't forget the tiddlywinks (Boing!) and the water and wine—enough for the entire congregation, including people sitting on folding chairs behind the last row of pews. Save enough cream sherry for me, too, Father.

Or else.

Or else what? I've been a good boy.

Hot up here near the altar…Work up a sweat waiting for the good Father to—

"Let your light so shine that men may see your good works, and be grateful."

Okay, here we go. Game over.

Father Hepplewhite's wristwatch read twelve thirty when we entered the Sacristy after the "Hark! The Herald Angels Sing" recessional. He shook hands with me, thanked me for being "a marvelous help," wished me Merry Christmas. He then went out to greet the congregation.

I still felt the tangy-sweet taste of communion wine in my mouth; still felt its warmth in my stomach. The communion wine cabinet was attached to the wall above the vestments bureau. I opened the cabinet door. One bottle of cream sherry. I lifted the bottle down, tipped it so that the light shone on the bottle's bluish glass, and checked its contents: half-filled. I listened, waited. No footsteps coming near. Quickly I unscrewed the cap, took one, then a second swig of the sherry and then returned the bottle, cap screwed back on, to its proper place in the cabinet and closed the door. A nice, sliding warmth all the way down. Something for a Merry Christmas!

My last duty was to extinguish the altar candles. I lifted the long-handled candle snuffer from beside the vestment bureau and walked out to the Sanctuary. A murmur of footsteps and conversation from the rear of the church. People in line—I picked out Mom, Dad, and Granddad ready to greet 'the good Father' and wish him a Merry Christmas. Most of the pews sat empty.

I entered the Sanctuary. I glanced at the gold Cross braced to the granite wall above the altar. The Cross gleamed, unsmeared under lights. I bowed, stepped up to the altar, and extinguished one at a time the three candles on the Epistle side.

The sweet-tangy taste of sherry tingled the inside my mouth. *Did 'the good Father' stash chewing gum in the Sacristy?*

I stepped down from the altar, bowed again, but didn't regard the Cross. I stepped up to extinguish the three candles on the Gospel side.

When I raised the candle snuffer, I felt a sudden calm come over me. It was like warm soothing water through my body. The sensation lightened me, made me feel that the problems in my life would disappear and drift away. Like a warm cloak, a restful happiness enveloped me.

I waited for more. A touch?

Nothing.

I put out the first candle and raised the snuffer above the second. Still nothing more.

I extinguished the second and last candles.

Nana, I thought as I stepped down from the altar and bowed in front of it.

Nana.

19

"Can I talk to you?"

I had ridiculed him behind his back. On the sly I had swigged communion wine from the Sacristy cabinet. Tonight, mockery and sneakiness were not my motives. I would be honest and sincere with Father Hepplewhite.

"Can I talk to you, please?"

His handshake was pliable, soft bread-like as always. The skin of his neck folded like thin flaps over his white collar.

"Let me take your coat, David," he offered. "We can talk in the den. Would you like some cocoa?"

My jacket over his right arm, 'the good Father' walked from the rectory vestibule through a short hallway to the kitchen. In black trousers, black shirt, and white collar, in this house, the St. Thomas rectory, he looked out of place. No robe, no white cord, no chasuble.

This was my first time in the rectory. The living room bulked with stiff chairs and sofas, tables and lamps. No music, no TV. Quiet. Only one religious object in it: a wooden crucifix fixed to the wall above the fireplace mantle but no charred logs in the hearth. Jesus had to depend on old radiator heat to keep warm.

"Follow me," said Father Hepplewhite, and carried two cups of cocoa as he led the way down the hall past the kitchen that smelled of butter and cocoa to the den—all books; three walls ceiling to floor of shelves of books. Beneath one window a wooden roll-top desk and chair. Maybe 'the good Father' composed his sermons at the desk.

"Have you read all these?" I asked.

He smiled but kept his lips closed. "Many. Do you need a book for a book report?"

I laughed more out of surprise at his joke than at the question. Maybe Father Hepplewhite *did* have a sense of humor.

He handed me a cup of cocoa and, as he sat down in his desk chair, invited me to sit in a brown leather chair angled toward him. The cushion seemed to sigh as I sat on it; I hoped Father Hepplewhite didn't think I had made a rude noise. Eye-level to my right was a shelf of hard-covers and paperbacks--many with religious titles, something called *The Story of One Man*, another *The Final Three Hours*.

I'm a prisoner, I thought: *Jesus on my right, Hepplewhite like a judge in front of me.* The cocoa tasted smooth and warm, but I didn't know where to rest the cup. Hold it on my lap? Put it on the floor? I wanted to hold something; I clutched the cup against my belt buckle.

Father Hepplewhite asked about my parents and Granddad and our Christmas. They were fine...Christmas a little different, not as cheerful, without my grandmother, I admitted, but it had been okay.

He nodded and smiled again without opening his mouth. Then: "Well, what did you want to talk about, David?"

"I don't know. It's—It's strange."

"Tell me." He sipped cocoa and set the cup on the desk next to his arm.

I let go of it, of everything: the deaths of Skip's mom and dad, the touch on my shoulder, the feeling of peace at the lake when Ross nearly went over the spillway, my thoughts of Nana near the altar on Christmas Eve, my questions about the gypsy woman and God. Everything. It felt like a long confession but one that didn't include sneaking booze and wine. I hadn't broken any commandments...Told white lies, yes. Sneaked cream sherry, yes. Tonight I wanted answers.

All the time I spoke my hands shook. A voice in my head commanded, *"Don't spill the stupid cocoa!"*

Father Hepplewhite's expression didn't change. He held his cup of cocoa at belt level and studied me as if I was a problem; the line of his mouth did not move.

"What do you think?" I asked.

He crossed his legs and leaned back in his chair. "Are you *sure* that what you felt on your shoulder and what you felt near the altar were *not* in your imagination? Are you abso*lute*ly sure, David? Sometimes in an emotional moment—"

"They *weren't* in my imagination! I *felt* them. Don't you get it?"

He was preaching, rehashing my parents' explanations for events they didn't understand.

"Sometimes we're so caught up in the emotion of the moment," he continued, setting his cup on the floor beside him, "that we i*mag*ine something happening to us when it's not really happening to us at all."

"That's what my parents said, but I *felt something*. It was like a hand. It was *really there*. Then I had that calm feeling, and right after that I thought of my grandmother. What the heck does it all mean?"

He sighed, crossed his legs again, and folded his hands in his lap. "I'm not quite sure, David. But I do think both of those experiences are wonderful mysteries. As to the gypsy woman you described," he shook his head, "I know of no woman in Lorrence like her." He smiled without parting his lips; the expression indicated that I was a little boy who should know the answer.

"What the heck's all *that* supposed to mean?" I thumped the cup of cocoa on the floor under the bookshelves. A wave of cocoa rose to the top but didn't spill over the edge.

"I mean that I'm not sure what it was that happened to you. Perhaps it was your imagination, but perhaps not. What you described sounds beautiful. Beautiful and lovely mysteries, which is what sacraments are, are they not? Faith in God is a lovely mystery."

"I don't know who or what God is." Without apology I stood my ground.

"I think you *do* know," Father Hepplewhite stated, as if I should understand by now who and what God represented in my life. "From all of your Sunday School classes and Catechism, and from all the times you've served at Holy Communion, I'm sure you know."

"Then why isn't He giving me answers?" Little waves sloshed in my stomach. My throat tightened. I forced back tears, determined not to cry in front of this man I had addressed as Father. Beautiful mystery? Faith? Enough. No more.

This minister had one more explanation: "Maybe God has already given you answers."

"But—"

"You want me to be more specific, David. I can't. I wish I could but I can't. You have to trust. Trust in God, trust in your faith."

"Not if I don't want to," I said.

He blinked at me as if he did not hear me correctly. "I'm sorry?" he said and took a hard-cover book from the shelf to his left and handed it to me. The book's title was *The Miracles in Faith.* "Reading this may help you," he said.

"I don't want it." I tossed it back to him. He caught it in his lap. "It's probably a bunch of crap."

I left the house, the first time I had ever walked out on anyone.

20

Lost Ground

I quit.

Two nights later, my father at a bank employees meeting, my mother answered the downstairs phone. I was about to go to my room to review World History notes for a quiz on the assassination of Kaiser Wilhelm. As I started up the stairs, something about my mother's voice—the way she expressed "He *what?* No, I didn't."—made me stop. My heart sped, my breath quickened, I took the stairs two at a time. I knew who the call was from. and I knew my mother would open my door even though it was closed.

Five minutes later she knocked once and opened the door.

"Just what do you think you were doing walking out on Father Hepplewhite? I just got off the phone with him, and believe me, he was *very* upset. Very."

I was sitting up in bed, my back against a pillow, the World History text open, face down beside me, my notebook propped against my legs. Without taking my eyes off my notes, I said, "I didn't like what he told me."

"Look at me, David. I can accept the fact you haven't gotten the answers you've wanted to your questions. I don't like your arguments, and to tell the truth it bothers me when you ask questions about things Dad and I believe in. But you had no right, no right at all, to treat Father Hepplewhite the way you did. *I'm* embarrassed and ashamed of what you did and Dad will be, too."

"I'm not."

"Well, someday I hope you are. You think about what's really important for you and our church from now on. You think about what you should do out of respect for people and your obligations to them. You think about that."

She swung the door closed. It shook when it stuck in the door jam.

In the next day's mail I saw the March acolyte schedule envelope, unopened, on the living room desk. The envelope was addressed to me.

I crumpled the envelope and foul-shot it underhand into the trash container under the desk.

After dinner that night my mother asked me if I had checked the schedule. It was the first time she had spoken to me since she had come to my room the night before.

"I'm not doing it," I said.

"Why?"

"I don't want to. Don't keep asking me to." I got up from the table.

"Then call Father Hepplewhite and tell him."

"What's this about?" my father said.

Directly to me she said, "If you don't want to be an acolyte anymore, tell him yourself."

"Don't worry, I will." I had said it more in anger than in truth. I didn't care if I ever saw Hepplewhite or heard from him again.

"What's going on?" My father pushed his plate to the side.

I didn't answer.

"Tell him," my mother ordered me.

I faced him. "I quit being an acolyte."

"In a pig's neck you will."

I felt myself slip, lose ground, but I determined not to back down.

I walked away. I didn't turn back when he called "David!" I went up to my room and slammed the door.

Later, after I turned out my lamp, I heard a one-two knock on my door.

"David?"

I was lying in bed facing away from the door as he opened it. My mother and father's shadows silhouetted on Mickey Mantle, Duke Snider, Jackie Robinson, and other greats on the wall.

"Are you awake?" my mother said.

What the hell do you think? my imaginary sarcastic voice burned to say out loud.

Somehow they knew I wasn't asleep. My mother sat at the end of the bed, her weight unthreatening. Dad's voice came from in front of the door. "Why'd you quit?" he asked.

I still didn't answer. Resistance slid out of me.

My mother asked, "Why don't you want to be an acolyte? It's something we think you need to do."

I kept my face turned to my pillow. "Are you gonna believe what I tell you?"

I counted to five before they answered nearly simultaneously, "Yes."

I poured out everything again. "It really happened. All of it. If you don't believe me, too bad. From now on I do things on my own."

They stayed near me for a while but said nothing more. I wanted to be left alone, yet I wanted them near me.

Minutes? A half hour or more? How long they stayed in the room I couldn't determine. I didn't know if my mother kissed me or not. I didn't hear them open and close the door. I didn't wipe away the tears from my eyes.

———————

He looked younger in black trousers, black shirt and white collar than he had appeared in vestments for a funeral Mass. Clean shaven, the tart scent of shaving lotion around him, thick black hair combed straight back from his forehead. Broad thick hands that reminded me of boxers' hands I had seen in sport magazines. Father Bradeen removed his glasses and shook hands with me. "Please come in," his grip firm, stronger than Hepplewhite's. A minty aroma, but no beer, drifted on his breath.

"We can talk in my office. Please, this way." His left hand lightly touching the back of my jacket, he extended his right arm toward the hallway straight ahead and an open door. A gold watchband looped around his right wrist.

Father Bradeen's office was high-ceilinged, book shelves floor to ceiling fortified two walls, a window and a framed painting of the Virgin Mary on the wall behind his desk. Mary cupped her right hand beneath her heart that was ringed with a golden light. She gazed out toward the hallway we had entered from.

"I'm sorry you have to sit on a wooden chair," Father Bradeen said, pointing to the classroom-type chair in front of his desk, "but a leg broke on the nice cushioned chair I've had here. I sent it out for repair, so I'm afraid that's the best I can offer you," he waved toward the replacement, "unless you want to sit behind my desk. But that would feel rather strange to you, wouldn't it?" He paused and smiled before he sat behind the desk. "Are you one of us? Catholic? I don't think I've seen you before."

"Episcopalian."

"Well, you're close."

The slatted wooden seat felt as hard as Sunday School chairs on my rear end.

"Your name is David?"

"Yes."

"What brings you here, David?"

I stated "I'm friends with Skip Malloy."

Father Bradeen leaned forward, elbows on the green desk blotter, and folded his hands under his chin. His face showed everything he had come to know about Skip and his family. "I see," he said. "How are Skip and his sister doing?"

"Okay so far." I explained that my parents and I had visited Skip and Liz and their aunt before Christmas.

"And from what you gather, he's doing all right? He's adjusted to the new school and everything? Not everything, I'm sure, but..."

Father Bradeen pushed back from the desk, rested his hands on the arms of the chair, and shook his head. "It was a terrible thing...an absolutely terrible thing. But it's good that he has you as a friend."

Should I ask him for advice about Liz? I wondered. I decided not to. Liz was not why I was sitting in front of him.

I flicked a glance at the Virgin Mary above him. I wanted to see if her eyes in any way looked down at me. They didn't. I didn't think that the gypsy woman's eyes had looked at me, either.

"What can I help you with, David?" Father Bradeen asked.

Before I explained what had happened to me last summer, I asked questions. "How come you say the Catholic service in Latin?"

"It's the language of the Church." He smiled, his lips closed like Father Hepplewhite's smile. "Next?"

"Do you think most people understand it?"

"If those people were brought up Catholic, I think they understand most of it. What they need to know. They've heard it all their lives if they attended Mass regularly." He smiled again. "Do you go to church regularly, David?"

"No. Only when I was an acolyte. I'm not anymore."

"Ah, I see." He leaned back in his chair. "Why only when you were an acolyte?"

"My parents told me I had to give something back to the church. But I'm not an acolyte anymore, so I don't go."

"And why is that?"

Not again, I thought. Father Bradeen was giving me the third degree. I felt as if I had to defend myself on a witness stand. I didn't like feeling that way. "Because: I don't get anything out of it."

"So, you're giving up, are you?" His lips moved in a slight, closed-mouth smile. He seemed to be enjoying this interrogation.

"I'm not giving up," I said. "I just don't like being told I have to go." I pointed at the picture of Mary and tried to change the subject. "Why does she have her hand under her heart?"

Without looking at the picture, Father Bradeen said, "Mary is the Immaculate Mother of Jesus. She was chosen among women, by God, to be Jesus's mother."

"What women?"

"All women."

"All the women in the world? Come on."

That question and my evident disbelief unsettled Father Bradeen. Maybe I was gaining back some ground. He shifted in his chair so that his right elbow leaned on the chair's arm.

"What's so special about Mary?" I almost laughed but thought better of it. *Not here. Not yet.*

"God recognized Mary as a pure woman who would nurture and love His son and bear the pain of His suffering." Bradeen studied me. "How are you doing with this theology so far? Does it sound familiar?"

"Some of it, yeah."

"The Catholic and Episcopal Churches are quite similar to each other, you know."

"I know. My Sunday School teachers told me all about it." Then I stated four simple words which I hoped would make him give me answers I wanted: "I just don't know…"

"What don't you know, David?"

I jounced my right leg. The floor mumbled but Father Bradeen's desk didn't shake. I wasn't going to stop even if he asked me to halt my nervous leg. I needed to explain everything again. I spilled all of it to this priest who gave me confidence to speak my mind and demand reasons I hope I could understand and believe in. My life was like a bunch of math and science questions I couldn't figure out.

When I finished, I kept moving my leg like a piston.

"I think you should take a long and deep breath, David. Your leg is moving about fifty miles an hour. Slow down." He smiled.

"I'm sorry." I immediately wanted to retract my apology. I didn't want to be sorry about anything anymore. I didn't take back the words I thought cowardly. I flexed my ankles. That slowed me down.

Father Bradeen narrowed his eyes. Maybe he thought I was telling a bunch of lies. Maybe he was trying to scare me into telling him the truth. Maybe he was just wondering what he was going to say. I looked right back at him.

Don't tell me the same old crap I've heard from Hepplewhite and Mom and Dad and Granddad, the belligerent voice complained in my head. No more!

"David, are you *sure*—are you *absolutely sure* that what you've just explained to me is the absolute truth. *The* absolute truth. Swear to God?"

"Yes. Swear to God."

"Not too loud, please…Well," he said taking a deep breath, "at least you didn't experience a vision or hear voices." He stood and regarded the painting of the Virgin Mary, and then spoke directly to me. "You weren't raised from the dead, you didn't come back to life, you didn't turn water into wine. You felt the sensation of a hand touch you. You felt a calmness go through your body. These aren't miracles, David. And the gypsy woman? I have no idea who you mean. So," he said, bending toward me and slipping his hands into his trousers pockets, "my *suspicion* is—not my *belief*, only my *suspicion*—you had some amazing experiences."

"That's all? That's it?"

"That's what I think."

"But come *on*: what touched me?"

"I don't know, and I don't want to hazard a guess. It would be unfair of me to tell you exactly what caused those events, because I don't *exactly* know. For your own sake, I'm thankful you experienced them. I think the touch and the feeling of calm gave you—

"You sound just like Hepplewhite. It's bullshit! Nothin' but bullshit!"

I walked out again.

I was on my own: again.

————

"You're quiet," Janice said to me on Long Avenue one early March afternoon as I walked her home from school. "What's the matter?"

"Nothing." I scuffed a twisted cigarette wrapper on the sidewalk.

Her complexion pinked from the chilly wind against our faces. She wore a tan coat with wide lapels and wide belt tied at the waist. She lowered her head and tightened her arms around the books she cradled against her coat.

Because of the experiences we had shared being close, I once more felt older, more aware of things in the world than other kids our age did; at the same time, not knowing certain things made me feel less confident. I couldn't be the strong and assured young man I wanted to be.

"Are you gonna tell me what's the matter?"

It took until we reached Taylor Avenue to explain everything and to answer Janice's questions. When I revealed I had walked out on Father Hepplewhite and Father Bradeen, she confronted me like a school principal. "You *didn't*," she said.

"I did. So what."

"That's like walking out on church."

"I don't care. I don't care if I ever go back into a church."

Janice said nothing more until we reached her front steps. "Come on in," she said. "Nobody's home."

While she went upstairs. I put my books and jacket on a chair near the front door. It felt strange being alone in the house with her. I listened for Melinda's and Mr. and Mrs. Taggart's voices as I usually did when I came there. Today, Melinda had gone to an ice cream and soda shop with friends, their parents were still at work. I leaned against the family room archway the casual way Mr. Taggart had done. Mid-afternoon now, sunlight laying a pale sheen on the sofa, chairs, and lamp tables.

Downstairs, Janice switched on an end table lamp, flipped on the TV to *Bandstand* and made peanut butter and grape jelly sandwiches and chocolate milk. Like a waitress she brought them on a tray to the coffee table in front of the sofa. She smoothed her brown, tan, and white plaid skirt over her knees as she sat down. When she tucked her legs beneath her, her stockings rubbed together. I quick-imagined the paleness of her thighs, and though I hadn't seen them since last summer at the beach and tee at Halcyon Lake, I thought about smoothing my hand up and down her legs. I felt myself stiffen.

I took a bite of a sandwich as Dick Clark announced, "Here's a song that sold over one million records in a matter of days. Can you believe it? Elvis Presley: 'Too Much'."

"Too loud," Janice said. She picked up half a sandwich from the tray, stepped to the TV, lowered the volume, and returned to the sofa. I wasn't sure if she knew that the swip-swip sound of her stockings had already excited me. If she was aware, she didn't let on. She chewed a couple bites, glanced at the dancers and then confronted me again. "What happened to you, it seems really strange…At the same time real. I think you should talk to Father Hepplewhite again."

"Forget it." I drank some chocolate milk and put the glass down on the table. "Don't tell anybody else what I told you."

We finished our snacks. Janice lowered the volume again. "So I can hear my sister before she comes in," she said.

We stretched out on the sofa, I on the inside, Janice on the cushions' edge. When we broke from a kiss I saw dancers jitterbug by the studio's camera. The couples and the music danced in an imaginary world, their faces, blouses and skirts, trousers and sport jackets costumes in a TV play in which no one spoke, or if they did speak, we didn't hear them. Janice beside me was not imaginary. Kissing her again and smoothing my hand across the front of her sweater blocked out everything else. Time slipped back to us when she put her hand above my heart and slowly sat up.

"We better take a break." She glanced below my belt and then shifted her eyes away.

We heard rapid footsteps on the front porch.

"Mel," Janice said. She slid an inch or two away from me but our shoulders still touched.

Melinda peeked into the family room "My my, the little lovers," she complained, then trotted up the stairs. A door slammed.

"One of her moods," Janice said.

"Guess I better go."

"Can you stay for dinner?" she asked.

I stayed.

21

"I'm not your guardian…I'm your friend."

Dear Mom and Dad,
Please don't be upset. I'm not doing anything wrong.
You can trust me. I've gone to see Skip.
I'll call you when I get there. I'll be back on Sunday.
David

March air crisp as a fall morning, sky grayish-white when I left the house. Blue jays and starlings yacked in backyard trees of houses along Willowyn Terrace. Clothes stuffed in my gym bag, Aunt Ceil's phone number and money in my wallet, I walked fast, my breath clouding the air, my mind on getting away from Hepplewhite and Bradeen and all the empty beliefs and prayers they preached, and all the obligations my parents had stressed to me. Nothing was working for me. Nothing was getting better for me, except being with Janice. She would understand what I was doing, where I was going, and why.

Maybe Granddad, too.

I glanced over my shoulder. No prowling police car, nobody. The way I wanted it.

A light shone in Granddad's kitchen. Checking over my shoulder, I scooted to the back door and knocked twice.

He peeked through the curtains and then slowly opened the door. "David," he said, clearing his throat. "What brings you here at this hour?

You going on a class trip? Come in, it's chilly."

I dropped my gym bag on the floor mat. "I'm going to Mount Howard to see Skip."

He tied the cord to his navy blue bathrobe, studied me and smiled. "Your mother and father don't know about this, do they. You sure you know what you're doing?"

"I'm going, Granddad."

He scuffed back into the kitchen in his bedroom slippers. I thought he would try to persuade me not to go. Instead, he cleared his throat again and asked, "How much money do you have?"

After I told him how much he said, "That'll get you as far as Mechanicsville, not Mount Howard. Wait here." He padded slowly through the dining room and, sliding his hand along the banister, walked slowly up the stairs.

I spied through the front curtains. Street and sidewalks lay empty.

"Here's twenty-five more," Granddad said, and handed me two tens and a five dollar bill. "I can't stop you, but you don't look like you're running away. Promise you'll be careful and you'll call your mother when you get there. Have a good trip."

"Thanks, Granddad."

I was careful: careful to catch a 6:05 bus for Philadelphia; careful to get off the bus at the Reading Terminal at seven o'clock; careful to cash in a dollar bill for change to make a phone call to Skip; careful to buy a ticket for the 7:46 train to Reading.

At the first phone booth I saw, I dropped in two quarters and dialed Ceil Kinsale's number.

Liz answered.

"It's David," I said.

"David? Where *are* you?"

"Philadelphia. I just bought a ticket to Reading. Can you pick me up there?"

The Reading station crammed with people and smelled like an unemptied waste basket of paper and food scraps. I imagined myself a running-back again as I toted my gym bag and cut through the crowd toward benches. I aimed for an unoccupied bench.

I set down the bag in front of the bench and immediately heard a familiar voice as if it funneled through a cheerleader's megaphone. "Jeez, Harper, you numbnut, are you *blind?*"

Skip crept out from behind Liz, who stood six feet behind me. "Harper, you sonovagun, great to see you, but damned if I'm gonna hug you! We gotta get outa here fast. Your parents called. Cops're out looking for you all over the place."

Jolly old Skip again: Through thick lenses his magnified eyes still beamed at me.

I caught Liz's familiar perfume even though she took my hands and held me at arm's length. "Oh, it's *good* to see you!"

She lay her hand on his arm. "Believe only half of what this kid says. Your mother did call me, not the police. She and your dad'll drive up Sunday to bring you home. I invited them to stay for dinner."

It was nearly an hour's ride in Ceil Kinsale's smoky gray Chrysler coupe from Reading to Mount Howard. The day didn't feel like a school day, more like a vacation day. The dashboard clock read twenty of ten. Third period at Lorrence High. World History. My teacher, a Korean War vet, would be lecturing about the Treaty of Versailles and the rise of the Nazi party. When I returned to class on Monday, I'd have to get notes from somebody reliable.

We turned off a two-lane highway and climbed a winding narrow road into the mountains. Strips of snow between metal guardrails looked like long, curved, frozen car grills either side of the road. Puffy, dirigible-shape clouds scudded across the sky and blocked the sun. On the driver's side, if Liz had rolled down her window and extended her arm, she might have scratched the snow and ice-covered hillside. After a sharp downhill we passed a cluster of red brick houses and a gas station whose bubble-head pumps looked like cartoon characters.

I asked how things were with Marty and his job at the lumber company. Business would pick up when the weather warmed, Liz said. "People start planning home repairs and additions then, and that means buying lumber." She turned to Skip beside her and said, "Tell David about the summer job

Marty has for you."

"Stacking lumber'n stocking shelves. Says it'll help me stay in shape for football."

"You gonna try out again?"

"Damn right."

"Watch those four-letter words, brother."

"I will if you'll let me drive when we get home."

So far, Liz didn't seem to be troubled by anything. Maybe she had gotten over the fear of being hugged by Marty and all of what made her remember her father's hands.

This time the South Kenton Street cleared sidewalks reminded me of Willowyn Terrace in front of St. Thomas'. Thinking about St. Thomas' reminded me of Father Hepplewhite, and the more I thought about him and the church, I muttered a four-letter word. Liz and Skip apparently didn't hear it.

"Let me drive in. Please?" asked Skip when we reached 233 South Kenton.

He and Liz changed places by her moving up and over, Skip sliding under.

Slowly he guided Aunt Ceil's Chrysler along the driveway's two concrete strips to the white-boarded garage. Parallel to the house, he accelerated, then braked suddenly as if a child had darted in front of the car.

He grinned at Lizzie and me: "Here we are!"

Inside the house Lizzie claimed she had already eaten breakfast—cereal and tea. She excused herself to "fix my face so I can look presentable at work."

Aunt Ceil, her lit filtered cigarette in an ashtray on the kitchen counter, created a late-morning breakfast for Skip and me; a full meal like the ones Nana (*Was it you near the altar?*) had prepared when I had stopped in Saturday mornings: orange juice, steak and scrambled eggs, home fries, toast with strawberry jam, and hot cocoa—a meal, according to Aunt Ceil, "any self-respecting Pennsylvania coal miner would be pleased to have set before him."

After she served us, she inhaled, exhaled smoke through the corner of her mouth, and said, "You two clean up after yourselves. Wash and dry your own dishes, wipe the crumbs off the table." She put the back of her right hand over her mouth, coughed, and left the kitchen. The cough hacked on like a chain reaction; one cough slinked into another as she went upstairs. We heard a door close.

"Happens all the time," Skip said. "Mom used to hate it when she and the old man came up here and had to listen to it. Aunt Ceill'll probably cough herself to death someday."

Skip poked at the home fries. I wondered if he was thinking about the coincidence of his remark.

Liz came into the kitchen as we finished our breakfast. She was lively, happy, joked with us about "playing hooky".

"I have a good reputation, don't worry," said Skip.

She asked me if I was serious about any girl.

"Yeah, pretty serious," I said.

She kissed me on the cheek. "She's lucky, David." She ducked out the back door, backed the Chrysler out the driveway, and left for the lumberyard.

Skip chewed a corner of toast and jam and said, "You picking up speed, Harper, with Janice?"

I mentioned that Janice and I had gone to some dances and movies. I didn't really want to talk about us, though. My relationship with her was between Janice and me, nobody else.

Skip and I cleared the table and did the dishes.

"Let's check what's goin' on at dear old Mount Howard High," he recommended.

Skip's high school still reminded me of an old hospital or factory: drab, institutional red brick, square windows, heavy doors. I pictured an ambulance squealing to a stop at the front steps, men in white coats jumping out with a stretcher and rushing inside.

We scooted through the school. No teacher we encountered questioned us. Three students hailed Skip "Hey, Malloy, you takin' the day off or somethin'?"

"Somethin'," Skip replied.

The smells within the walls were no different from those in Lorrence High, the hallway floors painted the same shade of gray, the fluorescent lighting giving the same overhead unshaded glare.

Hungry again, we walked to a sand-colored brick building my father and Marty had entered the Sunday before Christmas. In Mazio's Skip and I bought two "cold" subs, two root beers, and consumed our lunch at a scratched and initialed wood counter across from the deli case. Mazio's air—counter included—saturated with aromas of salad oil, oregano, garlic, and sliced meats. The 'sub' shop was a hundred percent better than a dry, stuffy classroom.

Holding his half sub in both hands, his mouth full, Skip managed, "Damn, this's good!"

After I had chewed two chunks of mine I asked, "How's Lizzie?"

Skip paused in chewing, he finished, and swallowed. "Doin' all right. She an' Marty don't always see eye-to-eye on things but she's okay.'

I figured not to push any further about Liz. Maybe I'd learn more when I saw her with Marty later that weekend.

"You still see that girl you told me about? The one you said you could talk to?"

"Cori. Smarter than half the teachers," he believed. Cori made Shakespeare clear as Mazio's front window. She helped him understand Geometry, too. "The Geometry teacher guy—He's an old military instructor, used to teach at West Point. He can't come down to our level. The way Cori explains theorems and all that stuff, she makes it all make sense."

"You talk with her about last summer?" A comment too late to withdraw, I cringed.

Skip waited.

"I told her. Made her swear not to tell nobody else. Not even her parents. I met them, they're okay, but you never know. Cori I can trust. She's sincere." He shook his head as if he disagreed with advice someone had given him. Apparently my friend didn't want to talk anymore about Cori or last summer. Not now. Maybe not even for the rest of the weekend.

Finished our subs and root beers, we walked outside into a handful of men in front of Kinsale's Pub. Men in work pants and brown or black and red hunting jackets. Some men bare-headed, some in black or brown woolen caps. One of the men inhaled a cigarette, took it between two fingers from his lips and exhaled. He was unshaven, salt 'n pepper whiskers like crusty stubs. "How come you kids hangin' 'round here? How come you ain't in school?"

The other men looked at him as if he had set us up for a joke. They chuckled, waited for our answer.

"We're twenty-one," Skip replied.

The unshaven questioner nodded to the other men. "Twenty-one my ass. They're kids." To us he said, "You look a fast sixteen, you ask me."

"My next birthday," I said.

One of the men wearing a red and black hunting jacket stepped forward. He pushed back from his forehead a black-billed cap and said, "You oughta be in school learnin' somethin', 'steada' hangin' around here."

A third man mumbled, "Whud'ya' mean, Clint? We ain't so bad."

All four men laughed, the tension broken.

The unshaven man dragged on his cigarette, exhaled, dropped it to the sidewalk and squished it under his right boot. He murmured something to the other three. They shrugged, nodded. The unshaven man asked us, "You kids wanna come in, see where grown men hang out'n see what's goin' on?"

What went on in Kinsale's Pub: a smoky room with a 12-inch black & white TV shelved above the bar and tuned to a game show. Two men shot pool, a broad-faced bartender with thick brown hair combed straight back served beers to three men seated on stools at the bar, a woman with short red hair and wearing a black apron over a white shirt, sleeves rolled to the elbows, served a sandwich and beer to a man alone at the bar. The man leaned over his sandwich and picked up one half of it in one hand. His other hand curled like a gravy spoon in his lap.

What else went on was three of the four men escorted Skip and me to a round table covered with a green and white checkered oilcloth. The man named Clint took off his hunting jacket and laid it slowly, neatly, on the back of a chair. He told Skip to bring two empty chairs for us from another empty table.

The bartender called to the men, "I'm sending Rolley here with your beers. Don't give them kids any. I wanna keep my license. Serious, you guys."

"We got your back, Timmy," replied Clint. He chuckled as if he had made a personal joke.

Rolley, the unshaven man who had first interrogated us, set the tray in the center of the table. The brown jacket he wore was unzipped, the padded lining frayed. Each man helped himself to a beer.

"Don't try anything. You kids're too young for this stuff," Rolley said. He sat down, kept his jacket on. The other men kept their caps on, hunting jackets unbuttoned or unzipped. As the conversation continued, I noticed Rolley blinked often and smiled at the same time.

Clint pushed his cap higher on his forehead and raised his glass in toast to the other three men. "First pint in this hand today," he said, chuckled again, and drank two gulps.

"Numbnuts here, he thinks he's not too young to drink," Skip told the men.

"Thanks," I said.

"What's your story, kid? Beer?" This question came from a man whose name I had not heard and who sat beside Clint. He hunched forward in his chair, ready for my answer.

"He tried the hard stuff," Skip replied.

"I can speak for myself. I wasn't the first, you know. You got me started trying it."

"Yeah, and I made my confession. Now it's your turn."

The man who had wondered what I had tried now nodded toward Skip. The man then asked me, "This know-it-all your friend?"

Immediately I answered, without sarcasm: "Yeah, he's my friend."

"So what'd you try, young man?" Clint asked me. He sniffed, scrunched up his mouth and took another gulp of beer.

I told them. I directed most of my explanation to Clint and the man beside him. I did not look at all at Skip.

"So whud you think, after you tried this stuff? And believe me, you ain't tried much," Clint laughed while the other men agreed.

"I don't know…just wanted to see what it was like. Got sick only once."

"You'll get sick as a dog or worse, you keep it up." This came from

Rolley. The other men lost their smiles. They looked at Rolley, then at me. He scratched the side of his face with his index finger. "You'll get so thirsty, you'll drink anything, and then you'll get so sick in that little gut of yours you won't wanna puke, it'll hurt so much. And then you'll wanna die.

"But maybe you're not ready to go that far yet." Through the rest of his speech he blinked as if his eyes were on a timer. He tightened his voice, held his thumb and forefinger as close as the eye of a needle, and he moved his head left and right like a slow pendulum. "Maybe you just wanna keep taking little nips here, little nips there from your old man's stock eh? Is that where you are? You wanna keep taking a little bit wherever you can? You wanna try some here?" Rolley stood up. He didn't move away from the table. He sniffed, looked down at me. "Come on, numbnuts, or whatever the hell your name is. You want somethin'? I'll square it with Timmy." He nodded toward the bar.

"No," I said.

"Why not?" Rolley said.

"Never mind. I don't want to."

"Yes you do," Rolley insisted. "You say you don't but you really do. I know you do. I started out like you." He smiled but not in apology for his personal revelation.

"He said he doesn't want any," Skip said.

"Your friend speaks."

"Let it go, Rolley," said Clint. "They get the message."

"He's too young to get the message," Rolley said. He sat down and sipped his beer.

The men were quiet, eyes on the green and white oilcloth and on their beers. They did not raise their eyes at Skip and me.

I anticipated, though, that the next minute when we pushed back our chairs and left that the four men watched us. Absolutely sure. The nerves at my back signaled all I needed to know that they were watching us leave.

"Why the hell'd you do that for?" I groused to Skip as we walked past a hardware store window.

"Felt like it."

"Thanks a lot."

Seconds later, he said, "You needed to hear that stuff."

"What are you? My guardian or something?"

"You need one?"

"No!"

"Good. I'm not your guardian, Harper. I'm your friend. Let's keep it that way."

We kicked around in the after-school hours. We tossed a football, watched "Bandstand," and listened to records in his bedroom. With an allowance he received from Liz and Marty, he had "bulged out" his collection of 45s. Skip put on an Elvis Presley EP. The record changer dropped it into place. "Wella whena my blue moon turns to gold again..." Skip sang along softly and stretched out on his bunk again, hands clasped behind his head the way he had when I had visited him that afternoon after his mother and father's funeral.

I noticed that the photograph of his mother and father together now stood on his bureau and rosary beads looped around the post of his lower bunk.

"How many times you think Elvis's done it?" he asked.

"I dunno...Probably a thousand."

"Let's figure it out. Say he was a virgin until he turned eighteen. That was when—January eighth, nineteen fifty-four? That leaves twenty-three days in January," he went on and calculated exactly 1192 days had passed since Elvis probably lost his virginity. "'*Given that*,' as my Geometry teacher says, and *given that* Elvis likes to do it at least once a night, maybe twice—"

"Maybe twice," I agreed.

"Yeah, probably twice. Maybe *three* times!"

Upon further calculation, we concluded Elvis Presley had probably "done it" 1223 times.

"And on the one thousand two hundred and twenty-fourth day he rested," proclaimed Skip.

Liz and Marty treated us to a spaghetti dinner at the Buckboard Inn ten miles from Mount Howard that evening. Aunt Ceil begged off; she wanted to watch a detective show and the Friday night fights. Saturday night it was pizza after a basketball game: Lebanon Valley College vs. Lafayette. Sitting at the pizza parlor table with Liz, Marty, and Skip, I thought they appeared like family, more like a wife, a husband, and a son than a brother and a sister and boyfriend. At times Marty nudged Liz's arm when he asked her if she wanted another Coke or when he laughed at some plays at the game. Liz didn't pull away from him.

They made me feel I belonged with them. I still felt drawn to Liz, I liked Marty, a tall, former basketball player who'd give a kid an autograph.

But did you shoot Ralph Malloy on purpose? Or did you tell the truth that night?, the questions like a wound that didn't hurt anymore but still wouldn't heal.

As I chewed pizza, Marty asked me if I had any sports lined up in the future.

"Just football," I replied.

"Just football?" He raised his eyebrows. "Only football? My man, you've got the build to be a starting guard on a basketball court and you're probably fast enough to play infield or outfield in baseball." He wiped a paper napkin across his mouth, lifted his bottle of beer, and took two swallows.

"I dunno," I said. I explained that after playing only the last few innings of Little League baseball, only two seasons of Babe Ruth, and I hadn't tried out for jayvee baseball.

"What're you waiting for?" Marty's eyes challenged me.

"Yeah, Harper, what're you waiting for?" Skip chimed in. "Time to give 'em hell again."

"You never know till you get out there and give it a shot." Marty took the next to last slice of pizza from the pan in the middle of our table.

Liz put her hand on Marty's arm.

"I know, I know," he said. He chewed pizza and then turned to me. His voice softer, he leaned forward and said, "Look, David: you strike me as a smart kid, so's Skip. Both you guys've been through a lot since last summer. Now you got to think about your future. Next few years're gonna go pretty fast, just like that." He snapped his fingers, chewed the last of his slice, and swallowed. "Don't wake up one day and wonder 'Why the heck didn't I take a chance and go out for baseball? I could've made it.' It doesn't have to be a sport, but you get the idea."

Sleet smacked the windshield of Marty's Bel Air on the way back to

Mount Howard. Marty slowed his speed to 40 mph on the two-lane highways, 25 or less on the sharp curves.

None of us said anything until, sleet still pelting the car, we turned into Aunt Ceil's driveway.

"Thank goodness you're home," she called down from the upstairs hallway. "I was about to call the state police, see if you went off the road somewhere." She coughed; it sounded like a rattle that stopped after about twenty seconds.

Marty put his hand on the stairway banister. "We did go off, Ceil, but all of us lifted the car and carried it back to the road. You sleep well, Ceil. Don't forget to put out that cigarette." In a lower voice he said to us, "She likes it when I kid around with her."

"Be careful when you drive home," Liz said to Marty.

"Make a bed for me?" Marty asked smiling, and touched her arm.

She turned away and seemed to withdraw from us. "Don't," she said quietly.

The illuminated hands and numbers on the clock on Skip's bureau read five after eleven. He tuned in his night-table radio to WKBW from Buffalo. Ray Charles' "I Got a Woman" pounded out. Skip turned up the volume. Sleet spattered the house.

"I wonder if this is what it's like for him—Ray Charles," he said after we stretched out in the bunks, he lower, I upper, lights switched off. "I wonder if it's like this when you're blind, nothing but dark."

"Dark or just a blank? Just—nothing."

"Probably like when you close your eyes," he said.

I closed my eyes. I sensed Skip had closed his. Everything blank. Everything.

"I don't think I could take being blind," he went on. "All the things you wouldn't see...I wouldn't be able to see Cori."

I heard him turn over below me.

"You know what I'd miss?" he asked more seriously. "I'd miss seeing my sister's face and Marty ducking through a doorway. Weird, 'idn it?"

"Not really. I'd miss seeing my mom and dad and Granddad. My grandmother...I still think about her," I said. I didn't tell him about what I had felt near the altar Christmas Eve. Then, realizing what I else I had said, I wanted to take back mention of Mom and Dad. I wanted to crawl away, dissolve inside the bedroom walls.

Before I could say anything more, Skip said, "I can still see Mom and the old man. Still hear'em."

"What's it like?"

"Just like they always were: the old man's drinkin' a beer, Mom's watchin' TV, or else they're yelling their heads off at each other. Sometimes I make up conversations for them, get the two of them talking to each other."

"What happens?"

"Same old shit. Sooner or later they start yelling. Mom goes to the bedroom, the old man goes out for a ride and comes home smashed. The way it always was."

The sound of sleet softened. Wind swished it against the house. I closed my eyes, but in my imagination again I saw flashing blue lights of a police car in front of the house on Jessup Avenue. I saw Dad step away from the crowd.

On WKBW Fats Domino pumped out "Blueberry Hill."

"With all the pounding he does, you'd think he'd lose weight."

"Depends what kind've pounding," I said.

He laughed, "Harper, you're *disgusting*," and I laughed along with him: "Can't help it."

"Oh Jesus!"

"I don't think He's around," I said.

"Nope. Prob'ly not. Haven't seen Him lately. Aunt Ceil pushes Lizzie and me to go to Mass, though. So, we go."

Skip turned again. In a lower voice he said, "Lizzie's changed."

I told him I had noticed a change in Liz last summer.

In a tone as quiet as the air above us, he said, "It's what the old man did to her and Lorraine." These ordinary words made me cringe. My body turned cold, the same shivering cold I experienced the night of Liz's birthday party.

Skip breathed. Sleet ticked against the window and the side of the house.

"Sometimes I'm glad he's dead. Sometimes…I dunno. Then: "You want to come to ten o'clock Mass tomorrow?"

I felt myself lose ground, the way I had slipped when Mom and Dad had come to my room to ask me why I didn't want to be an acolyte anymore.

"I mean, I'm not forcing you. You don't have to if you don't want to."

"I know…I quit being an acolyte."

"Why?"

"It's a pain. I finally got up the courage to talk to Bradeen. Told him everything."

"What'd he say?"

"Same stuff Hepplewhite told me, just different words. Haven' seen the gypsy woman, either."

I listened to the wind blow sleet against the window. The sound made me feel safe.

"It's strange when I think about my mom and the old man," Skip said, his voice slow, as if he drifted toward sleep. "Almost like they're here, if I want'em to be. I can do that."

I pictured Skip below me, his face without glasses, thinking. "I'm like a god," he said more passionately. "I create them in my imagination…Make 'em talk…I always hope what happens turns out better than it really did, but it doesn't."

I thought of the pictures Granddad had given me. I had looked at them and wondered about the lives of aunts and uncles I had never known. I thought about Nana again. I missed her. I visualized her face footsteps away from me near the altar.

"Where do you think they are?" I asked.

"My parents?" He gave out a long sigh. "I know my mom's in Heaven, not in limbo. She's definitely in Heaven. I don't know about the old man." As he spoke the words his voice changed and trembled. "I guess he's with her."

Then all of his anguish and anger and sorrow flooded out of him. "I hate that son of a bitch for what he did to my mom and Lorraine and Lizzie…*the sonovabitch, I hated him… I wanted him dead in Hell*." Skip sobbed for what seemed a long time, as long as the sleet blew like sand against the side of the house and drifted away. I wanted to comfort him, tell him that everything would be all right someday. Those words were only letters arranged to define, not express, comfort and assurance. I could not express the language Skip needed.

Beyond the closed bedroom door, a shadow moved in the sliver of the hallway light beneath the door. It seemed to wait, and then it moved away, the floorboards faintly creaking. Had Lizzie been listening to us? I waited for the click of a door opening or closing. None came. Only the shadow and sound of footsteps passing outside Skip's bedroom, followed by footsteps descending the stairs. Then, quiet.

Skip quieted. He coughed and cleared his throat. "I'm sorry...I meant it after it all happened but now...I dunno, Harper. I hope she's all right. Him? I dunno. He's gotta pay for it."

He coughed again and turned over, his voice toward the wall.

Sleet sprayed the side of the house. The sliver of light beneath the door seemed like a border not to trespass.

"I hate him. I know I'm supposed to love him, goddamn it. He's my father! He beat the shit out of my mother and did god knows what to Lizzie. How can a man...?"

Voices wailed on the radio. I paid no attention to the songs or the disc jockey. It must have been close to midnight. Mom and Dad would arrive the following morning. I'd go home with them, I'd go back to school, but school seemed as far away as Christmas now.

I heard Skip's slow, deliberate breathing, as if he was drifting toward sleep.

"You still awake?" he asked.

"Still awake...I was thinking about Lorraine. You heard anything about her?"

"Not much. She came here with her boyfriend after Christmas. Lizzie didn't say much about her afterwards."

It seemed another long time before Skip said, "Sorry I lost it. I'm still tryin' to get it all straightened out. Sorry I was a wise ass yesterday at the bar, too."

"You needed to be a wise ass," I said.

In the dark I saw his arm reach up alongside my bunk. I reached down. We clasped hands.

"Still my best friend, Harper," he said.

"Best friends," I said.

Part IV: FOUND

22

Finding a Way

10:00 Mass? We didn't attend. Aunt Ceil let us to sleep in. By eleven o'clock Sunday morning we, Marty included but not Liz, had finished breakfast. Five minutes later Mom and Dad pulled into the driveway. No long conversation of how was the drive?, any sign of snow?, or Can you stay for dinner? Mom and Dad frowned at the low gray sky. Dad wanted to stay within the speed limit back to Lorrence right away rather than chance repeating another precarious trip through mountains in sleet or snow. Weather wasn't the only reason my parents didn't want to stay. If they had thought I was a "mixed-up runaway teenager," they wanted me in the safe confines of home.

I waited to see if Liz would come downstairs to say goodbye. She didn't. Marty left, the changing gears of his Chevy working as fast and smooth as Jerry Zanger's Mercury.

"Give'em hell," Skip called to me from the back steps.

I woke up under Lorrence's overcast sky. The town looked the same as when I had left two days before. The same town where I had lived and slept in for almost sixteen years. The same quiet, dull, ordinary town I had witnessed before the previous spring when Ralph Malloy's hands and cruelty had violated this ordinary town. The same town I believed I was growing away from. Looking down Willowyn Terrace at the houses and at

St. Thomas Church, I knew I didn't want to be stuck in Lorrence for another summer. I had begun the next phase of my life. I felt older, perhaps wiser but not better than Jack MacAdams or Guy Ross or anybody else. Just different from them. Older. I had accomplished something I could not name or define, but I knew it was important.

"Granddad wants to see you," Mom said as I carried my gym bag upstairs. She stood at the bottom of the stairs, one hand on the banister. "I told him you'd come over or you'd call him. Father Hepplewhite would like to talk to you, too."

"I don't wanna talk to him. Next time he calls, tell him I'm out of town."

"Tell him yourself. And don't be sarcastic."

I closed my bedroom door.

The very next night I answered a front door knock-knock. There he stood—black overcoat and black hat—under the porch light—like a mob figure out of a 30's and 40's gangster movie. Bugsy Hepplewhite? Doughface Hepplewhite? Mad Dog Hepplewhite? Did he pack a pistol inside his overcoat pocket? Was he going to grab me, stuff me in the trunk of his car, dump me on a country road so I'd have to find my way home?

Nope. Good old Father Hepplewhite smiled and said, "Hello, David."

Come on in, Mad Dog, was my imaginary greeting. *Seen any gypsies lately?*

I held the inside door open for him. I caught aromas of shaving lotion and toothpaste as his overcoat brushed my shoulder.

Mom and Dad shook hands with him. Father Hepplewhite responded as if they were old friends he had not seen in a long time.

"David, would you take Father Hepplewhite's coat?" Dad asked.

"That's all right," said the 'good Father.' "I'll keep it with me."

He draped the coat over his right arm and eased down into Dad's favorite chair. I sat on the sofa, directly across from the man who had spouted mystery and faith instead of concrete answers to my questions. My mouth felt dry as a communion wafer. I had to be strong; hold my ground.

The black overcoat looped over his arm signaled 'the good Father' planned to stay only a few minutes.

My parents excused themselves back to the kitchen to finish putting away dishes. Part of their scheme to put me on the spot.

Father Hepplewhite smiled as if one of us had to apologize. I wasn't going to apologize for anything. He would not, *could* not, make me apologize for walking out on him and quitting my acolyte duties.

Plates clacked in the kitchen, cabinet doors clicked open, snapped closed. I pictured Mom and Dad whispering to each other.

The rector of St. Thomas cleared his throat. "David, one evening some weeks ago you came to see me. Tonight I thought I would visit you. I'd like you to come back as an acolyte."

His crossed ankles, black socks, and black shoes annoyed me. I tried to think of a response that once and for all would send him away so that he would never ask me to do anything for the church again. I couldn't put necessary words together. The necessary words hid behind my parents' low voices in the kitchen, somewhere in the clink of silverware and the soft slide of drawers opening and closing.

"You and I had an interesting talk that night," Father Hepplewhite continued.

"Yeah, I thought so," I managed.

"Yes, I'm sure. And I've thought about what you described to me. Those experiences, including the feelings you experienced in church Christmas Eve, must weigh heavily on you. You didn't know what to think about that sensation of a touch, did you," he said, "or what you felt at the lake and near the altar." All the while he kept his hands folded and offered me a thin smile as if he was about to spring a trap.

"I wanna know for sure. Nobody gives me a straight answer, just the same old stuff."

Mom and Dad came into the room and sat on the sofa beside me. I shifted as close as I could into the corner away from them. Dad leaned over and nudged me with his elbow, as if he wanted to kid around with me. I stayed where I wanted to be.

"You're a very lucky and very special boy, David," said Father Hepplewhite.

"Me? I don't think so."

"You are. From my experience, what you described that happened to you hasn't happened to any boy that I'm aware of, or adults, for that matter. That's why it's so special. It wasn't a miracle that you experienced. It was something marvelous."

"Father Bradeen told me the same thing."

"Oh?" 'The good Father' moved his topcoat to the right arm of the chair. "You spoke with him?"

"I thought he could give me the answers I wanted. He didn't. Nobody has."

"We can't, David."

I didn't expect my mother's response. I had almost forgotten she was sitting on the sofa next to Dad. The tone of her voice sounded close to an apology. Once I heard it, I began to accept it.

"We want to but we can't. We don't know," she said.

Father Hepplewhite held his overcoat and stood slowly and winced, as if he had pain in his legs. "Perhaps we can talk again about what happened to you," he said to me. "When you're ready. I'd like to hear your thoughts. In the meantime, would you give some thought to coming back as an acolyte?"

"Maybe," I said, more to move him toward the front door and leave the house than to accept his invitation.

Dad turned toward me. I ignored him.

"Well, I'm glad you'll consider it," 'the good Father' said.

"Would you stay for a cup of tea?" Mom asked him.

"Thank you, Grace, but some other time," he said.

Dad helped Father Hepplewhite with his overcoat, and he and Mom escorted him to the front door.

"Goodnight, David," said Father Hepplewhite. "I hope to see you soon."

I wanted to tell him, *Don't count on it*. It churned in me to punch the sofa, fling a cushion where 'Mad Dog' had established himself. I didn't say, punch, or fling anything. And I didn't like myself very much for saying "Maybe." I had had too many *maybe's* in my life. I should have had the guts to say *No!* But Mom and Dad would have accused me of being rude. I didn't want another argument. I wanted to be left alone.

Father Hepplewhite had made a major indentation on the chair's cushion. What would Skip have said about Hepplewhite's ass? Big impression?

My mother crossed her arms. "You could have been more polite."

"I answered him. I want him to leave me alone."

Mom and Dad didn't bother me anymore that night.

––––––––––

School stretched long and slow like one enormous yawn. Teachers frowned, tired of looking at the same pimpled and frustrated faces they had ruled since September; tired of asking us to open our textbooks to this page or that; tired of asking us to take notes on this war, that treaty, this story, this lab. On warm spring days my teachers didn't mind if I arrived a couple minutes late after walking Janice to her classes. I didn't work hard, didn't take books home, didn't study for tests. When I looked out classroom windows at rain-dampened oak and maple limbs and clearing sky, I remembered Marty Bannon's advice: Go for it. In Skip's words, "Give 'em hell."

Skip's words came true when Guy Ross caught me at my locker in an empty hallway one afternoon after school.

"Heard you went up to see ol' Alfred E.," he said. His smile sneered.

Jack MacAdams stood five yards behind Ross.

"How's ol' Alfie doing?" Ross asked me.

Something ignited in me again. I had saved this no-good bastard from broken bones or worse. I had turned down his parents' money for saving him. I wished I had taken that money. I looked at Guy Ross's face, chin pimples erupting to life, that sneery smile back over his teeth. I fantasized my right fist smashing his mouth, my left bashing his jaw. Would I be a coward, ignore this chance to lash out at insults about my best friend? Would my retaliation, whatever its shape, change Ross's behavior for the better?

I couldn't walk away. I had to do something, say something.

First, I scrambled for words. Second, I slammed my locker door.

Ross blinked.

I didn't yell. I didn't pounf my fists against him. As strong and steady as

I could, I said, "Shut the hell up, Ross. You never gave Skip a chance, you never knew what he was going through. You and MacAdams there, you never gave a *damn* about him. You had the so-called guts to make fun of him, but you had no guts at all when it counted. You're a piece 'a shit, Ross. A goddamn piece 'a shit. You say one more lousy thing about Skip Malloy, I'll smash your face and break your hands!"

"Whoa!" MacAdams walked away.

Ross and I stared at each other. He narrowed his eyes. I didn't move. I didn't blink. If he threw the first punch, I'd deck him, pound his head on the hallway floor the way I had slammed it on the tee.

I waited.

He didn't raise a fist. He only snickered as if to say 'What's the use?' then turned his back on me and followed MacAdams.

"Bastard!" I whispered.

When I walked home that afternoon I wondered why I felt I had lost something.

————

I took Marty Bannon's advice. I joined the jayvee baseball team coached by Mr. Erskine. I pitched and played left field.

After using me in left field during inevitable losses and wins and as mop-up man when our pitching staff depleted itself, the season came down to third place Lorrence vs. second place Kenner's Point.

The last home game of the season: a warm, late May afternoon under a high sky. "It'll be tough judging fly balls," Coach Erskine cautioned us before the game. "No background except that high blue to see the ball against."

That sky was probably one reason why our opposition had scored eleven runs against us by the end of the top of the fifth inning. The other reason was that Kenner's Point's line-up, some who had bruised and knocked me around last November, hit practically everything our first two pitchers threw. Singles, doubles, triples found the gaps in our infield and outfield. On the same dirt under the same sky, we scribbled only three runs in four innings.

Home half of the fifth, Coach Erskine nodded to me. "Harper, get loose." He clapped his hands twice.

My stomach tightened, my arm extended tightly from my shoulder as I warmed up. Before this game I had thrown only at batting practice, nothing in regulation. What did Erskine want me to do in this one, a sure win for our friendly visitors? Major League relievers who came in, in such one-sided situations as this were "mop-up" pitchers. That was my role today: official mop-up man.

Top of the sixth: Coach Erskine walked me to the mound and handed me the ball. He scuffed dirt in front of the pitcher's slab. "Don't worry about the score, don't try to strike everybody out. You've got eight guys behind you. Do the best you can. Throw to the target."

I scanned the outfield and infield, conscious of life outside and inside baselines before I threw my first pitch: Mom, Dad, and Granddad standing beside Dad's Plymouth beyond the right field foul line; clusters of other parents sitting in lawn chairs or standing beside cars deep in first and third baseline foul territory; chatter of infielders, the hard feel of the ball in my right hand and the comfortable, raised red stitches my right index and second finger found—*There...there*—before I went into my wind-up. All of it. *There...there...Okay. Give 'em hell!*

Strange. I expected I'd throw overhand, the way I had pitched in batting practice, the motion I used warming up. For a reason I couldn't explain, I delivered that first pitch three-quarter sidearm. Somehow that motion seemed natural. The first batter leaned away and learned it was a strike.

He fouled the next two, then struck out swinging. The next two batters grounded out.

Coach Erskine clapped his hands in front of our bench as we jogged off the field. "Good pitching, Harper! Okay, you guys, let's get some runs!"

We tried. The first batter walked, the second, our center fielder, drove a single to right. Runners on first and third, no outs, bottom of the sixth: the situation when I picked up a 33-ounce Louisville Slugger.

In the on-deck circle I practice swung, conscious of two girls who sat on the ground in front of an equipment shed. The man and woman beside them were Mr. and Mrs. Taggart, the girls Melinda and Janice.

"Come on, David, hit one!" Melinda's squawk.

I set my feet in the left-hand batter's box.

Later that night Janice told me she had warned Melinda not to yell anything when I came to bat. "'It'll take his mind off the game and make him nervous,' I told her. I'm sorry. She embarrassed me and probably you."

It didn't matter.

I saw the first pitch clearly, a smear of red stitches and scuffed white that dipped down and—

Hit the damn thing!

I did. A dribbler between the second baseman and the second base bag. I dug toward first. Horns blared, voices yelled, and I pounded my right foot on the first base bag one second after the ball thacked into the first baseman's glove. Out number one in an inning of a game we still lost.

"But you drove home a run," Granddad reminded me that night at dinner, "and you moved the runner from first to second. He scored, too. Remember? Not bad." He patted my knee. "Not bad at all."

Coach Erskine had given me a similar compliment in the locker room after the game, another loss for us. "Well, you got baptized today. You held your own. Knocked in a run and held them scoreless. A good day's work."

Mom and Dad reacted as if I had single-handedly won a state championship. It was good to hear their compliments, but their words made me feel like a little boy who had earned great respect. I didn't want to feel like a little boy. "I wish we had hit better," I said.

"Well, you did your best," Dad said. "If everybody swings the bat, the runs will come."

I heard Marty Bannon's encouragement in my head.

———

Janice: I hadn't told my parents I had given her a friendship ring at Christmas. I had told no one.

"Are we ever going to meet this young lady? It would be nice if you invited here for dinner sometime," my mother said to me one night before I met Janice at the movies.

"I guess so." But my relationship with her was my business, no one else's. We had our own life. We were a couple like other high school couples who walked to class together, ate lunch together and spent time together on weekends.

I didn't follow through with my mother's recommendation.

Janice and I talked: homework, movies we wanted to see, songs we liked, records we wanted to buy. We talked about Skip, about what had happened to him the summer before, and about what we could do for him if he visited Lorrence this coming summer. We talked about our futures. College for Janice, a major in Biology or Chemistry. "I like studying how things grow and develop," she said one day as we walked up Long Avenue after one of my games. She nudged my arm. "How about you? You *do* want to go to college, don't you?"

"Sure, but I've got no idea what I want to study."

She looked across at me. "You're good at helping people, David. You helped Skip last summer. You want to find out the answers to things, too."

"But I can't figure out things I need to know," I said.

"Dad said he'd be happy to talk with you about different colleges sometime," she said. "He likes you."

We paused at the top of Long Avenue's hill. A block away Sunrise Auditorium stood empty. That afternoon on the side lot where Skip had been the human dodge ball, kids played tackle football. I flashed the two of us running like hell down the sidewalk across from where Janice and I now stood.

A cheer from the kids cut the air. No one hurt, no one in pain, one of them had scored a touchdown.

I glanced at Janice as we crossed Long Avenue to Taylor. Her white blouse lay open the first two buttons. The skin below her throat shone pale pink...*Her arms around me when we lay close together.* Whenever we talked about those times, her voice became secretive for only the two of us, and when we put our arms around each other again she whispered, "No one else, David. No one."

In front of her house she asked, "Are you going to be an acolyte again?"

"Yeah, I'll go to college for it."

"Come on, be serious. You shouldn't forget about what happened to you," she said. "There's got to be answers."

On my way home later I passed Skip's house. Some brown siding shingles hung loose at an angle, and the sun porch screen bulked inward, as if someone or something heavy had leaned into it. A realtor's 'For Sale' sign still stabbed the front lawn.

"Nobody wants to buy a house where a man murdered his wife," my father had said more than once.

————

"In the kitchen, Davy," Granddad called out after I opened the front screen door and stepped inside. Somehow he knew I was there.

The kitchen looked and smelled clean and polished. He told me he had "cranked up" his spring-cleaning spree this week. Now he washed and dried his hands on a hand towel. He needed a haircut, I noticed; gray hair curled over his ears and the back of his shirt collar.

"How'd you know it was me?" I said.

"I could tell by the sound of the door closing." He rubbed his hands together as if he was ready to perform magic tricks. Then he set a cup of tea for himself and a glass of chocolate milk for me on the kitchen table. "There you are!" he said.

It was good to be with Granddad again. He wouldn't scheme to persuade me to do chores, he wouldn't lecture me about what I should or not do in my life. When I confided things to him, he believed me. Nana had believed me, too.

I didn't tell him about Father Hepplewhite's visit. He probably had heard about 'Mad Dog's' visit from Mom and Dad. I said nothing about my visit with Father Bradeen and my run-in with Guy Ross. I described my trip to Mount Howard—the train ride, the dinners—and I told him how Aunt Ceil, Liz, and Skip seemed like a family. I didn't tell him about Skip breaking down. Those situations were private.

"How's Skip? Is he doing all right?"

"I think so." Skip was doing the best he could, I explained. Before I left to come home that weekend, we had made plans for me to visit him again that summer. He didn't want to come back to Lorrence in the near future. Maybe someday.

Granddad looked closely at me "How about you, Davy? he said. "I been thinkin' about that little episode of yours last summer. You doing all right?"

"I'm okay," I said, without mentioning the men outside Kinsale's and without telling him how I felt every time saw Dad's liquor bottles lined up on the pantry floor. I hadn't touched them, hadn't opened them. Sometimes I had wanted to sneak a drink, but I had made a promise. I didn't want to repeat last summer all over again.

"I'll take you at your word," Granddad said.

"I'm still working on other stuff."

"Anything I can help you with?" He knew I had more to say. "I heard the good Father Hepplewhite dropped in to discuss matters with you," he said.

"I don't want to be an acolyte anymore. It won't do me any good."

Granddad cleared his throat again and stirred his tea. He disagreed with my decision, I was sure. "You got to believe in something, David. Otherwise, you don't really have much in your life."

Another sermon: I didn't want to hear it.

"After Nana, I felt something like you're going through now. I looked for answers—Why this, why that—but didn't find much. Going back to church didn't give me all the answers, but it helped. I made a connection. There's something there, David."

"What?"

"I can't name it. I just know it's there."

"Yeah, but why the hell do I have to go to church to find it?"

Surprised, perhaps shocked at the tone of my question, Granddad shook his head. Maybe he was upset at me, maybe confused by my questions. Worse, maybe I had hurt his feelings. He didn't answer me right away.

He drank the rest of his tea. Without the TV or radio on, the house seemed too quiet.

He set down his cup and wiped the back of his hand across his mouth. Without looking directly at me. With an edge of disappointment he said, "Stay here. I got something to show you."

He went upstairs. A minute later put a black and white photograph matted in cardboard in front of me on the table. "There: I found this one yesterday," he said. "Nana and me. The baby she's holding is your mother. That was taken the day she was baptized. I want you to have it."

I looked at the picture—the upper left corner taped, the tape thin and yellow, the edge brittle. Nana and Granddad stood in front of a church I had not seen before, but its stone front reminded me of St. Thomas Church. My grandparents weren't looking at the camera's eye. They weren't laughing or smiling. They were looking at my infant mother wrapped in a white blanket in Nana's arms as if she was a gift they would hold and care for and love forever.

Granddad stood behind me and placed his hand on my shoulder. "Nice, huh?" he said.

"Yeah," I said, my face turned away from him. I think he understood why.

On a Friday afternoon in late May I dropped off my school books on my bed. Downstairs on the living room desk was a letter addressed to me; the address in the upper left corner was 233 South Kenton Street, Mount Howard, Pa., the handwriting Skip's.

"Not good news," the letter began. From there I read only to the end of the first paragraph. Liz had broken up with Marty. "Just didn't work out," Skip wrote. "When I asked her why, she said Marty wanted to get too serious. He didn't think things through. They don't agree on a lot of stuff. That's all she says."

More broken stuff, I thought.

I only glanced at the other two paragraphs and then stuffed the letter in my hip pocket. I didn't feel like staying in the house, I didn't even want to see Janice. Not yet.

I didn't want to think now about Liz, Marty, and Skip. Nothing I could do.

I rode my bike out to St. Mary's Cemetery, entered between the granite pillars that framed the entrance, and pedaled up the unpaved roadway. At the junction where the road forked, a statue of the Virgin Mary looked down upon me, her arms extended in welcome, a bouquet of fresh flowers at her feet. I had the strange sensation that, even though her figure was stone, her eyes were watching me. Mary knew I was there. Maybe she understood the reason why.

I rested my bike on the edge of the lawn on my right, the grass recently mowed, clippings left to dry. Flowers decorated the ground in front of gravestones or stood in vases on the base. Some names on the stones were familiar; grandparents of students from the high school, parents of people Mom and Dad had known from their high school years. Many names were strange to me.

Where are they now? I wondered, probably to no one. *Heaven, or some other world, some other place, a place without a name, without ties to anyone on earth, without a god. Who really knows for sure what happens to us after we die?*

Granddad had slowly walked up and down stairs; he had winced when I had asked him "...why do I have to go to church to find it?" I hadn't meant to hurt his feelings. I just wanted an answer. Maybe I'd never find that answer. Maybe I'd never learn all the answers to my questions.

Spying a maroon Mercury thirty yards ahead of me jarred back to the present. Arms folded, leaning back against the passenger door: Jerry Zanger. He seemed to stare at a tombstone on the ground in front of him.

I walked toward the car. The polished body gleamed in sunlight, the rear fender bright silver, taillights deep red. The car didn't threaten me like it had when it had prowled streets and chugged by Our Lady Queen of Heaven last summer.

Jerry Zanger turned, startled, challenged by my footsteps.

He studied me, I studied him. His brown curly hair hung across his forehead, his white T-shirt blotched with sweat. He dragged on a cigarette, flicked the butt onto the grass and then stubbed it into the lawn. He didn't frown. His mouth showed the start of a curious smile.

"Harper," he said.

Fresh red and white geraniums were planted in front of a slate marble stone inches from his feet. The stone read:

Zanger

Alice: 1887 – 1953 Martin: 1884 – 1950

"Somethin' you wanna ask?" he said.

"No."

He studied me again. He cocked his head toward a plot of stones farther up the road. "They're up there, near that fence," he said.

"You saw the graves?" I asked.

"I just told you where they are." He motioned with his head, a move that demanded I leave him alone.

The sun warmed my face and neck. The wind swayed limbs of pines and oaks along the wrought-iron fence that bordered the cemetery. The road curved like a horseshoe. To the right the gravesites were spaced farther apart from each other, some stones gray, others white. A charcoal gray stone caught my attention. I walked to it. Carved on the front was the six-letter name I had come to find: **MALLOY**. Centered near the bottom of the stone was an inscription: *Ralph James, 1912 – 1956,* and *Helen Marie, 1914 – 1956.*

Skip had been baptized William Thomas James Malloy. Part of his name was on this stone. Had he seen his father's marker and not told me about it? Maybe he wasn't ready to talk about it yet. That was all right.

I was ready.

I knew I should say a prayer. I bowed my head, waited, thought. Nothing but jumbled words, beginnings of questions, beginnings of prayers. Nothing that made sense. I looked beyond Mr. and Mrs. Malloy's gravestone to the other stones whose names stared back at me.

"Can you help Liz?" I said, only loud enough so I could to hear my own words. "She needs help. Skip still loves you."

I waited, listened, though I was unsure what I waited and listened for. Maybe a voice? A touch? The wind stirred the trees again, but the leaves shaking and the rumbling of a car engine not far away were the only sounds I heard, nothing more.

"You shouldn't be here," I said softly. "Neither one of you. It shouldn't've happened. Skip's doing all right but not Liz and Marty. Liz needs your help."

Mrs. Malloy had been kind and generous to me; more than a mother who had made sandwiches, dinners, and iced tea; more than a mother who had hosted sleepovers. She had asked how I was doing, had wanted me to remember her to Mom and Dad. She had wanted friends.

What had I ever done for her? Had I helped her? Not much. Not when I should have.

I looked around me. On the ground were stones and pebbles. I found an egg-shaped stone, smoothed sand from it, and placed it under Mrs. Malloy's name.

"Thank you," I said.

"And she thanks *you*."

The woman stood about five yards behind me. I had not seen her there seconds before. I had not seen her near the Zanger gravestones. She wore a long dress swirled with blue and gold, black and red, a gold crucifix pendant around her neck, and a scarf of red, green, and black. Barefoot. Thick black hair streaked with white on the left side. She held no rosary beads.

I waited for her to speak. She seemed to wait for me.

"Who are you?" I asked.

"Consider me your friend."

"Are you a gypsy?"

"No," she replied, in a near smile.

"You look like one."

"I'm not a gypsy, David."

"How do you know my name?"

"I've seen you, and I've listened to you. I know you, David."

"Then who *are* you. Some missionary woman?"

"In a way, yes. I'm a kind of missionary woman."

"So are you real?"

"You see me, do you not?"

I wanted to challenge her but I didn't want my questions to sound rude. "Do you *know* me? Really know me? Do you know what *hap*pened to me and Skip last summer?"

"Yes, I do. But I can't give you all the answers you want."

"So why are you here?"

She didn't answer. She smiled in ways that Father Hepplewhite and

Father Bradeen had smiled when I had tried to pin them down to clear, concrete answers to my questions.

I looked at Mrs. Malloy's name. "How do you know she thanks me?"

"I just know. Please believe me," she said, and placed her right hand over her heart.

"Did you know her?"

"I know many people here. They visit me in their own way, and I visit them in my own way." She spoke with a lilt in her voice, as if she was reading a prayer she believed in.

"How do they visit you?"

"How is not important, David. They find their way."

I took a step toward her. Her face appeared both old and young. She did not show fear of me; I did not feel afraid of her. I stepped within arm's reach of her.

"Tell me who you are."

She touched my arm and then drew her hand away. Her touch was warm and calm. "I'm someone you can trust," she said.

"Then tell me what happened to me at Skip's church."

"You can trust in what those feelings felt like to you, David. They were given to you, no one else."

"Who gave them to me?"

"Trust the feelings in your heart, David. You will. You'll find your way."

She began to walk away.

"Who *are* you?" I called out to her.

She turned to me. Her face was calm, her eyes were kind. Again she put her hand over her heart. "I am part of the mystery you've been seeking," she said.

She walked on toward the road, toward the statue of the Virgin Mary where the road forked, and toward the cemetery entrance. The colors of her long dress shimmered in sunlight. The air in her wake smelled of grass and flowers. I followed her, wanted to ask her more questions. Somehow, though, she had begun to reveal what I had been searching for since last summer.

When I reached my bike it was not lying on the grass where I had left it. It rested against the base of the pillar below the Virgin Mary. Jerry Zanger and his Mercury were not in sight. The woman I had spoken with had disappeared.

Dad's dull gray Plymouth hunched like an inferior machine in our driveway. The inside front door of the house hung open. I didn't want to go in, not right away.

As usual, Willowyn Terrace lay quiet. Houses still, cars in driveways, windows and doors open. Nobody on their porches, nobody in their yards. No cars in front of St. Thomas. The church appeared small. Nothing going on there.

Maybe I'll see her again. Maybe.

Should I go in my house? Probably. Nothing else to do.

Or I could go somewhere else. The more I thought about that, the more I wanted to go, just *go somewhere* where I could think. About Jerry Zanger. Would he talk to me again, or would he ignore me, go his own way? What did it matter to me what he did? But there was something more in Zanger than the bullying jerk who had taunted and beaten Skip. Something...Maybe Zanger was a decent guy after all. Maybe he had something inside him he didn't want people to know about.

About Janice: about going out with her that summer. I'd get a job for spending money for the movies and for school clothes next September. Save for a car and college.

What the hell did I want to do after college?

I thought of Dad's stock on the kitchen pantry floor. Of Rolley and Clint and the other men at Kinsale's. What good would it do me to sneak more of that stuff? I might try to. I might get away with it, I might not. I didn't want to break another trust again. I had broken too many already.

I looked again at St. Thomas'. Would the gypsy be there? Could I talk with her again?

I am part of the mystery you've been seeking.

I walked up the front steps.

I showed Mom and Dad the letter from Skip. Together they read it.

"What do you think happened?" Dad asked my mother.

243

"I don't know. It's too bad. Maybe they can reconcile," she said, "but I don't know. There may be things going on we won't know about. It's just too bad."

She gave the letter back to me. "Tell Skip we're thinking of Liz and him, and Marty, too."

I told them I had gone to St. Mary's Cemetery.

My mother stood now in the living room – dining room archway, Dad next to the post at the bottom of the stairs. Their faces showed more questions. I said nothing else. I moved around Dad and started up the stairs to my room.

"David, wait," he said. His eyes challenged me, but out of the corner of my eye I saw Mom shake her head at him.

He asked, "Did you go to Mr. and Mrs. Malloy's grave?"

"Yes."

I wouldn't tell them about the woman I had spoken with there. In a special and private way she belonged to me.

At the same time I wanted to pound the wall and kick the spindles from under the banister. Instead, I turned again to go upstairs.

"David?"

Mom stood beside Dad. When I saw the expression on her face, I remembered the picture of Nana and Granddad holding her. I tried to fight it back. I couldn't. The second I felt her arms around me, I broke. I didn't want to but I couldn't help it. I released all of it for Mr. and Mrs. Malloy, for Skip and Liz, for Nana. For everything I didn't know answers to.

Dad stood beside me, his arm around my back the way he had last summer in front of Skip's house. I didn't want to remember that scene of the crowd and police lights and voices. Maybe I was supposed to remember all of it. That's the way things were: fate. Maybe I had to put more trust in my heart.

––––––––––

You haven't heard from me in a long time. I'm sorry, but I didn't want to talk to You. You know why. You may not want to listen to me now. Anyway, I'm here.

You haven't seen me in church lately, either. You know the reason for that. I'm not trying to start an argument, I'm not trying to be a wise guy. I just haven't felt like going. That's not a sin, is it?

Maybe I've been wrong in all this. Maybe I should've talked to You more and tried to find out from You more about how life really is. Maybe I should believe You really did touch my shoulder at the funeral and help me at the lake. I just don't know.

I'm not sure if You can help me now or not. I saw the woman this afternoon at the cemetery. You probably know her. She told me I'd have to find my own way, so here's what I'm willing to do. I'll be an acolyte again. I'll try and think more about what Father Hepplewhite, Father Bradeen, and Granddad told me. Granddad said he made a connection. I guess that's what I'm trying to do. Maybe he's right. Maybe I'll get a few more answers if I think about that and some other things. I'll talk to You again. I hope You'll listen.

I hope You can help Liz, Skip, and Marty. Tell Nana I said hello and that Granddad says he'd like to dance with her again sometime.

Goodnight.

Epilogue

It's been many years since those events in Lorrence. The town where I now live lies far from Lorrence, far from Mount Howard. It is surrounded by hills my wife and I and our children and grandchildren have hiked, but the trails are slowly vanishing; in their place construction equipment truck dirt roads, bulldozed building lots, and newly-framed houses. When the wind from the hills is strong, I hear the whine and grind of machines and the pound of hammers. Sometimes I think of Guy Ross and Jack MacAdams in high houses that overlook the northern New Jersey towns where they live. Sometimes I wonder if Jerry Zanger still manages a service station in Lorrence: "Zanger's Gas and Convenience," the sign read the last time I drove by.

He stayed. Then I chastise myself for my judgment of him—indeed, for judgment of anyone at all—and for living too much in the past instead of in the quick present.

Voices of the past shadow me.

"You're good at helping people," Janice Taggart had once encouraged me.

Maybe.

Janice and I survived high school but not higher education. She transitioned away from Lorrence, asserted herself in pre-med at Northwestern, specialized in pediatrics, and met a resident who specialized in family medicine and who became her husband. Eventually, they settled in the Far West, the Pacific Ocean in view from their back deck. Janice and I see each other at class reunions. We dance while our spouses chat.

One of life's ironies: Janice and her husband, by mutual decision, remain childless. Apparently ever mindful of the needs of others, they devote their lives to caring for other people's children. Father Hepplewhite would be pleased.

Like her sister, Melinda, too, moved away. After high school she enrolled in a secretarial school in Boston, then switched to a career in business management. Janice's twin has never married. She avoids class reunions.

I often think of the woman who sat behind me at the Malloy funeral and whom I encountered at St. Mary's Cemetery; the woman whose face looked both old and young. I had doubted Father Hepplewhite and Father Bradeen. I do not doubt the woman who said I would find my way.

"Best friends," I once expressed to Skip.

Our friendship remains.

A friendship—a long, enduring friendship—is like two countries close yet far apart from each other. Skip and I share that territory. After he graduated from Mount Howard High School, he enlisted in the army. He wrote me from Fort Dix during Basic Training. "I think I'm one of the smartest guys here," he said in the letter, "considering most of the other jugheads in my squad are high school drop-outs. Some of them can't even find Pennsylvania on a map!

"How's life with you?"

My life was, to use a term from a college Psych class, one of "stasis." In that condition I envied Skip's opportunity for adventure; one that took him from the United States, to England, to Germany; from the New World to the Old and back again. We both escaped being sucked into a civil war in Southeast Asia, Skip because he did not re-up, instead entered and graduated college on the GI Bill; I because my vocation as a guidance counselor was, at the time, considered "necessary" at home.

Meanwhile, I stayed in my old world longer than I wanted to. While most of the Lorrence High School Class of 1959, like Janice, went away to school or, like Skip, joined the military, I "stayed". I lived at home, commuted to Forgeville State College, majored in History, minored in English, and took as many courses as the college offered in Psychology. "The more I read about the human mind," I wrote to Janice and Skip, "the more I want to study it. I want to find out what makes people tick and help them find their way out of their problems."

Was I successful? That depends.

As a counselor I helped middle and high school students select courses and tried to give them strategies to help them resolve personal problems. I left serious issues of substance abuse, criminal threatening and other behaviors on school property to the local police. Retired now from public education, I counsel adults with child-raising and marital issues at a local mental health agency. I come home tired, sometimes "wiped out." I "empty my head" by talking and sorting out the day with Kathryn, my wife. I sometimes question the worth of my counseling but my colleagues and Kathryn sustain me.

Successful in my job? Helpful to others?

Maybe.

I wish I could have done more to help Liz.

Years ago when I visited Skip in Mount Howard I did not hear Liz and Marty's raised and troubled voices. I knew little of the tension between them. I learned more when I read a letter from Skip during his time in the army. I can't recall the letter's exact content; I do, however, remember these lines: "Marty tried hard to make it work. He could only make it work to a point. Beyond that, no dice. After Aunt Ceil died, Liz wanted to be on her own, by herself."

Skip didn't divulge anything more about Liz and Marty's relationship. I respected that desire for privacy. But knowing what Ralph Malloy had committed upon his daughter and upon Lorraine Wyles, and remembering the tragedies thereafter, I drew my own conclusions. My conclusions may be flawed. Then again…

Kathryn and I receive annual Christmas greetings from Liz. She tells us about her travels—Alaska, England, Scotland, and Ireland among her destinations—but her 233 South Kenton Avenue, Mount Howard address remains the same. She is godmother to Skip and Cori's three children.

The last I heard about Lorraine Wyles was that she had joined a hippie commune in upper New York State. I doubt the commune exists anymore, and I wonder where her life brought her after the 60s "revolution." I look for Lorraine in photographs of Woodstock Nation and in the feature documentary of the festival. I still haven't found her. I keep looking…

"There's something there, David," Granddad had assured me.

Granddad passed away in his sleep the winter of my first year of being a history teacher / part-time guidance counselor. Granddad's kindness succeeded him. The house where he and Nana had lived became his legacy to my parents. After thirty years of renting houses, they became owners of their first and only home.

I returned to be an acolyte for Granddad's funeral service. As I listened to frail Father Hepplewhite express his homily of eternal rest, I did not expect a touch upon my shoulder. I didn't anticipate it, didn't wish for it. I did not need the touch. I suppose I have found, as the woman I met at the Malloys' grave believed, my way. I had come to accept Father Hepplewhite's interpretation of the touch as "a marvelous mystery:" Something I wouldn't always understand, but something I would continue to wonder about. In the Sanctuary during the service for Granddad, I felt neither blessed nor conflicted. I did, however, feel at peace as reasonably as I could, with myself, my friends and family, with God, though not with all of the world.

"If you don't have that sense of peace within yourself," I have advised troubled clients, "you'll be at odds with the rest of the world for the rest of your life."

Skip agrees. "I still see it in my sister, I saw it in me," he said to me one summer day.

Though we live hundreds of miles apart, our families spend New Year's Eve and one week together every summer. The last week of July we occupy a rental on the Jersey shore, the house with a wrap-around deck footsteps from the beach. There, we entertain our children, grandchildren, and friends. We hosted my parents, too, when they were still alive and healthy. In the early 80s my mother and father died within weeks of each other, that fateful turn of events, I think, rather fitting. "I can't see Dad living without Mom," Kathryn said after my father passed on.

One morning last summer Skip and I sipped coffee on the deck. The tide was out, and early risers—dog walkers and joggers—followed their routines along the sand. Skip and I have both "gone gray," and lines crinkle our faces. He wears contact lenses now instead of thick-lensed glasses. I still remember the dance at Sunrise Auditorium and the police presence in front of his house. So does he.

"Had a dream last night about the old man. He said he was sorry." Skip ran his left index finger along the rim of his cup.

"Did you believe him?" I asked.

"I want to..."

He looked out at the tide and the people on the beach. "Helluva long time to come to terms with the sonova bitch," he said slowly. "When I was overseas I thought a lot about what he was and what happened that summer. I started drinking again...get plowed and stagger back to base, sleep it off, then play the whole goddamn business all over again in my head. Couldn't get rid of it. Not even after I came home and got my degree and started counseling kids. Some of them went through the same kind of shit I did. There I was. I had to help myself if I was going to be any good to them."

"Who'd you talk to?" I asked.

"Myself. Had good conversations with myself. Still do," he chuckled, and sipped his coffee. "I talked to Liz and Cori...I asked Lizzie if she remembered ever seeing our parents in a tender moment. Only once, she said. She saw them hug each other and kiss on the front porch glider one night. Me, I never saw them give each other any affection at all. Always the old man was saying shit like 'Get me another beer,' or 'Is that all you're good for?' And Mom and me cleaning up his messes." Skip shook his head and half-smiled. "Not like things were at your house, Harper. You were lucky. You had it easy."

"I guess I did," I said. "Except for a few trips to the kitchen pantry."

"Yeah...Not such a Boy Scout after all, were you."

We shared a laugh.

"I used to talk to you, too," Skip said. "I'd ask myself 'What would numbnuts say?'"

"What *did* I say?"

"Same thing one of my shrinks told me: 'You went through it. Now get to a place where you can let go of it. Put it where it won't hurt you anymore. If you don't, you're never gonna be any good to yourself, your family, or anybody else.'"

Skip finished his coffee, set down his cup, and extended his hand across the table. Once more, and not for the last time, we clasped hands.

ABOUT THE AUTHOR

Raised in Pitman, New Jersey, John T. "Jack" Hitchner graduated from Glassboro State College (now Rowan University) and Dartmouth College. He has also studied at the University of Bath in the United Kingdom.

For over 35 years he taught English in public schools in New Jersey and New Hampshire, until retiring from public education in 2001. Since 1989, he has been an adjunct instructor in English at Keene State College, where he teaches Creative Writing and Coming of Age in War and Peace.

His publications include two chapbooks of poetry—*Not Far From Here*, 2010, and *Seasons and Shadows*, 2011. *How Far Away, How Near*, a collection of short fiction, appeared in 2012.

His poem "My Father in Winter" was awarded the Robert Penn Warren Free Verse Prize by *The Anthology of New England Writers*. He has also been a Featured Poet in the noted poetry journals *the Aurorean* and *Long Story Short*.

He lives with his wife Patricia in New Hampshire.

The Acolyte is his first novel.